The native moved slowly, letting the beast edge in on him. It pawed the ground, and snorted through a pair of breather holes below the horns. Then the native leaped in the air, and chanted something unintelligible. As he came down in the dirt, the animal moved sharply, and charged across the cleared space. People in its line of attack stepped back quickly; and the native leaped agilely out of the way.

It went that way for over an hour.

The ristable charged, and the native leaped out of its path.

Then, when Derr was convinced it would go on this way till darkness . . . the dance changed. Radically.

The native settled down cross-legged in the dirt, and clasped his hands to his chest. He settled down, and the bull charged.

Great God! thought Derr in horror, *he's sitting there, letting it gore him. He's . . .*

—from "Final Trophy"
by Harlan Ellison

STARHUNTERS:VOL. III

created by

DAVID DRAKE

BLUEBLOODS

BAEN BOOKS

BLUEBLOODS

Copyright © 1990 by David Drake

A Baen Books Original

Baen Publishing Enterprises
260 Fifth Avenue
New York, N.Y. 10001

ISBN: 0-671-69866-4

Cover art by Pat Ortega

First printing, March 1990

Distributed by
SIMON & SCHUSTER
1230 Avenue of the Americas
New York, N.Y. 10020

Printed in the United States of America

DEDICATION

To Phil Thomas

Though I never thought I'd be dedicating a book
to a union organizer.

Contents

Introductions by David Drake

Acknowledgments

Among the many people who've helped me put together this volume are Marty Greenberg and Charles Waugh; Karl Edward Wagner, MD; Harlan Ellison; Sandra Miesel; Phil Thomas; Dan Breen and his staff, particularly Rick McGee and Kevin Maroney; and Perry Knowlton. All of them friends.

I used to think there were good guys and bad guys. Bad things happened because the bad guys did them. As I got older, I learned that a lot of the 'bad things' weren't bad from every viewpoint; often, they weren't unrelievedly bad even in my better-informed opinion.

More important, the people who did them were almost never bad guys in their own minds, at least at the time the events occurred. After the fact, long after the fact, maybe they had second thoughts. Maybe British soldiers had nightmares about Amerind babies dying because of the smallpox-ridden blankets the troops had distributed as part of the treaty. Maybe Japanese veterans weep to remember cutting open the bellies of pregnant women during the Rape of Nanking.

But at the time, they were doing something they thought was necessary, something that was beneficial to the cause in which they believed. Often, like the bomber pilots who obeyed Churchill's personal orders to turn Dresden into an inferno as a warning to the Russians who were about to take the city, they are instruments of a policy of which they know nothing.

They aren't bad guys. We aren't bad guys. But God knows, we've done bad things, a lot of us.

Goal-directed people make policy. They look at the

1

big picture and decide what's required if the North
American colonists are to be kept safe from Indians;
how the huge subject population of conquered China
can be prevented from rising against the small garri-
sons which will remain along the lines of communication; how Joe Stalin, Satan in a moustache, can be
contained after the war.

The guys at the sharp end tend to be task oriented,
doing the job that's in front of them and not looking
beyond it. That's the only way they could do a lot of the
jobs which policy decides must be done, for the good of
the People or the Cause or Profit.

The guys at the sharp end on both sides are a lot
alike. Without them, none of the policy makers could
achieve their necessary goals.

And a lot of the guys get very good at the business
they do—on both sides.

THE FURIES

Roger Zelazny

As an afterthought, Nature sometimes tosses a bone to those it maims and casts aside. Often, it is in the form of a skill, usually useless, or the curse of intelligence.

When Sandor Sandor was four years old he could name all the one hundred forty-nine inhabited worlds in the galaxy. When he was five he could name the principal land masses of each planet and chalk them in, roughly, on blank globes. By the time he was seven years old he knew all the provinces, states, countries and major cities of all the main land masses on all one hundred forty-nine inhabited worlds in the galaxy. He read Landography, History, Landology and popular travel guides during most of his waking time; and he studied maps and travel tapes. There was a camera behind his eyes, or so it seemed, because by the time he was ten years old there was no city in the galaxy that anyone could name about which Sandor Sandor did not know *something*.

And he continued.

Places fascinated him. He built a library of street guides, road maps. He studied architectural styles and principal industries, and racial types, native life forms, local flora, landmarks, hotels, restaurants, airports and seaports and spaceports, styles of clothing and personal ornamentation, climatic conditions, local arts and crafts, dietary habits, sports, religions, social institutions, customs.

When he took his doctorate in Landography at the age of fourteen, his oral examinations were conducted via closed circuit television. This is because he was afraid to leave his home—having done so only three times before in his life and having met with fresh trauma on each occasion. And *this* is because on all one hundred forty-nine inhabited worlds in the galaxy there was no remedy for a certain degenerative muscular disease. This disease made it impossible for Sandor to manipulate even the finest prosthetic devices for more than a few minutes without suffering fatigue and great pain; and to go outside he required three such devices—two legs and a right arm—to substitute for those which he had missed out on receiving somewhere along the line before birth.

Rather than suffer this pain, or the pain of meeting persons other than his Aunt Faye or his nurse, Miss Barbara, he took his oral examinations via closed circuit television.

The University of Brill, Dombeck, was located on the other side of that small planet from Sandor's home, else the professors would have come to see *him*, because they respected him considerably. His 855-page dissertation, "Some Notes Toward a Gravitational Matrix Theory Governing the Formation of Similar Land Masses on Dissimilar Planetary Bodies," had drawn attention from Interstel University on Earth itself. Sandor Sandor, of course, would never see the Earth. His muscles could only sustain the gravitation of smaller planets, such as Dombeck.

And it happened that the Interstel Government, which monitors everything, had listened in on Sandor's oral examinations and his defense of his dissertation.

Associate Professor Baines was one of Sandor's very few friends. They had even met several times in person, in Sandor's library, because Baines often said he'd wanted to borrow certain books and then came and spent the afternoon. When the examinations were concluded, Associate Professor Baines stayed on the circuit for several minutes, talking with Sandor. It was during this time that Baines made casual reference to an almost useless (academically, that is) talent of Sandor's.

At the mention of it, the government man's ears had pricked forward (he was a Rigellian). He was anxious for a promotion and he recalled an obscure memo . . .

Associate Professor Baines had mentioned the fact that Sandor Sandor had once studied a series of 30 random photos from all over the civilized galaxy, and that the significant data from these same photos had also been fed into the Department's L-L computer. Sandor had named the correct planet in each case, the land mass in 29, the county or territory in 26, and he had correctly set the location itself within 50 square miles in 23 instances. The L-L comp had named the correct planet for 27.

It was not a labor of love for the computer.

So it became apparent that Sandor Sandor knew just about every damn street in the galaxy.

Ten years later he knew them all.

But three years later the Rigellian quit his job, disgusted, and went to work in private industry, where the pay was better and promotions more frequent. *His* memo, and the tape, had been filed, however . . .

Benedick Benedict was born and grew up on the watery world of Kjum, and his was an infallible power for making enemies of everyone he met.

The reason why is that while some men's highest pleasure is drink, and others are given to gluttony, and still others are slothful, or lechery is their chief delight, or *Phrinn*-doing, Benedick's was gossip—he was a loudmouth.

Gossip was his meat and his drink, his sex and his religion. Shaking hands with him was a mistake, often a catastrophic one. For, as he clung to your hand, pumping it and smiling, his eyes would suddenly grow moist and the tears would dribble down his fat cheeks.

He wasn't sad when this happened. Far from it. It was a somatic conversion from his paranorm reaction.

He was seeing your past life.

He was selective, too; he only saw what he looked for. And he looked for scandal and hate, and what is often worse, love; he looked for lawbreaking and unrest, for memories of discomfort, pain, futility, weakness. He saw everything a man wanted to forget, and he talked about it.

If you are lucky he won't tell you of your own. If you have ever met someone else whom he has also met in this manner, and if this fact shows, he will begin talking of *that* person. He will tell you of that man's or woman's life, because he appreciates this form of social reaction even more than your outrage at yourself. And his eyes and voice and hand will hold you, like the clutch of the Ancient Mariner, and in a sort of half dream-state; and you will hear him out and you will be shocked beneath your paralysis.

Then he will go away and tell others about you.

Such a man was Benedick Benedict. He was probably unaware how much he was hated, because this reaction never came until later, after he had said "Good day," departed, and been gone for several hours. He left his hearers with a just-raped feeling—and later fear, shame, or disgust forced them to suppress the occurrence and to try to forget him. Or else they hated him quietly, because he was dangerous. That is to say, he had powerful friends.

He was an extremely social animal; he loved attention, he wanted to be admired, he craved audiences.

He could always find an audience too, somewhere. He knew so many secrets that he was tolerated in important places in return for the hearing. And he was wealthy too, but more of that in a moment.

As time went on, it became harder and harder for him to meet new people. His reputation spread in geometric proportion to his talking, and even those who would hear him preferred to sit on the far side of the room, drink enough alcohol to partly deaden memories of themselves, and to be seated near a door.

The reason for his wealth is because his power extended to inanimate objects as well. Minerals were rare on Kjum, the watery world. If anyone brought him a sample he could hold it and weep and tell them where to dig to hit the main lode.

From one fish caught in the vast seas of Kjum, he could chart the course of a school of fish.

Weeping, he could touch a native rad-pearl necklace and divine the location of the native's rad-pearl bed.

Local insurance associations and loan companies kept Benedict Files—the pen a man had used to sign his contract, his snubbed-out cigarette butt, a plastex hanky with which he had mopped his brow, an object left in security, the remains of a biopsy or blood test—so that Benedick could use his power against those who renege on these companies and flee, on those who break their laws.

He did not revel in his power either. He simply enjoyed it. For he was one of the nineteen known paranorms in the one hundred forty-nine inhabited worlds in the galaxy, and he knew no other way.

Also, he occasionally assisted civil authorities, if he thought their cause a just one. If he did not, he suddenly lost his power until the need for it vanished. This didn't happen too often though, for a humanitarian was Benedick Benedict, and well-paid, because he was laboratory-tested and clinically-proven. He could psychometrize. He could pick up thought-patterns originating outside his own skull . . .

Lynx Links looked like a beachball with a beard, a fat patriarch with an eyepatch, a man who loved good food and drink, simple clothing, and the company of simple people; he was a man who smiled often and whose voice was soft and melodic.

In his earlier years he had chalked up the most impressive kill-record of any agent ever employed by Interstel Central Intelligence. Forty-eight men and seventeen malicious alien lifeforms had the Lynx dispatched during his fifty-year tenure as a field agent. He was one of the three men in the galaxy to have lived through half a century's employment with ICI. He lived comfortably on his government pension despite three wives and a horde of grandchildren; he was recalled occasionally as a consultant; and he did some part-time missionary work on the side. He believed that all life was one and that all men were brothers, and that love rather than hate or fear should rule the affairs of men. He had even killed with love, he often remarked at Tranquility Session, respecting and revering the person and the spirit of the man who had been marked for death.

This is the story of how he came to be summoned back from Hosanna, the World of the Great and Glorious Flame of the Divine Life, and was joined with Sandor Sandor and Benedick Benedict in the hunt for Victor Corgo, the man without a heart.

* * *

Victor Corgo was Captain of the *Wallaby*. Victor Corgo was Head Astrogator, First Mate, and Chief Engineer of the *Wallaby*. Victor Corgo *was* the *Wallaby*.

One time the *Wallaby* was a proud Guardship, an ebony toadstool studded with the jewel-like warts of fast-phase projectors. One time the *Wallaby* skipped proud about the frontier worlds of Interstel, meting out the Unique justice of the Uniform Galactic Code—in

those places where there was no other law. One time
the proud *Wallaby*, under the command of Captain
Victor Corgo of the Guard, had ranged deep space and
become a legend under legendary skies.

A terror to brigands and ugly aliens, a threat to
Code-breakers, and a thorn in the sides of evildoers
everywhere, Corgo and his shimmering fungus (which
could burn an entire continent under water-level within
a single day) were the pride of the Guard, the best of
the best, the cream that had been skimmed from all the
rest.

Unfortunately, Corgo sold out.

He became a heel.

. . . A traitor.

A hero gone bad . . .

After forty-five years with the Guard, his pension but
half a decade away, he lost his entire crew in an ill-
timed raid upon a pirate stronghold on the planet Kilsh,
which might have become the hundred-fiftieth inhabited world of Interstel.

Crawling, barely alive, he had made his way half
across the great snowfield of Brild, on the main land
mass of Kilsh. At the fortuitous moment, Death making
its traditional noises of approach, he was snatched from
out its traffic lane, so to speak, by the Drillen, a no-
madic tribe of ugly and intelligent quadrapeds, who
took him to their camp and healed his wounds, fed him,
and gave him warmth. Later, with the cooperation of
the Drillen, he recovered the *Wallaby* and all its arms
and armaments, from where it had burnt its way to a
hundred feet beneath the ice.

Crewless, he trained the Drillen.

With the Drillen and the *Wallaby* he attacked the
pirates.

He won.

But he did not stop with that.

No.

When he learned that the Drillen had been marked

for death under the Uniform Code he sold out his own species. The Drillen had refused relocation to a decent Reservation World. They had elected to continue occupancy of what was to become the hundred-fiftieth inhabited world in the galaxy (that is to say, in Interstel).

Therefore, the destruct-order had been given.

Captain Corgo protested, was declared out of order.

Captain Corgo threatened, was threatened in return.

Captain Corgo fought, was beaten, died, was resurrected, escaped restraint, became an outlaw.

He took the *Wallaby* with him. The *Happy Wallaby*, it had been called in the proud days. Now, it was just the *Wallaby*.

As the tractor beams had seized it, as the vibrations penetrated its ebony hull and tore at his flesh, Corgo had called his six Drillen to him, stroked the fur of Mala, his favorite, opened his mouth to speak, and died just as the words and the tears began.

"I am sorry . . ." he had said.

They gave him a new heart, though. His old one had fibrillated itself to pieces and could not be repaired. They put the old one in a jar and gave him a shiny, antiseptic egg of throbbing metal, which expanded and contracted at varying intervals, dependent upon what the seed-sized computers they had planted within him told of his breathing and his blood sugar and the output of his various glands. The seeds and the egg contained his life.

When they were assured that this was true and that it would continue, they advised him of the proceedings of courts martial.

He did not wait, however, for due process. Breaking his parole as an officer, he escaped the Guard Post, taking with him Mala, the only remaining Drillen in the galaxy. Her five fellows had not survived scientific inquiry as to the nature of their internal structures. The rest of the race, of course, had refused relocation.

Then did the man without a heart make war upon mankind.

Raping a planet involves considerable expense. Enormous blasters and slicers and sluicers and refiners are required to reduce a world back almost to a state of primal chaos, and then to extract from it its essential (*i.e.*, commercially viable) ingredients. The history books may tell you of strip-mining on the mother planet, back in ancient times. Well, the crude processes employed then were similar in emphasis and result, but the operations were considerably smaller in scale.

Visualize a hundred miles of Grand Canyon appearing overnight; visualize the reversal of thousands of Landological millenia in the twinkling of an eye; consider all the Ice Ages of the Earth, and compress them into a single season. This will give you a rough idea as to time and effect.

Now picture the imported labor—the men who drill and blast and slice and sluice for the great mining combines: Not uneducated, these men; willing to take a big risk, certainly though, these men—maybe only for one year, because of the high pay; or maybe they're careerists, because of the high pay—these men, who hit three worlds in a year's time, who descend upon these worlds in ships full of city, in space-trailer mining camps, out of the sky; coming, these men, from all over the inhabited galaxy, bringing with them the power of the tool and the opposed thumb, bearing upon their brows the mark of the Solar Phoenix and in their eyes the cold of the spaces they have crossed over, they know what to do to make the domes of atoms rise before them and to call down the tornado-probosci of suck-vortices from the freighters on the other side of the sky; and they. do it thoroughly and efficiently, and not without style, tradition, folksongs, and laughter—for they are the sweat-crews, working against time (which is money), to gain tonnage (which is money), and to beat their competitors to market (which is important, inasmuch as one worldsworth influences future sales for many months), these men, who bear in one hand the flame and in the other the whirlwind, who come down with their families and all their possessions, erect temporary metropoli, work their magic act, and go—after the vanishing trick has been completed.

Now that you've an idea as to what happens and who is present at the scene, here's the rub:

Raping a planet involves considerable expense.

The profits are more than commensurate, do not misunderstand. It is just that they could be even greater . . .

How?

Well— For one thing, the heavy machinery involved is quite replaceable, in the main. That is, the machinery which is housed within the migrant metropoli.

Moving it is expensive. Not moving it isn't. For it is actually cheaper, in terms of material and labor, to manufacture new units than it is to fast-phase the old ones more than an average of 2.6 times.

Mining combines do not produce them (and wouldn't really want to); the mining manufacturing combines like to make new units as much as the mining combines like to lose old ones.

And of course it is rented machinery, or machinery on which payments are still being made, to the financing associations, because carrying payments makes it easier to face down the Interstel Revenue Service every fiscal year.

Abandoning the units would be criminal, violating either the lessor-lessee agreement or the Interstel Commercial Code.

But accidents do happen . . .

Often, too frequently to make for comfortable statistics . . .

Way out there on the raw frontier.

Then do the big insurance associations investigate, and they finally sigh and reimburse the lien-holders.

. . . And the freighters make it to market ahead of schedule, because there is less to dismantle and march-order and ship.

Time is saved, commitments are met in advance, a better price is generally obtained, and a headstart on the next worldsworth is supplied in this manner.

All of which is nice.

Except for the insurance associations.

But what can happen to a transitory New York full of heavy equipment?

Well, some call it sabotage.

. . . Some call it mass-murder.

. . . Unsanctioned war.

. . . Corgo's lightning.

But it is written that it is better to burn one city than to curse the darkness.

Corgo did not curse the darkness.

. . . Many times.

The Day they came together on Dombeck, Benedick held forth his hand, smiled, said: "Mister Sandor . . ."

As his hand was shaken, his smile reversed itself. Then it went away from his face. He was shaking an artificial hand.

Sandor nodded, dropped his eyes.

Benedick turned to the big man with the eyepatch.

". . . And you are the Lynx?"

"That is correct, my brother. You must excuse me if I do not shake hands. It is against my religion. I believe that life does not require reassurance as to its oneness."

"Of course," said Benedick. "I once knew a man from Dombeck. He was a *gnil* smuggler, named Worten Wortan—"

"He is gone to join the Great Flame," said the Lynx. "That is to say, he is dead now. ICI apprehended him two years ago. He passed to Flame while attempting to escape restraint."

"Really?" said Benedick. "He was at one time a *gnil* addict himself—"

"I know. I read his file in connection with another case."

"Dombeck is full of *gnil* smugglers"—Sandor.

"Oh. Well, then let us talk of this man Corgo."

"Yes"—the Lynx.

"Yes"—Sandor.

"The ICI man told me that many insurance associations have lodged protests with their Interstel representatives."

"That is true"—Lynx.

"Yes"—Sandor, biting his lip. "Do you gentlemen mind if I remove my legs?"

"Not at all"—the Lynx. "We are co-workers, and informality should govern our gatherings."

"Please do," said Benedick.

Sandor leaned forward in his chair and pressed the coupling controls. There followed two thumps from beneath his desk. He leaned back then and surveyed his shelves of globes.

"Do they cause you pain?" asked Benedick.

"Yes"—Sandor.

"Were you in an accident?"

"Birth"—Sandor.

The Lynx raised a decanter of brownish liquid to the light. He stared through it.

"It is a local brandy"—Sandor. "Quite good. Somewhat like the *xmili* of Bandla, only non-addictive. Have some."

The Lynx did, keeping it in front of him all that evening.

"Corgo is a destroyer of property," said Benedick.

Sandor nodded.

". . . And a defrauder of insurance associations, a defacer of planetary bodies, a deserter from the Guard—"

"A murderer"—Sandor.

". . . And a zoophilist," finished Benedick.

"Aye"—the Lynx, smacking his lips.

"So great an offender against public tranquility is he that he must be found."

". . . And passed back through the Flame for purification and rebirth."

"Yes, we must locate him and kill him," said Benedick.

"The two pieces of equipment . . . Are they present?" —the Lynx.

"Yes, the phase-wave is in the next room."

". . . And?" asked Benedick.

"The other item is in the bottom drawer of this desk, right side."

"Then why do we not begin now?"

"Yes. Why not now?"—the Lynx.

"Very well"—Sandor. "One of you will have to open the drawer, though. It is in the brown-glass jar, to the back."

"I'll get it," said Benedick.

A great sob escaped him after a time, as he sat there with rows of worlds at his back, tears on his cheeks, and Corgo's heart clutched in his hands.

"It is cold and dim . . ."

"Where?"—the Lynx.

"It is a small place. A room? Cabin? Instrument panels . . . A humming sound . . . Cold, and crazy angles everywhere . . . Vibration . . . Hurt!"

"What is he doing?"—Sandor.

". . . Sitting, half-lying—a couch, webbed, about him. Furry one at his side, sleeping. Twisted—angles—everything—wrong. Hurt!"

"The *Wallaby*, in transit"—Lynx.

"Where is he going?"—Sandor.

"HURT!" shouted Benedick.

He dropped the heart into his lap.

He began to shiver. He wiped at his eyes with the backs of his hands.

"I have a headache," he announced.

"Have a drink"—Lynx.

He gulped one, sipped the second.

"Where was I?"

The Lynx raised his shoulders and let them fall.

"The *Wallaby* was fast-phasing somewhere, and Corgo was in phase-sleep. It is a disturbing sensation to fast-phase while fully conscious. Distance and duration grow distorted. You found him at a bad time—while under sedation and subject to continuum-impact. Perhaps, tomorrow will be better . . ."

"I hope so."

"Yes, tomorrow"—Sandor.

"Tomorrow . . . Yes.

"There *was* one other thing," he added, "a thing in his mind . . . There was a sun where there was no sun before."

"A burn-job?"—Lynx.

"Yes."

"A memory?"—Sandor.

"No. He is on his way to do it."

The Lynx stood.

"I will phase-wave ICI and advise them. They can check which worlds are presently being mined. Have you any ideas how soon?"

"No," I can not tell that.

"What did the globe look like? What continental configurations?"—Sandor.

"None. The thought was not that specific. His mind was drifting—mainly filled with hate."

"I'll call in now—and we'll try again . . . ?"

"Tomorrow. I'm tired now."

"Go to bed then. Rest."

"Yes, I can do that . . ."

"Good night, Mister Benedict."

"Good night . . ."

"Sleep in the heart of the Great Flame."

"I hope not . . ."

*   *   *

Mala whimpered and moved nearer her Corgo, for she was dreaming an evil dream: They were back on the great snowfield of Brild, and she was trying to help him—to walk, to move forward. He kept slipping though, and lying there longer each time, and rising more slowly each time and moving ahead at an even slower pace, each time. He tried to kindle a fire, but the snow-devils spun and toppled like icicles falling from the seven moons, and the dancing green flames died as soon as they were born from between his hands.

Finally, on the top of a mountain of ice she saw them.

There were three . . .

They were clothed from head to toe in flame; their burning heads turned and turned and turned; and then one bent and sniffed at the ground, rose, and indicated their direction. Then they were racing down the hillside, trailing flames, melting a pathway as they came, springing over drifts and ridges of ice, their arms extended before them.

Silent they came, pausing only as the one sniffed the air, the ground . . .

She could hear their breathing now, feel their heat . . .

Mala whimpered and moved nearer her Corgo.

For three days Benedick tried, clutching Corgo's heart like a Gipsy's crystal, watering it with his tears, squeezing it almost to life again. His head ached for hours after, each time that he met the continuum-impact. He wept long, moist tears for hours beyond contact, which was unusual. He had always withdrawn from immediate pain before; remembered distress was his forte, and a different matter altogether.

He hurt each time that he touched Corgo and his mind was sucked down through that subway in the sky; and he touched Corgo eleven times during those three days, and then his power went away, really.

*   *   *

Seated, like a lump of dark metal on the hull of the *Wallaby*, he stared across six hundred miles at the blazing hearth which he had stoked to steel-tempering heights; and he *felt* like a piece of metal, resting there upon an anvil, waiting for the hammer to fall again, as it always did, waiting for it to strike him again and again, and to beat him to a new toughness, to smash away more and more of that within him which was base, of that which knew pity, remorse, and guilt, again and again and again, and to leave only that hard, hard form of hate, like an iron boot, which lived at the core of the lump, himself, and required constant hammering and heat.

Sweating as he watched, smiling, Corgo took pictures.

When one of the nineteen known paranorms in the one hundred forty-nine inhabited worlds in the galaxy suddenly loses his powers, and loses them at a crucial moment, it is like unto the old tales wherein a Princess is stricken one day with an unknown malady and the King, her father, summons all his wise men and calls for the best physicians in the realm.

Big Daddy ICI (*Rex ex machina*-like) did, in similar manner, summon wise men and counsellors from various Thinkomats and think-repairshops about the galaxy, including Interstel University, on Earth itself. But alas! while all had a diagnosis, none had on hand any suggestions which were immediately acceptable to all parties concerned:

"A drug-induced countertrauma should work best."

"Bombard his thalamus with Beta particles."

"Hypno-regression to the womb, and restoration at a pretraumatic point in his life."

"More continuum-impact."

"Six weeks on a pleasure satellite, and two aspirins every four hours."

"There is an old operation called a lobotomy . . ."

"Lots of liquids and green leafy vegetables."

"Hire another paranorm."

For one reason or another, the principal balked at all of these courses of action, and the final one was impossible at the moment. In the end, the matter was settled neatly by Sandor's nurse Miss Barbara, who happened onto the veranda one afternoon as Benedick sat there fanning himself and drinking *xmili*.

"Why Mister Benedict!" she announced, plopping her matronly self into the chair opposite him and spiking her *redlonade* with three fingers of *xmili*. "Fancy meeting you out here! I thought you were in the library with the boys, working on that top secret hush-hush critical project called Wallaby Stew, or something."

"As you can see, I am not," he said, staring at his knees.

"Well, it's nice just to pass the time of day sometimes, too. To sit. To relax. To rest from the hunting of Victor Corgo . . ."

"Please, you're not supposed to know about the project. It's top secret and critical—"

"And hush-hush too, I know. Dear Sandor talks in his sleep every night—so much. You see, I tuck him in each evening and sit there until he drifts away to dreamland, poor child."

"Mm, yes. Please don't talk about the project, though."

"Why? Isn't it going well?"

"No!"

"Why not?"

"Because of *me*, if you must know! I've got a block of some kind. The power doesn't come when I call it."

"Oh, how distressing! You mean you can't peep into other persons' minds any more?"

"Exactly."

"Dear me. Well, let's talk about something else then. Did I ever tell you about the days when I was the highest-paid courtesan on Sordido V?"

Benedick's head turned slowly in her direction.

"Nooo . . ." he said. "You mean *the* Sordido?"

"Oh yes. Bright Bad Barby, the Bouncing Baby, they used to call me. They still sing ballads, you know."

"Yes, I've heard them. Many verses . . ."

"Have another drink. I once had a coin struck in my image, you know. It's a collectors' item now, of course. Full-length pose, flesh-colored. Here, I wear it on this chain around my neck.—Lean closer, it's a short chain."

"Very—interesting. Uh, how did all this come about?"

"Well—it all began with old Pruria Van Teste, the banker, of the export-import Testes. You see, he had this thing going for synthofemmes for a long while, but when he started getting up there in years he felt there was something he'd been missing. So, one fine day, he sent me ten dozen Hravian orchids and a diamond garter, along with an invitation to have dinner with him . . ."

"You accepted, of course?"

"Naturally not. Not the first time, anyway. I could see that he was pretty damn eager."

"Well, what happened?"

"Wait till I fix another *redlonade*."

Later that afternoon, the Lynx wandered out onto the veranda during the course of his meditations. He saw there Miss Barbara, with Benedick seated beside her, weeping.

"What troubles thy tranquility, my brother?" he inquired.

"Nothing! Nothing at all! It is wonderful and beautiful, everything! My power has come back—I can feel it!" He wiped his eyes on his sleeve.

"Bless thee, little lady!" said the Lynx, seizing Miss Barbara's hand. "Thy simple counsels have done more to heal my brother than have all these highly-paid medical practitioners brought here at great expense. Virtue lies in thy homely words, and thou art most beloved of the Flame."

"Thank you, I'm sure."

"Come brother, let us away to our task again!"

"Yes, let us!—Oh thank you, Bright Barby!"

"Don't mention it."

Benedick's eyes clouded immediately, as he took the tattered blood-pump into his hands. He leaned back, stroking it, and moist spots formed on either side of his nose, grew like well-fed amoebae, underwent mitosis, and dashed off to explore in the vicinity of his shelf-like upper lip.

He sighed once, deeply.

"Yes, I am there."

He blinked, licked his lips.

". . . It is night. Late. It is a primitive dwelling. Mud-like stucco, bits of straw in it . . . All lights out, but for the one from the machine, and its spillage—"

"Machine?"—Lynx.

"What machine?"—Sandor.

". . . Projector. Pictures on wall . . . World—big, filling whole picture-field—patches of fire on the world, up near the top. Three places—"

"Bhave VII!"—Lynx. "Six days ago!"

"Shoreline to the right goes like this . . . And to the left, like this . . ."

His right index finger traced patterns in the air.

"Bhave VII"—Sandor.

"Happy and not happy at the same time—hard to separate the two. Guilt, though, is there—but pleasure with it. Revenge . . . Hate people, humans . . . We adjust the projector now, stop it at a flareup.—Bright! How good!—Oh good! That will teach them!—Teach them to grab away what belongs to others . . . To murder a race!—The generator is humming. It is ancient, and it smells bad . . . The dog is lying on our foot. The foot is asleep, but we do not want to disturb the dog, for it is Mala's favorite thing—her only toy, companion, living doll, four-footed . . . She is scratching behind its ear with her forelimb, and it loves her. Light leaks down upon them . . . Clear they are. The breeze is warm, very, which is why we are unshirted. It stirs the tasseled hanging . . . No force-field or window-pane . . . Insects buzz by the projector—pterodactyl silhouettes on the burning world—"

"What kind of insects?"—Lynx.

"Can you see what is beyond the window?"—Sandor.

". . . Outside are trees—short ones—just outlines, squat. Can't tell where trunks begin . . . Foliage too thick, too close. Too dark out.—Off in the distance a tiny moon . . . Something like *this* on a hill . . ." His hands shaped a turnip impaled on an obelisk. "Not sure how far off, how large, what color, or what made of . . ."

"Is the name of the place in Corgo's mind?"—Lynx.

"If I could touch him, with my hand, I would know it, know everything. Only receive impressions *this* way, though—surface thoughts. He is not thinking of where he is now . . . The dog rolls onto its back and off of our foot —at last! She scratches its tummy, my love dark . . . It kicks with its hind leg as if scratching after a flea—wags its tail. Dilk is puppy's name. She gave it that name, loves it . . . It is like one of hers. Which was murdered. Hate people—humans. *She* is people. Better than . . . Doesn't butcher that which breathes for selfish gain, for Interstel. Better than people, my pony-friends, better . . . An insect lights on Dilk's nose. She brushes it away. Segmented, two sets of wings, about five milli-meters in length, pink globe on front end, bulbous, and buzzes as it goes, the insects—you asked . . ."

"How many entrances are there to the place?"—Lynx.

"Two. One doorway at each end of the hut."

"How many windows?"

"Two. On opposing walls—the ones without doors. I can't see anything through the other window—too dark on that side."

"Anything else?"

"On the wall a sword—long hilt, very long, two-handed—even longer maybe—three? four?—short blades, though, two of them—hilt is in the middle—and each blade is straight, double-edged, forearm-length . . . Beside it, a mask of—flowers? Too dark to tell. The blades shine, the mask is dull. Looks like flowers, though. Many little ones . . . Four sides to the mask, shaped like a kite, big end down. Can't make out features. It projects fairly far out from the wall, though. Mala is restless. Probably doesn't like the pictures—or maybe doesn't see them and is bored. Her eyes are different. She nuzzles our shoulder now. We pour her a drink in her bowl. Take another one ourself. She doesn't drink hers. We stare at her. She drops her head and drinks. —Dirt floor under our sandals, hard-packed. Many tiny white—pebbles?—in it, powdery-like. The table is wood, natural . . . The generator sputters. The picture fades, comes back. We rub our chin. Need a shave . . . The hell with it! We're not standing any inspections! Drink— one, two—all gone! Another!"

Sandor had threaded a tape into his viewer, and he was spinning it and stopping it, spinning it and stopping it. He checked his worlds chronometer.

"Outside," he asked, "does the moon seem to be moving up, or down, or across the sky?"

"Across."

"Right to left, or left to right?"

"Right to left. It seems about a quarter past zenith."

"Any coloration to it?"

"Orange, with three black lines. One starts at about eleven o'clock, crosses a quarter of its surface, drops straight down, cuts back at seven. The other starts at two, drops to six. They don't meet. The third is a small upside-down letter 'c'—lower right quarter . . . Not big, the moon, but clear, very. No clouds."

"Any constellations you can make out?"—Lynx.

". . . Head isn't turned that way now, wasn't turned toward the window long enough. Now there is a noise, far off . . . A high-pitched chattering, almost metallic. Animal. He pictures a six-legged tree creature, half the size of a man, reddish-brown hair, sparse . . . It can go on two, four, or six legs on the ground. Doesn't go down on the ground much, though. Nests high. An egg-layer. Many teeth. Eats flesh. Small eyes, and black—two. Great nose-holes. Pesty, but not dangerous to men—easily frightened."

"He is on Disten, the fifth world of Blake's System," said Sandor. "Night-side means he is on the continent Diden-lan. The moon Babry, well past zenith now, means he is to the east. A Mellar-mosque indicates a Mella-Muslim settlement. The blade and the mask seem Hortanian. I am sure they were brought from further inland. The chalky deposits would set him in the vicinity of Landear, which *is* Mella-Muslim. It is on the Dista River, north bank. There is much jungle about. Even those people who wish seclusion seldom go further than eight miles from the center of town—population 153,000—and it is least settled to the northwest, because of the hills, the rocks, and—"

"Fine! That's where he is then!"—Lynx. "Now here is how we'll do it. He has, of course, been sentenced to death. I believe—yes, I know!—there is an ICI Field Office on the second world—whatever its name—of that System."

"Nirer"—Sandor.

"Yes. Hmm, let's see . . Two agents will be empowered as executioners. They will land their ship to the northwest of Landear, enter the city, and find where the man with the strange four-legged pet settled, the one who arrived within the past six days. Then one agent will enter the hut and ascertain whether Corgo is within. He will retreat immediately if Corgo is present, signalling to the other who will be hidden behind those trees or whatever. The second man will then fire a round of fragmentation plaster through the unguarded window. One agent will then position himself at a safe distance beyond the northeast corner of the edifice, so as to cover a door and a window. The other will move to the southwest, to do the same. Each will carry a

two-hundred channel laser sub-gun with vibrating head.
—Good! I'll phase-wase it to Central now. We've got
him!"

He hurried from the room.

Benedick, still holding the thing, his shirt-front soak-
ing, continued:

" 'Fear not, my lady dark. He is but a puppy, and he
howls at the moon . . .' "

It was 31 hours and 20 minutes later when the Lynx
received and decoded the two terse statements:

EXECUTIONERS THE WAY OF ALL FLESH. THE WALLABY
HAS JUMPED AGAIN.

He licked his lips. His comrades were waiting for the
report, and *they* had succeeded—they had done their
part, had performed efficiently and well. It was the
Lynx who had missed his kill.

He made the sign of the Flame and entered the library.

Benedick knew—*he* could tell. The little paranorm's
hands were on his walking stick, and that was enough—
just that.

The Lynx bowed his head.

"We begin again," he told them.

Benedick's powers—if anything, stronger than ever—
survived continuum-impact seven more times. Then he
described a new world: Big it was, and many-peopled—
bright—dazzling, under a blue-white sun; yellow brick
everywhere, neo-Denebian, architecture, greenglass,
windows, a purple sea nearby . . .

No trick at all for Sandor:

"Phillip's World," he named it, then told them the
city: "Delles."

"This time *we* burn *him*," said the Lynx, and he was
gone from the room.

"Christian-Zoroastrians," sighed Benedick, after he
had left. "I think this one has a Flame-complex."

Sandor spun the globe with his left hand and watched it turn.

"I'm not preconning," said Benedick, "but I'll give you odds, like three to one—on Corgo's escaping again."

"Why?"

"When he abandoned humanity he became something less, and more. He is not ready to die."

"What do you mean?"

"I hold his heart. He gave it up, in all ways. He is invincible now, but he will reclaim it one day. Then he will die."

"How do you know?"

". . . A feeling. There are many types of doctors, among them pathologists. No less than others, they, but masters only of blackness. I *know* people, have known many. I do not pretend to know *all* about them. But weaknesses—yes, those I know."

Sandor turned his globe and did not say anything.

But they *did* burn the *Wallaby*, badly.

He lived, though.

He lived, cursing.

As he lay there in the gutter, the world burning, exploding, falling down around him, he cursed *that* world and every other, and everything in them.

Then there was another burst.

Blackness followed.

The double-bladed Hortanian sword, spinning in the hands of Corgo, had halved the first ICI executioner as he stood in the doorway. Mala had detected their approach across the breezes, through the open window.

The second had fallen before the fragmentation plaster could be launched. Corgo had a laser sub-gun himself, Guard issue, and he cut the man down, firing through the wall and two trees in the direction Mala indicated.

Then the *Wallaby* left Disten.

But he was troubled. How had they found him so

quickly? He had had close brushes with them before—
many of them, over the years. But he was cautious, and
he could not see where he had failed this time, could
not understand how Interstel had located him. Even his
last employer did not know his whereabouts.

He shook his head and phased for Phillip's World.

To die is to sleep and not to dream, and Corgo did
not want this. He took elaborate pains, in-phasing and
out-phasing in random directions; he gave Mala a golden
collar with a two-way radio in its clasp, wore its mate
within his death-ring; he converted much currency, left
the *Wallaby* in the care of a reputable smuggler in
Unassociated Territory and crossed Phillip's World to
Delles-by-the-Sea. He was fond of sailing, and he liked
the purple waters of this planet. He rented a large villa
near the Delles Dives—slums to the one side, Riviera
to the other. This pleased him. He still had dreams; he
was not dead yet.

Sleeping, perhaps, he had heard a sound. Then he
was suddenly seated on the side of his bed, a handful of
death in his hand.

"Mala?"

She was gone. The sound he'd heard had been the
closing of a door.

He activated the radio.

"What is it?" he demanded.

"I have the feeling we are watched again," she replied, through his ring. ". . . Only a feeling, though."

Her voice was distant, tiny.

"Why did you not tell *me?* Come back—now."

"No. I match the night and can move without sound.
I will investigate. There *is* something, if I have fear . . .
Arm yourself!"

He did that, and as he moved toward the front of the
house they struck. He ran. As he passed through the
front door they struck again, and again. There was an
inferno at his back, and a steady rain of plaster, metal,

wood and glass was falling. Then there was an inferno around him.

They were above him. This time they had been cautioned not to close with him, but to strike from a distance. This time they hovered high in a shielded globe and poured down hot rivers of destruction.

Something struck him in the head and the shoulder. He fell, turning. He was struck in the chest, the stomach. He covered his face and rolled, tried to rise, failed. He was lost in a forest of flames. He got into a crouch, ran, fell again, rose once more, ran, fell again, crawled, fell again.

As he lay there in the gutter, the world burning, exploding, falling down around him, he cursed *that* world and every other, and everyone in them.

Then there was another burst.

Blackness followed.

They thought they had succeeded, and their joy was great.

"Nothing," Benedick had said, smiling through his tears.

So that day they celebrated, and the next.

But Corgo's body had not been recovered.

Almost half a block had been hurled down, though, and eleven other residents could not be located either, so it seemed safe to assume that the execution had succeeded. ICI, however, requested that the trio remain together on Dombeck for another ten days, while further investigations were carried out.

Benedick laughed.

"Nothing," he repeated. "Nothing."

But there is a funny thing about a man without a heart: His body does not live by the same rules as those of others: No. The egg in his chest is smarter than a mere heart, and it is the center of a wonderful communications system. Dead itself, it is omniscient in terms of that which lives around it; it is not omnipotent, but it has resources which a living heart does not command.

As the burns and lacerations were flashed upon the screen of the body, it sat in instant criticism. It moved itself to an emergency level of function; it became a flag vibrating within a hurricane; the glands responded and poured forth their juices of power; muscles were activated as if by electricity.

Corgo was only half-aware of the inhuman speed with which he moved through the storm of heat and the hail of building materials. It tore at him, but this pain was cancelled. His massive output jammed non-essential neural input. He made it as far as the street and collapsed in the shelter of the curb.

The egg took stock of the cost of the action, decided the price had been excessively high, and employed immediate measures to insure the investment.

Down, down did it send him. Into the depths of sub-coma. Standard-model humans cannot decide one day that they wish to hibernate, lie down, do it. The physicians can induce *dauerschlaff* with combinations of drugs and elaborate machineries. But Corgo did not need these things. He had a built-in survival kit with a mind of its own; and it decided that he must go deeper than the mere coma-level that a heart would have permitted. So it did the things a heart cannot do, while maintaining its own functions.

It hurled him into the blackness of sleep without dreams, of total unawareness. For only at the border of death itself could his life be retained, be strengthened, grow again. To approach this near the realm of death, its semblance was necessary.

Therefore, Corgo lay dead in the gutter.

People, of course, flock to the scene of any disaster.

Those from the Riviera pause to dress in their best catastrophe clothing. Those from the slums do not, because their wardrobes are not as extensive.

One though, was dressed already and was passing nearby. "Zim" was what he was called, for obvious reasons. He had had another name once, but he had all but forgotten it.

He was staggering home from the *zimlak* parlor where he had cashed his Guard pension check for that month-cycle.

There was an explosion, but it was seconds before he realized it. Muttering, he stopped and turned very slowly in the direction of the noise. Then he saw the flames. He looked up, saw the hoverglobe. A memory appeared within his mind and he winced and continued to watch.

After a time he saw the man, moving at a fantastic pace across the landscape of Hell. The man fell in the street. There was more burning, and then the globe departed.

The impressions finally registered, and his disaster-reflex made him approach.

Indelible synapses, burnt into his brain long ago, summoned up page after page of The Complete Guard Field Manual of Immediate Medical Actions. He knelt beside the body, red with burn, blood and firelight.

". . . Captain," he said, as he stared into the angular face with the closed dark eyes. "Captain . . ."

He covered his own face with his hands and they came away wet.

"Neighbors. Here. Us. Didn't—know . . ." He listened for a heartbeat, but there was nothing that he could detect. "Fallen . . . On the deck my Captain lies . . . fallen . . . old . . . dead. Us. Neighbors, even . . ." His sob was a jagged thing, until he was seized with a spell of hiccups. Then he steadied his hands and raised an eyelid.

Corgo's head jerked two inches to his left, away from the brightness of the flames.

The man laughed in relief.

"You're alive, Cap! You're still alive!"

The thing that was Corgo did not reply.

Bending, straining, he raised the body.

" 'Do not move the victim'—that's what it says in the Manual. But you're coming with me, Cap. I remember now . . . It was after I left. But I remember . . . All. Now I remember, I do . . . Yes. They'll kill you another time—if you do live . . . They will, I know. So I'll have to move the victim. Have to . . .—Wish I wasn't so fogged . . . I'm sorry, Cap. You were always good, to the men, good to me. Ran a tight ship, but you were good . . . Old *Wallaby*, happy . . . Yes. We'll go now, killer. Fast as we can. Before the Morbs come.—Yes. I remember . . . you. Good man, Cap. Yes."

So, the *Wallaby* had made its last jump, according to the ICI investigation which followed. But Corgo still dwelled on the dreamless border, and the seeds and the egg held his life.

After the ten days had passed, the Lynx and Benedick still remained with Sandor. Sandor was not anxious for them to go. He had never been employed before; he liked the feeling of having co-workers about, persons who shared memories of things done. Benedick was loathe to leave Miss Barbara, one of the few persons he could talk to and have answer him, willingly. The Lynx liked the food and the climate, decided his wives and grandchildren could use a vacation.

So they stayed on.

Returning from death is a deadly slow business. Reality does the dance of the veils, and it is a long while before you know what lies beneath them all (if you ever really do).

When Corgo had formed a rough idea, he cried out: "Mala!"

. . . The darkness.

Then he saw a face out of times gone by.

"Sergeant Emil . . . ?"

"Yes, sir. Right here, Captain."

"Where am I?"

"My hutch, sir. Yours got burnt out."

"How?"

"A hoverglobe did it, with a sear-beam."

"What of my—pet? A Drillen . . ."

"There was only you I found, sir—no one, nothing, else. Uh, it was almost a month-cycle ago that it happened . . ."

Corgo tried to sit up, failed, tried again, half-succeeded. He sat propped on his elbows.

"What's the matter with me?"

"You had some fractures, burns, lacerations, internal injuries—but you're going to be all right, now."

"I wonder how they found me, so fast—again . . . ?"

"I don't know, sir. Would you like to try some broth now?"

"Later."

"It's all warm and ready."

"Okay, Emil. Sure, bring it on."

He lay back and wondered.

There was her voice. He had been dozing all day and she was part of a dream.

"Corgo, are you there? Are you there, Corgo? Are you . . ."

His hand! The ring!

"Yes! Me! Corgo!" He activated it. "Mala! Where are you?"

"In a cave, by the sea. Every day I have called to you. Are you alive, or do you answer me from Elsewhere?"

"I am alive. There is no magic to your collar. How have you kept yourself?"

"I go out at night. Steal food from the large dwellings with the green windows like doors—for Dilk and myself."

"The puppy? Alive, too?"

"Yes. He was penned in the yard on that night . . . Where are you?"

"I do not know, precisely . . . Near where our place was. A few blocks away—I'm with an old friend . . ."

"I must come."

"Wait until dark. I'll get you directions. —No. I'll send him after you, my friend . . . Where is your cave?"

"Up the beach, past the red house you said was ugly. There are three rocks, pointed on top. Past them is a narrow path—the water comes up to it, sometimes covers it—and around a corner then, thirty-one of my steps, and the rock hangs overhead, too. It goes far back then, and there is a crack in the wall—small enough to squeeze through, but it widens. We are here."

"My friend will come for you after dark."

"You are hurt?"

"I was. But I am better now. I'll see you later, talk more then."

"Yes—"

In the days that followed, his strength returned to him. He played chess with Emil and talked with him of their days together in the Guard. He laughed, for the first time in many years, at the tale of the Commander's wig, at the Big Brawl on Sordido III, some thirty-odd years before . . .

Mala kept to herself, and to Dilk. Occasionally, Corgo would feel her eyes upon him. But whenever he turned, she was always looking in another direction. He realized that she had never seen him being friendly with anyone before. She seemed puzzled.

He drank *zimlak* with Emil, they ventured off-key ballads together . . .

Then one day it struck him.

"Emil, what are you using for money these days?"

"Guard pension, Cap."

"Flames! We've been eating you out of business! Food, and the medical supplies and all . . ."

"I had a little put away for foul weather days, Cap."

"Good. But you shouldn't have been using it. There's

quite a bit of money zipped up in my boots.—Here. Just a second . . . There! Take these!"

"I can't, Cap . . ."

"The hell, you say! Take them, that's an order!"

"All right, sir. But you don't have to . . ."

"Emil, there is a price on my head—you know?"

"I know."

"A pretty large reward."

"Yes."

"It's yours, by right."

"I couldn't turn you in, sir."

"Nevertheless, the reward is yours. Twice over. I'll send you that amount—a few weeks after I leave here."

"I couldn't take it, sir."

"Nonsense, you will."

"No, sir. I won't."

"What do you mean?"

"I just mean I couldn't take that money."

"Why not? What's wrong with it?"

"Nothing, exactly . . . I just don't want any of it. I'll take this you gave me for the food and stuff. But no more, that's all."

"Oh . . . All right, Emil. Any way you like it. I wasn't trying to force . . ."

"I know, Cap."

"Another game now? I'll spot you a bishop and three pawns this time."

"Very good, sir."

"We had some good times together, eh?"

"You bet, Cap. Tau Ceti—three months' leave. Remember the Red River Valley—and the family native life-forms?"

"Hah! And Cygnus VII—the purple world with the Rainbow Women?"

"Took me three weeks to get that dye off me. Thought at first it was a new disease. Flames! I'd love to ship out again!"

Corgo paused in mid-move.

"Hmm . . . You know, Emil . . . It might be that you could."

"What do you mean?"

Corgo finished his move.

"Aboard the *Wallaby*. It's here, in Unassociated Territory, waiting for me. I'm Captain, and crew—and everything—all by myself, right now. Mala helps some, but—you know, I could use a First Mate. Be like old times."

Emil replaced the knight he had raised, looked up, looked back down.

"I—I don't know what to say, Cap. I never thought you'd offer me a berth . . ."

"Why not? I could use a good man. Lots of action, like the old days. Plenty cash. No cares. We want three months' leave on Tau Ceti and we write our own bloody orders. We take it!"

"I—I do want to space again, Cap—bad. But—no, I couldn't . . ."

"Why not, Emil? Why not? It'd be just like before."

"I don't know how to say it, Cap . . . But when we—burnt places, before—well, it was criminals—pirates, Code-breakers—you know. Now . . . Well, now I hear you burn—just people. Uh, non-Code-breakers. Like, just plain civilians. Well—I could not."

Corgo did not answer. Emil moved his knight.

"I hate them, Emil," he said, after a time. "Every lovin' one of them, I hate them. Do you know what they did on Brild? To the Drillen?"

"Yessir. But it wasn't civilians, and not the miners. It was not *everybody*. It wasn't every lovin' one of them, sir.—I just couldn't. Don't be mad."

"I'm not mad, Emil."

"I mean, sir, there are some as I wouldn't mind burnin', Code or no Code. But not the way you do it, sir. And I'd do it for free to those as have it coming."

"Huh!"

Corgo moved his one bishop.

"That's why my money is no good with you?"

"No, sir. That's not it, sir. Well maybe part . . . But only part. I just couldn't take pay for helping someone I—respected, admired."

"You use the past tense."

"Yessir. But I still think you got a raw deal, and what they did to the Drillen was wrong and bad and—evil—but you can't hate everybody for that, sir, because *everybody* didn't do it."

"They countenanced it, Emil—which is just as bad. I am able to hate them all for that alone. And people are all alike, all the same. I burn without discrimination these days, because it doesn't really matter *who*. The guilt is equally distributed. Mankind is commonly culpable."

"No, sir, begging your pardon, sir, but in a system as big as Interstel not everybody knows what everybody else is up to. There are those feeling the same way you do, and there are those as don't give a damn, and those who just don't know a lot of what's going on, but who would do something about it if they knew, soon enough."

"It's your move, Emil."

"Yessir."

"You know, I wish you'd accepted a commission, Emil. You had the chance. You'd have been a good officer."

"No, sir. I'd not have been a good officer. I'm too easy-going. The men would've walked all over me."

"It's a pity. But it's always that way. You know? The good ones are too weak, too easy-going. Why is that?"

"Dunno, sir."

After a couple moves:

"You know, if I were to give it up—the burning, I mean—and just do some ordinary, decent smuggling with the *Wallaby*, it would be okay. With me. Now. I'm tired. I'm so damned tired I'd just like to sleep—oh, four, five, six years, I think. Supposing I stopped the burning and just shipped stuff here and there—would you sign on with me then?"

"I'd have to think about it, Cap."

"Do that, then. Please. I'd like to have you along."

"Yessir. Your move, sir."

It would not have happened that he'd have been found by his actions, because he *did* stop the burning; it would not have happened—because he was dead on ICI's books—that anyone would have been looking for him. It happened, though—because of a surfeit of *xmili* and good will on the part of the hunters.

On the eve of the breaking of the fellowship, nostalgia followed high spirits.

Benedick had never had a friend before, you must remember. Now he had three, and he was leaving them.

The Lynx had ingested much good food and drink, and the good company of simple, maimed people, whose neuroses were unvitiated with normal sophistication—and he had enjoyed this.

Sandor's sphere of human relations had been expanded by approximately a third, and he had slowly come to consider himself at least an honorary member of the vast flux which he had only known before as humanity, or Others.

So, in the library, drinking, and eating and talking, they returned to the hunt. Dead tigers are always the best kind.

Of course, it wasn't long before Benedick picked up the heart, and held it as a connoisseur would an art object—gently, and with a certain mingling of awe and affection.

As they sat there, an odd sensation crept into the pudgy paranorm's stomach and rose slowly, like gas, until his eyes burned.

"I—I'm reading," he said.

"Of course"—the Lynx.

"Yes"—Sandor.

"Really!"

"Naturally"—the Lynx. "He is on Disten, fifth world of Blake's System, in a native hut outside Landear—"

"No"—Sandor. "He is on Phillip's World, in Delles-by-the-Sea."

They laughed, the Lynx a deep rumble, Sandor a gasping chuckle.

"No," said Benedick. "He is in transit, aboard the *Wallaby*. He has just phased and his mind is still mainly awake. He is running a cargo of ambergris to the Tau Ceti system, fifth planet—Tholmen. After that he plans on vacationing in the Red River Valley of the third planet—Cardiff. Along with the Drillen and the puppy, he has a crewman with him this time. I can't read anything but that it's a retired Guardsman."

"By the holy Light of the Great and Glorious Flame!"

"We know they never did find his ship . . ."

". . . And his body was not recovered. —Could *you* be mistaken, Benedick? Reading something, someone else . . . ?"

"No."

"What should we do, Lynx?"—Sandor.

"An unethical person might be inclined to forget it. It is a closed case. We *have* been paid and dismissed."

"True."

"But think of when he strikes again . . ."

". . . It would be because of us, our failure."

"Yes."

". . . And many would die."

". . . And much machinery destroyed, and an insurance association defrauded."

"Yes."

". . . Because of us."

"Yes."

"So we should report it"—Lynx.

"Yes."

"It is unfortunate . . ."

"Yes."

". . . But it will be good to have worked together this final time."

"Yes. It will. Very."

"Tholmen, in Tau Ceti, and he just phased?"—Lynx.

"Yes."

"I'll call, and they'll be waiting for him in T.C."

". . . I told you," said the weeping paranorm. "He wasn't ready to die."

Sandor smiled and raised his glass with his flesh-colored hand.

There was still some work to be done.

When the *Wallaby* hit Tau-Ceti all hell broke loose.

Three fully-manned Guardships, like onto the *Wallaby* herself, were waiting.

ICI had quarantined the entire system for three days. There could be no mistaking the ebony toadstool when it appeared on the screen. No identification was solicited.

The tractor beams missed it the first time, however, and the *Wallaby's* new First Mate fired every weapon aboard the ship simultaneously, in all directions, as soon as the alarm sounded. This had been one of Corgo's small alterations in fire-control, because of the size of his operations: no safety circuits; and it was a suicide-ship, if necessary: it was a lone wolf with no regard for *any* pack: one central control—touch it, and the *Wallaby* became a porcupine with laser-quills, stabbing into anything in every direction.

Corgo prepared to phase again, but it took him forty-three seconds to do so.

During that time he was struck twice by the surviving Guardship.

Then he was gone.

Time and Chance, which govern all things, and sometimes like to pass themselves off as Destiny, then seized upon the *Wallaby*, the puppy, the Drillen, First Mate Emil, and the man without a heart.

Corgo had set no course when he had in-phased.
There had been no time.

The two blasts from the Guardship had radically altered the *Wallaby's* course, and had burnt out 23 fast-
phase projectors.

The *Wallaby* jumped blind, and with a broken leg.

Continuum-impact racked the crew. The hull repaired
rents in its skin.

They continued for 39 hours and 23 minutes, taking
turns at sedation, watching for the first warning on the
panel.

The *Wallaby* held together, though.

But where they had gotten to no one knew, least of
all a weeping paranorm who had monitored the battle
and all of Corgo's watches, despite the continuum-impact
and a hangover.

But suddenly Benedick knew fear:

"He's about to phase-out. I'm going to have to drop
him now."

"Why?"—the Lynx.

"Do you know where he is?"

"No, of course not!"

"Well, neither does he. Supposing he pops out in the
middle of a sun, or in some atmosphere—moving at
that speed?"

"Well, supposing he does? He dies."

"Exactly. Continuum-impact is bad enough. I've never
been in a man's mind when he died—and I don't think
I could take it. Sorry. I just won't do it. I think I might
die myself if it happened. I'm so tired now . . . I'll just
have to check him out later."

With that he collapsed and could not be roused.

So, Corgo's heart went back into its jar, and the jar
went back into the lower righthand drawer of Sandor's
desk, and none of the hunters heard the words of
Corgo's answer to his First Mate after the phasing-out:

"Where are we?—The Comp says the nearest thing is

a little pingpong ball of a world called Dombeck, not noted for anything. We'll have to put down there for repairs, somewhere off the beaten track. We need projectors."

So they landed the *Wallaby* and banged on its hull as the hunters slept, some five hundred forty-two miles away.

They were grinding out the projector sockets shortly after Sandor had been tucked into his bed.

They reinforced the hull in three places while the Lynx ate half a ham, three biscuits, two apples and a pear, and drank half a liter of Dombeck's best Mosel.

They rewired shorted circuits as Benedick smiled and dreamt of Bright Bad Barby the Bouncing Baby, in the days of her youth.

And Corgo took the light-boat and headed for a town three hundred miles away, just as the pale sun of Dombeck began to rise.

"He's here!" cried Benedick, flinging wide the door to the Lynx' room and rushing up to the bedside. "He's—"

Then he was unconscious, for the Lynx may not be approached suddenly as he sleeps.

When he awakened five minutes later, he was lying on the bed and the entire household stood about him. There was a cold cloth on his forehead and his throat felt crushed.

"My brother," said the Lynx, "you should never approach a sleeping man in such a manner."

"B-but he's here," said Benedick, gagging. "Here on Dombeck! I don't even need Sandor to tell!"

"Art sure thou hast not imbibed too much?"

"No, I tell you he's here!" He sat up, flung away the cloth. "That little city, Coldstream—" He pointed through the wall. "—I was there just a week ago. I *know* the place!"

"You have had a dream—"

"Wet your Flame! but I've not! I held his heart in these hands and saw it!"

The Lynx winced at the profanity, but considered the possibility.

"Then come with us to the library and see if you can read it again."

"You better believe I can!"

At that moment Corgo was drinking a cup of coffee and waiting for the town to wake up. He was considering his First Mate's resignation:

"I never wanted to burn anyone, Cap. Least of all, the Guard. I'm sorry, but that's it. No more for me. Leave me here and give me passage home to Phillip's—that's all I want. I know you didn't want it the way it happened, but if I keep shipping with you it might happen again some day. Probably will. They got your number somehow, and I couldn't *ever* do *that* again. I'll help you fix the *Wallaby*, then I'm out. Sorry."

Corgo sighed and ordered a second coffee. He glanced at the clock on the diner wall. Soon, soon . . .

"That clock, that wall, that window! It's the diner where I had lunch last week, in Coldstream!" said Benedick, blinking moistly.

"Do you think all that continuum-impact . . . ?"—the Lynx.

"I don't know"—Sandor.

"How can we check?"

"Call the flamin' diner and ask them to describe their only customer!"—Benedick.

"*That* is a very good idea"—the Lynx.

The Lynx moved to the phone-unit on Sandor's desk.

Sudden, as everything concerning the case had been, was the Lynx's final decision:

"Your flyer, brother Sandor. May I borrow it?"

"Why, yes. Surely . . ."

"I will now call the local ICI office and requisition a laser-cannon. They have been ordered to cooperate with us without question, and the orders are still in effect. My executioner's rating has never been suspended. It appears that if we ever want to see this job completed we must do it ourselves. It won't take long to mount the gun on your flyer.—Benedick, stay with him every minute now. He still has to buy the equipment, take it back, and install it. Therefore, we should have sufficient time. Just stay with him and advise me as to his movements."

"Check."

"Are you sure it's the right way to go about it?"—Sandor.

"I'm sure . . ."

As the cannon was being delivered, Corgo made his purchases. As it was being installed, he loaded the light-boat and departed. As it was tested, on a tree stump Aunt Faye had wanted removed for a long while, he was aloft and heading toward the desert.

As he crossed the desert, Benedick watched the rolling dunes, scrub-shrubs and darting *rabbophers* through his eyes.

He also watched the instrument-panel.

As the Lynx began his journey, Mala and Dilk were walking about the hull of the *Wallaby*. Mala wondered if the killing was over. She was not sure she liked the new Corgo so much as she did the avenger. She wondered whether the change would be permanent. She hoped not . . .

The Lynx maintained radio contact with Benedick.

Sandor drank *xmili* and smiled.

After a time, Corgo landed.

The Lynx was racing across the sands from the opposite direction.

They began unloading the light-boat.

The Lynx sped on.

"I am near it now. Five minutes," he radioed back.

"Then I'm out?"—Benedick.

"Not yet"—the reply.

"Sorry, but you know what I said. I won't be there when he dies."

"All right. I can take it from here"—the Lynx.

Which is how, when the Lynx came upon the scene, he saw a dog and a man and an ugly but intelligent quadruped beside the *Wallaby*.

His first blast hit the ship. The man fell.

The quadruped ran, and he burnt it.

The dog dashed through the port into the ship.

The Lynx brought the flyer about for another pass.

There was another man, circling around from the other side of the ship, where he had been working.

The man raised his hand and there was a flash of light.

Corgo's death-ring discharged its single laser beam.

It crossed the distance between them, penetrated the hull of the flyer, passed through the Lynx' left arm above the elbow, and continued on through the roof of the vehicle.

The Lynx cried out, fought the controls, as Corgo dashed into the *Wallaby*.

Then he triggered the cannon, and again, and again and again, circling, until the *Wallaby* was a smouldering ruin in the middle of a sea of fused sand.

Still did he burn that ruin, finally calling back to Benedick Benedict and asking his one question.

"Nothing"—the reply.

Then he turned and headed back, setting the autopilot and opening the first-aid kit.

". . . Then he went in to hit the *Wallaby's* guns, but I hit him first"—Lynx.

"No"—Benedick.

"What meanest thou 'no'? *I* was there."

"So was I, for awhile. I *had* to see how he felt."

"And?"

"He went in for the puppy, Dilk, held it in his arms, said to it, 'I am sorry.' "

"Whatever, he is dead now and we have finished. It is over"— Sandor.

"Yes."

"Yes."

"Let us then drink to a job well done, before we part for good."

"Yes."

"Yes."

And they did.

While there wasn't much left of the *Wallaby* or its Captain, ICI positively identified a synthetic heart found still beating, erratically, amidst the hot wreckage.

Corgo was dead, and that was it.

He should have known what he was up against, and turned himself in to the proper authorities. How can you hope to beat a man who can pick the lock to your mind, a man who dispatched forty-eight men and seventeen malicious alien life-forms, and a man who knows every damn street in the galaxy.

He should have known better than to go up against Sandor Sandor, Benedick Benedict and Lynx Links. He should, he should have known.

For their real names, of course, are Tisiphone, Alecto and Maegaera. They are the Furies. They arise from chaos and deliver revenge; they convey confusion and disaster to those who abandon the law and forsake the way, who offend against the light and violate the life, who take the power of Flame, like a lightning-rod, in their two too mortal hands.

There are basically two methods of hunting your prey: you can chase after it, or you can wait for it to come to you.

Either system works perfectly well, if both the hunter and the prey are adapted to it. Big cats stalk and rush their prey; crocodiles wait with cold-blooded patience until an antelope—or a fisherman—puts his leg within one bone-crushing snap of the reptile's jaws.

Human hunters use both techniques, making their choice on the basis of cultural and economic factors—as well as whim. Where hunting is weekend recreation, as it is for the overwhelming majority of American deer-hunters, the choice is pretty clear: active hunting, tramping through the woods looking for hoofprints or droppings, is a lot more fun than sitting in a blind being nibbled by insects while you wait for deer to make the suicidal error of wandering into your line of fire.

On the other hand, if you talk to the guys at your local sporting-goods store, you'll find that the fellows who consistently, year after year, get their bag limit do so by finding a good spot and waiting for the deer. They aren't necessarily more knowledgeable about deer than their active brethren, nor are they always better shots. They just have different priorities.

Spiders use both techniques also: some wait in webs, while others—the tarantulas and wolf spiders—prowl the grass. Even among the web spiders, however, the males are free-wandering hunters who only approach a web for the purpose of mating with the female which makes it her lair.

Web spiders are therefore an even better yardstick with which to measure the efficiency of active and passive techniques than are human hunters.

Male spiders are tiny, fragile-looking creatures in comparison to the sleek bulk of the females who wait impassively in their webs for the prey that fate will bring them.

THE MIRROR

Arthur Porges

"A magnificent old house," the agent said expansively. "Just the thing for a large family—with taste. Not one of these ticky-tacky modern cracker boxes with no room to breathe."

In his heart, Mr. Avery agreed completely, but knew he mustn't let his feelings show. Not if a bargain was to be made. So he tried to look shrewd and tightfisted, much as a dormouse might counterfeit ferocity. His was not a poker face; it registered emotions quite similar to those that once flickered in contrasty muggings across the silent screen. He yearned for the huge house, all gingerbread, with its cornices, attics, and above all, the thirty-by-forty foot living room that boasted a seventeen-foot ceiling and a fireplace big enough for half a redwood tree. And there were ten acres of brushy land, offering wonderful privacy. What a spot for the kids! With five of them, all active, outgoing, creative, and impulsive—just like Dad—finding a suitable house was no simple matter. Yes, this one, almost hidden by towering, leafy oaks was a prize—a lucky stroke.

"It's not bad," he said cautiously, quite unaware that his soft, brown eyes shone like beacons. "But, after all, Mr. Doss, the place has been shut up for over thirty years, and what with the stories, that would scare most customers off. Everybody isn't as free from superstition as I am, you know."

"Nothing to all the talk," the agent assured him. "The owner just didn't care to rent or sell. He inherited the property at a fairly early age, but never lived there— probably because it was too big for one person alone. That's reasonable enough. One man in a thirty-room house! Of course," he added quickly, seeing that a question was trembling on Avery's lips, "it needs some work, but that's why the ad called it a 'fixer-upper.' A handy man will get a real bargain, whereas if we had to call in regular contractors . . ."

Mr. Avery was not merely a dedicated do-it-yourselfer, he was a remarkably good one, having a knack for cabinet work, masonry, electrical outlets, and even plumbing. He looked forward with pleasant anticipation to the job of renovating the house. The family could stay in the old one, several hundred miles away, while he toiled in peace, making the nest ready for them. There was no need to consult Lottie; she knew his taste was impeccable and that he definitely headed the family. Mr. Avery, in fact, often thought of himself as a modern paterfamilias in the Victorian tradition, and imposed the image rather successfully on his brood.

He and the agent soon agreed on terms, with Doss giving a little, very graciously, and Avery yielding much more than necessary, but feeling no pain, so skilfully was he manipulated.

There followed a period of intense and enjoyable activity on his part, as he began to put the old house in order. There were rotten boards and panels to be re- placed; stairs that quivered at even a light tread; wallpaper to be hung; gallons of paint needed inside and out; and furniture, including suitable antiques, to be bought.

Finally there was the interesting puzzle of the mirror.

This enormous installation was let into the wall above the fireplace, also a giant, intricately carved and decorated. For some reason, the glass had been covered with many brush strokes of heavy, black enamel. After thirty years of drying, the stuff refused to soften even under the most potent chemicals, and Avery was reduced to a kind of slow, tiresome scraping and chipping that made his wrists ache.

He mentioned the mirror to the only man in town who remembered anything about the house, but learned little that was new. Instead the fellow rehashed the story of the murders.

"Nasty business," the old man said, delighted, obviously, to have a fresh victim. "Colton had a big family— eight kids—but one was out that night. Anyhow, Colton went nuts and killed all of 'em, and then jumped out an upper window to the flagstones, and he died, too. Son that was out—he came home found them all dead— ones inside all chopped or torn to bits, they say. So horrible the coroner never did talk about it in court. Boy sealed up the house right after. Don't think it was his idea—just a kid. Old Wright, the coroner, he musta told him to. All pretty mysterious. Some think Colton didn't do it—that house is haunted." He spat. "Me, I wouldn't live there for a million."

"Did the coroner have the mirror painted over, too?"

"Dunno about that. Didn't know 'twas done. Painted over, y' say? Now I did hear once that some of the kids claimed they saw things in it."

"I've got it pretty well cleaned," Avery said dryly. "And it's just a mirror. In fact, my family will love it. I've always wanted one that big over the fireplace. Might even make up some good stories about it." He winked. "Stolen, basically, from Lewis Carroll." The old man looked at him blankly, and Avery coughed. Maybe the guy would recognize a name like *Herzog* or *The Spy Who Came in From the Cold*, but he wouldn't bet on that, either. Probably the sports page was his limit . . .

As Avery expected, his family was enthusiastic about the house. Even children brought up to be more worldly and cynical would have enjoyed exploring such a pile, with its many fascinating nooks, storerooms, attics, cupboards, and crawl-spaces. Since they ranged in age from five to thirteen, the Avery kids were fully able to make the most of the place. They walked, ran, jumped, and climbed until they knew every inch of the house.

There was only one disappointment: the mirror was still a mess. The lowest layers of paint were particularly resistant; they seemed to have been rushed on to form a grating, with regular horizontal and vertical strokes. In time, of course, Avery would get the glass clear, but for the present, there were more urgent matters requiring his attention. The well, in particular, was acting up in spite of the new electric pump Avery installed; perhaps the casing had a leak. And water was certainly more important than the mirror.

But the time did come, finally, when he could give the glass his full attention, and by using a heavier blade plus a steaming device, Avery removed the last of the black enamel.

Although the mirror was obviously quite old, it gave a clear, undistorted reflection. With his family grouped around a blazing fire, Avery talked, with verve and imagination, about the looking-glass world to be seen—in part—over the mantel. To one side was an archway identical to their own, but they could see only part way into its shadowy depths.

Mr. Avery's fancies, which owed so much to Carroll, found an intent audience; even his wife listened. The oldest boy, Larry, more science-minded at thirteen, showed less interest until his father, with shrewd premeditation, raised the question: why are left and right interchanged, but not up and down? That puzzle kept Larry occupied for the rest of the tale.

Janie, who was eight, had a complaint.

"The looking-glass room is just like ours," she pouted.

"Not really," her father said. "See the picture on the wall? In our room, the man's on the left; in there, he's on the right. Besides," he added quickly, aware that the distinction didn't impress her markedly—how could it at her age?—"we don't know what's in the rest of the house, through the archway and in all the other rooms. They may be altogether different. And the ones who live there stay out of this room which we can see." He was too perceptive and intelligent to invent any unpleasant tenants; the worst was a fat, elfish creature named Gnolfo, who robbed the refrigerator in the kitchen and could never be seen from this location. Once during the story Avery pretended to glimpse Gnolfo peering through the arch, and Bill verified it, adding rather uneasily, that the elf was small and hairy—but Bill was only five and not held to be a competent witness by his siblings . . .

It was a charming tableau for a paterfamilias: the five children, all look-alikes in their dark hair and big, brown eyes, but with different temperaments. Janie and Marcia were impish and apt to be challenging, while the three boys were more physical, taking Avery's logic as dependable even when the girls intuitively doubted. And Lottie—she belonged in the picture, too, he felt. Almost a Victorian wife: meek, biddable, sweet, and yet no lightweight mentally. She knew many classics, and played the piano like a concert artist. If only she didn't like Poulenc and some even more wild moderns so much—that didn't fit—yes, he was a lucky fellow to have such a family. Father had been so taken with his first three grandchildren that he'd put a nice sum of money in trust, and now Avery didn't need to do much work as a lawyer—lend the old family name to Winslow, Talcott, and Avery and show up at the office a few hours each week.

"Where does Gnolfo stay?" Brian demanded, standing close to the mirror. He was ten, and mature enough to act as a babysitter for his juniors, a job usually ducked by Larry as unworthy of a thirteen-year-old. Both boys were strong and vigorous, and Larry owned a .22, which he could shoot with considerable skill. Any prowler who came looking for trouble while the parents were away might be in for a shock, Avery thought, looking approvingly at Brian's sturdy body and resolute, if rather bovine, eyes.

"Upstairs," he told his son. "Not that it's laid out just like ours; I rather think it isn't. But then, we'll never know, will we?"

"Maybe we could get through some time," Janie suggested half-heartedly. She wasn't at all sure, at eight, that the mirror had another side facing a different world. Yet older people knew so many things kids hadn't learned yet, how *could* one be sure Daddy was making it up?

"It's possible—some day," Mr. Avery agreed, smiling. "Alice did, and she was a real girl—Alice Liddell." And when Larry, expecting this once to catch his father out, scoffed, he was shown, much to his annoyance, the facts in the encyclopedia. The squelch did wonders for Avery's status; the younger children would now just as soon doubt the next day's sunrise.

"The story will be continued tomorrow," Mr. Avery said at nine-thirty. "Now it's bedtime, except for Larry; he gets his extra half-hour."

"Not tomorrow, dear," Lottie reminded him. "We're going to the Randalls', remember?"

"I forgot, confound it," he said, irritated. He enjoyed his role at the fireside, monarch of all he surveyed. The one alotted him in other homes was considerably less exalted, thanks to his dormouse appearance and total lack of interest in modern matters. Then he said crisply: "Larry will be in charge, and all of you must stay in the house; I don't want anybody outside when there are no neighbors handy like in our old place. Anyhow, we'll be back by midnight. See that they're in bed at the usual time, son. And be there yourself before eleven."

Neither he nor his wife had any misgivings when they left the following evening. Although the house was isolated to a degree, the heavy doors locked, as did the windows. Larry was a manly fellow, and the .22 could be taken from the closet without his father's permission in an emergency.

After dinner, previously prepared by their mother, the children gathered in the living room, where a nice fire burned. If they felt reluctant to run about the upper floors while alone, it was perfectly natural. By day the children tended to split up into groups, pairs or even individuals, according to mood or type of play, but at night even a courageous thirteen-year-old had no pressing business in the dark attics above . . .

"Tell us about the looking-glass rooms," Bill lisped. "And the fat little boy with the funny name."

Larry felt flattered; it was seldom they treated him so like a second father. But he doubted his capacity as a bard.

"Well," he said uneasily, "there's not much to tell. It's a whole big house just like ours—"

"Daddy said it isn't," Janie interrupted.

"I mean it has other rooms, some on the same floor and some upstairs. But Gnolfo, he likes the kitchen, where the food is." He did his best from then on, but knew his audience was restive. He had almost lost them completely; only Bill watched the glass, when suddenly the child gave a squeak of dismay.

"I saw something!" Bill cried. "It was in the arch there."

"Don't be silly," Larry said. "If it was there, it would be in our arch here, too."

"Why?" Marcia demanded. "Who said so? That's a different room, actually; Daddy said so."

"I saw it," Bill said, his chubby face pale and strained. "I don't like that—that Nolfy. He's hairy and funny and jumps around . . ."

"Where did he go?" Brian asked.

"He came right into the looking-glass room, and over to the fireplace—*his* ol' fireplace, where you can't see it."

"Great!" Larry said in a sardonic voice. "You're the clever one." He grinned at the others. "Billy knows we can't prove Gnolfo's not behind the mantel—that's part of the looking-glass room we can't see." Then his face went blank with thought. "Wait a minute. If we had another mirror, and moved it back from the fireplace a few feet, and then looked in the big mirror—sure, then we'd see their fire. And that's one even Dad didn't think of!" he added proudly.

"Mom's got a pretty big mirror on her dresser," Brian said. "You and me could carry it down here easy, I bet."

"That's right," Larry said. "And that's just what we'll do. You kids wait here, and in a minute you'll see all the rest of the looking-glass room. We'll have some fun with Dad tomorrow, too."

He and Brian raced up the stairs, too excited to have any fear of the dark landing, and soon returned carrying the dresser mirror, lifted from its gimbals by four strong, eager hands.

They maneuvered it to the center of the room, while the other children darted in and out to keep tabs on the reflection. Finally Larry found a spot where, on peering into the bigger one, they could see in the smaller one's reflection, the fireplace of the looking-glass room.

Marcia saw it first, and whimpered; Bill began to scream; and Larry just froze, his eyes pits of horror.

The thing crouching there may have felt the children's collective gaze, for it rose to its full height of some three feet to glare at them. It had teeth and talons and great blank eyes, pitiless as the sun; dark, matted hair covered its body, which rippled continually with a terrible vitality like that of a centipede. Then it was on the mantel, first on the looking-glass side, and almost immediately on theirs . . .

When the Averys came into the house at eleven-forty and saw the living room, Lottie began to scream—shrill, toneless, repetitive notes that sounded like mechanical whistles. She kept them up for hours, even under heavy doses of morphine, and was silent only in death, two days later.

Mr. Avery looked at the remains of his children, and knew that all but one were dead. Janie's eyes showed that she was still alive, but it also held a wordless plea, as if she understood what was best; and her father, without knowing why, did what had to be done, giving the child release. Only then did he begin to whimper in a high, quavering voice nothing like his normal rich baritone. Later, he was indicted for murder, but a vegetable cares little about such things. . . .

A BRINK REALTY
SPECIAL!
HOUSE FOR SALE
OR LEASE
OWNER WILL SACRIFICE!
IDEAL FOR LARGE FAMILY

One of the more startling revelations I got from my first course in criminal law was that actions are not in themselves criminal. One must have the intention to commit a crime at the time the action takes place (mens rea, if you want the Latin of it).

That doesn't mean that you have to know that what you're doing is a crime; that comes under the tag, "Ignorance of the law is no excuse." In other words, If you come from a culture in which citizens as a matter of course slaughter sheep in the street and let the storm drains take care of the blood and offal, you are still guilty of a crime (a number of crimes including, I suppose, littering) if you do this same thing in a posh district of London. Of course, if you're the Iranian ambassador, you won't be charged because you have diplomatic immunity—which is not limited to diplomats from countries conforming to Western notions of civilization; but that's another matter.

The concept of criminal intent addresses what you thought you were doing, not whether or not you knew it was against the law. That is, if you thought you were backing up the car; and, unbeknownst to you, your neighbor's dog happened to be sleeping under the car;

you haven't committed a crime even though you have destroyed your neighbor's chattel.

You haven't committed murder if it was your neighbor and not his dog under the car, either. Always assuming that you didn't willfully crush the victim into the pavement.

That's where the insanity defense comes in. Like it or not, the concept is simple: somebody who's too crazy to know what he's doing can't willfully do anything. That doesn't mean that somebody who's shot up the mall, thinking that he was defending Earth from the invading Martians, ought to be loose on the street; and it certainly doesn't mean that there isn't grand scope for abuse.

But somebody who honestly doesn't know what he's doing can't be guilty of a crime.

There aren't a lot of good SF stories dealing with the law. This is one of the exceptions.

PRIVATE EYE

Henry Kuttner

The Forensic Sociologist looked closely at the image on the wall screen. Two figures were frozen there, one in the act of stabbing the other through the heart with an antique letter cutter, once used at Johns Hopkins for surgery. That was before the ultra-microtome, of course.

"As tricky a case as I've ever seen," the sociologist remarked. "If we can make a homicide charge stick on Sam Clay, I'll be a little surprised."

The tracer engineer twirled a dial and watched the figures on the screen repeat their actions. One—Sam Clay—snatched the letter cutter from a desk and plunged it into the other man's heart. The victim fell down dead. Clay started back in apparent horror. Then he dropped to his knees beside the twitching body and said wildly that he didn't mean it. The body drummed its heels upon the rug and was still.

"That last touch was nice," the engineer said.

"Well, I've got to make the preliminary survey," the sociologist sighed, settling in his dictachair and placing his fingers on the keyboard. "I doubt if I'll find any evidence. However, the analysis can come later. Where's Clay now?"

"His mouthpiece put in a *habeas mens*."

"I didn't think we'd be able to hold him. But it was worth trying. Imagine, just one shot of scop and he'd have told the truth. Ah, well. We'll do it the hard way, as usual. Start the tracer, will you? It won't make sense till we run it chronologically, but one must start somewhere. Good old Blackstone," the sociologist said, as, on the screen, Clay stood up, watching the corpse revive and arise, and then pulled the miraculously clean paper cutter out of its heart, all in reverse.

"Good old Blackstone," he repeated. "On the other hand, sometimes I wish I'd lived in Jeffrey's time. In those days, homicide was homicide."

Telepathy never came to much. Perhaps the developing faculty went underground in response to a familiar natural law after the new science appeared—omniscience. It wasn't really that, of course. It was a device for looking into the past. And it was limited to a fifty-year span; no chance of seeing the arrows at Agincourt or the homunculi of Bacon. It was sensitive enough to pick up the "fingerprints" of light and sound waves imprinted on matter, descramble and screen them, and reproduce the image of what had happened. After all, a man's shadow can be photographed on concrete, if he's unlucky enough to be caught in an atomic blast. Which is something. The shadow's about all there is left.

However, opening the past like a book didn't solve all problems. It took generations for the maze of complexities to iron itself out, though finally a tentative check-and-balance was reached. The right to kill has been sturdily defended by mankind since Cain rose up against Abel. A good many idealists quoted, "The voice of thy brother's blood crieth unto me from the ground," but that didn't stop the lobbyists and the pressure groups. Magna Carta was quoted in reply. The right to privacy was defended desperately.

And the curious upshot of this imbalance came when the act of homicide was declared nonpunishable, unless intent and forethought could be proved. Of course, it was considered at least naughty to fly in a rage and murder someone on impulse, and there was a nominal punishment—imprisonment, for example—but in practice this never worked, because so many defenses were possible. Temporary insanity. Undue provocation. Self-defense. Manslaughter, second-degree homicide, third degree, fourth degree—it went on like that. It was up to the State to prove that the killer had planned his killing in advance; only then would a jury convict. And the jury, of course, had to waive immunity and take a scop test, to prove the box hadn't been packed. But no defendant ever waived immunity.

A man's home wasn't his castle—not with the Eye able to enter it at will and scan his past. The device couldn't interpret, and it couldn't read his mind; it could only see and listen. Consequently the sole remaining fortress of privacy was the human mind. And that was defended to the last ditch. No truth-serum, no hypoanalysis, no third-degree, no leading questions.

If, by viewing the prisoner's past actions, the prosecution could prove forethought and intent, O.K.

Otherwise, Sam Clay would go scot-free. Superficially, it appeared as though Andrew Vanderman had, during a quarrel, struck Clay across the face with a stingaree whip. Anyone who has been stung by a Portuguese man-of-war can understand that, at this point, Clay could plead temporary insanity and self-defense, as well as undue provocation and possible justification. Only the curious cult of the Alaskan Flagellantes, who make the stingaree whips for their ceremonials, know how to endure the pain. The Flagellantes even like it, the pre-ritual drug they swallow transmutes pain into pleasure. Not having swallowed this drug, Sam Clay very naturally took steps to protect himself—irrational steps, perhaps, but quite logical and defensible ones.

Nobody but Clay knew that he had intended to kill Vanderman all along. That was the trouble. Clay couldn't understand why he felt so let down.

The screen flickered. It went dark. The engineer chuckled.

"My, my. Locked up in a dark closet at the age of four. What one of those old-time psychiatrists would have made of that. Or do I mean obimen? Shamans? I forget. They interpreted dreams, anyway."

"You're confused. It—"

"Astrologers! No, it wasn't either. The ones I mean went in for symbolism. They used to spin prayer wheels and say 'A rose is a rose is a rose,' didn't they? To free the unconscious mind?"

"You've got the typical layman's attitude toward antique psychiatric treatments."

"Well, maybe they had something, at that. Look at quinine and digitalis. The United Amazon natives used those long before science discovered them. But why use eye of newt and toe of frog? To impress the patient?"

"No, to convince themselves," the sociologist said. "In those days the study of mental aberrations drew potential psychotics, so naturally there was unnecessary mumbo-jumbo. Those medicos were trying to fix their own mental imbalance while they treated their patients. But it's science today, not a religion. We've found out how to allow for individual psychotic deviation in the psychiatrist himself, so we've got a better chance of finding true worth. However, let's get on with this. Try ultraviolet. Oh, never mind. Somebody's letting him out of that closet. The devil with it. I think we've cut back far enough. Even if he was frightened by a thunderstorm at the age of three months, that can be filed under Gestalt and ignored. Let's run through this chronologically. Give it the screening for . . . let's see. Incidents involving these persons: Vanderman, Mrs.

Vanderman, Josephine Wells—and these places: the office, Vanderman's apartment, Clay's place—"

"Got it."

"Later we can recheck for complicating factors. Right now we'll run the superficial survey. Verdict first, evidence later," he added, with a grin. "All we need is a motive—"

"What about this?"

A girl was talking to Sam Clay. The background was an apartment, grade B-2.

"I'm sorry, Sam. It's just that . . . well, these things happen."

"Yeah. Vanderman's got something I haven't got, apparently."

"I'm in love with him."

"Funny. I thought all along you were in love with me."

"So did I . . . for a while."

"Well, forget it. No, I'm not angry, Bea. I'll even wish you luck. But you must have been pretty certain how I'd react to this."

"I'm sorry—"

"Come to think of it, I've always let you call the shots. Always."

Secretly—and this the screen could not show—he thought: Let her? I wanted it that way. It was so much easier to leave the decisions up to her. Sure, she's dominant, but I guess I'm just the opposite. And now it's happened again.

It always happens. I was loaded with weight-cloths from the start. And I always felt I had to toe the line, or else. Vanderman—that cocky, arrogant air of his. Reminds me of somebody. I was locked up in a dark place, I couldn't breathe. I forget. What . . . who . . . my father. No, I don't remember. But my life's been like that. He always watched me, and I always thought some day I'd do what *I* wanted—but I never did. Too late now. He's been dead quite a while.

He was always so sure I'd knuckle under. If I'd only defied him once—

Somebody's always pushing me in and closing the door. So I can't use my abilities. I can't prove I'm competent. Prove it to myself, to my father, to Bea, to the whole world. If only I could—I'd like to push Vanderman into a dark place and lock the door. A dark place, like a coffin. It would be satisfying to surprise him that way. It would be fine if I killed Andrew Vanderman.

"Well, that's the beginning of a motive," the sociologist said. "Still, lots of people get jilted and don't turn homicidal. Carry on."

"In my opinion, Bea attracted him because he wanted to be bossed," the engineer remarked. "He'd given up."

"Protective passivity."

The wire taps spun through the screening apparatus. A new scene showed on the oblong panel. It was the Paradise Bar.

Anywhere you sat in the Paradise Bar, a competent robot analyzer instantly studied your complexion and facial angles, and switched on lights, in varying tints and intensities, that showed you off to best advantage. The joint was popular for business deals. A swindler could look like an honest man there. It was also popular with women and slightly passé teleo talent. Sam Clay looked rather like an ascetic young saint. Andrew Vanderman looked noble, in a grim way, like Richard Coeur-de-Leon offering Saladin his freedom, though he knew it wasn't really a bright thing to do. *Noblesse oblige*, his firm jaw seemed to say, as he picked up the silver decanter and poured. In ordinary light, Vanderman looked slightly more like a handsome bulldog. Also, away from the Paradise Bar, he was redder around the chops, a choleric man.

"As to that deal we were discussing," Clay said, "you can go to—"

The censoring juke box blared out a covering bar or two.

Vanderman's reply was unheard as the music got briefly louder, and the lights shifted rapidly to keep place with his sudden flush.

"It's perfectly easy to outwit these censors," Clay said. "They're keyed to familiar terms of profane abuse, not to circumlocutions. If I said that the arrangement of your chromosomes would have surprised your father . . . you see?" He was right. The music stayed soft.

Vanderman swallowed nothing. "Take it easy," he said. "I can see why you're upset. Let me say first of all—"

"Hijo—"

But the censor was proficient in Spanish dialects. Vanderman was spared hearing another insult.

"—that I offered you a job because I think you're a very capable man. You have potentialities. It's not a bribe. Our personal affairs should be kept out of this."

"All the same, Bea was engaged to me."

"Clay, are you drunk?"

"Yes," Clay said, and threw his drink into Vanderman's face. The music began to play Wagner very, very loudly. A few minutes later, when the waiters interfered, Clay was supine and bloody, with a mashed nose and a bruised cheek. Vanderman had skinned his knuckles.

"That's a motive," the engineer said.

"Yes, it is, isn't it? But why did Clay wait a year and a half? And remember what happened later. I wonder if the murder itself was just a symbol? If Vanderman represented, say, what Clay considered the tyrannical and oppressive force of society in general—synthesized in the representative image . . . oh, nonsense. Obviously Clay was trying to prove something to himself, though. Suppose you cut forward now. I want to see this in normal chronology, not backward. What's the next selection?"

"Very suspicious. Clay got his nose fixed up and then went to a murder trial."

He thought: I can't breathe. Too crowded in here. Shut up in a box, a closet, a coffin, ignored by the spectators and the vested authority on the bench. What would I do if I were in the dock, like that chap? Suppose they convicted? That would spoil it all. Another dark place—If I'd inherited the right genes, I'd have been strong enough to beat up Vanderman. But I've been pushed around too long.

I keep remembering that song.

Stray in the herd and the boss said kill it,
So I shot him in the rump with the handle of a skillet.

A deadly weapon that's in normal usage wouldn't appear dangerous. But if it could be used homicidally —No, the Eye could check on that. All you can conceal these days is motive. But couldn't the trick be reversed? Suppose I got Vanderman to attack me with what he thought was the handle of a skillet, but which I knew was a deadly weapon—

The trial Sam Clay was watching was fairly routine. One man had killed another. Counsel for the defense contended that the homicide had been a matter of impulse, and that, as a matter of fact, only assault and battery plus culpable negligence at worst, could be proved, and the latter was canceled by an Act of God. The fact that the defendant inherited the decedent's fortune, in Martial oil, made no difference. Temporary insanity was the plea.

The prosecuting attorney showed films of what had

happened before the fact. True, the victim hadn't been killed by the blow, merely stunned. But the affair had occurred on an isolated beach, and when the tide came in—

Act of God, the defense repeated hastily.

The screen showed the defendant, some days before his crime, looking up the tide-table in a news tape. He also, it appeared, visited the site and asked a passing stranger if the beach was often crowded. "Nope," the stranger said, "it ain't crowded after sundown. Gits too cold. Won't do you no good, though. Too cold to swim then."

One side matched *Actus non facit reum, nisi mens sit rea*—"The act does not make a man guilty, unless the mind be also guilty"—against *Acta exteriora indicant interiora secreta*—"By the outward acts we are to judge of the inward thoughts." Latin legal basics were still valid, up to a point. A man's past remained sacrosanct, provided—and here was the joker—that he possessed the right citizenship. And anyone accused of a capital crime was automatically suspended from the citizenship until his innocence had been established.

Also, no past-tracing evidence could be introduced into a trial unless it could be proved that it had direct connection with the crime. The average citizen did have a right of privacy against tracing. Only if accused of a serious crime was that forfeit, and even then evidence uncovered could be used only in correlation with the immediate charge. There were various loopholes, of course, but theoretically a man was safe from espionage as long as he stayed within the law.

Now a defendant stood in the dock, his past opened. The prosecution showed recordings of a ginger blonde blackmailing him, and that clinched the motive and the verdict—guilty. The condemned man was led off in tears. Clay got up and walked out of the court. From his appearance he seemed to be thinking.

*   *   *

He was. He had decided that there was only one possible way in which he could kill Vanderman and get away with it. He couldn't conceal the deed itself, nor the actions leading up to it, nor any written or spoken word. All he could hide were his own thoughts. And, without otherwise betraying himself, he'd have to kill Vanderman so that his act would appear justified. Which meant covering his tracks for yesterday as well as for tomorrow and tomorrow.

Now, thought Clay, this much can be assumed: If I stand to lose by Vanderman's death instead of gaining, that will help considerably. I must juggle that somehow. But I mustn't forget that at present I have an obvious motive. First, he stole Bea. Second, he beat me up.

So I must make it seem as though he's done me a favor—somehow.

I must have an opportunity to study Vanderman carefully, and it must be a normal, logical, waterproof opportunity. Private secretary. Something like that. The Eye's in the future now, after the fact, but it's watching me—

I must remember that. *It's watching me now!*

All right. Normally, I'd have thought of murder, at this point. That can't and shouldn't be disguised. I must work out of the mood gradually, but meanwhile—

He smiled.

Going off to buy a gun, he felt uncomfortable, as though that prescient Eye, years in the future, could with a wink summon the police. But it was separated from him by a barrier of time that only the natural processes could shorten. And, in fact, it had been watching him since his birth. You could look at it that way—

He could defy it. The Eye couldn't read thoughts.

He bought the gun and lay in wait for Vanderman in a dark alley. But first he got thoroughly drunk. Drunk enough to satisfy the Eye.

After that—

* * *

"Feel better now?" Vanderman asked, pouring another coffee.

Clay buried his face in his hands.

"I was crazy," he said, his voice muffled. "I must have been. You'd better t-turn me over to the police."

"We can forget about that end of it, Clay. You were drunk, that's all. And I . . . well, I—"

"I pull a gun on you . . . try to kill you . . . and you bring me up to your place and—"

"You didn't use that gun, Clay. Remember that. You're no killer. All this has been my fault. I needn't have been so blasted tough with you," Vanderman said, looking like Coeur-de-Leon in spite of uncalculated amber fluorescence.

"I'm no good. I'm a failure. Every time I try to do something, a man like you comes along and does it better. I'm a second-rater."

"Clay, stop talking like that. You're just upset, that's all. Listen to me. You're going to straighten up. I'm going to see that you do. Starting tomorrow, we'll work something out. Now drink your coffee."

"You know," Clay said, "you're quite a guy."

So the magnanimous idiot's fallen for it, Clay thought, as he was drifting happily off to sleep. Fine. That begins to take care of the Eye. Moreover, it starts the ball rolling with Vanderman. Let a man do you a favor and he's your pal. Well, Vanderman's going to do me a lot more favors. In fact, before I'm through, I'll have every motive for wanting to keep him alive.

Every motive visible to the naked Eye.

Probably Clay had not heretofore applied his talents in the right direction, for there was nothing second-rate about the way he executed his homicide plan. In that, he proved very capable. He needed a suitable channel for his ability, and perhaps he needed a patron.

Vanderman fulfilled that function; probably it salved his conscience for stealing Bea. Being the man he was, Vanderman needed to avoid even the appearance of ignobility. Naturally strong and ruthless, he told himself he was sentimental. His sentimentality never reached the point of actually inconveniencing him, and Clay knew enough to stay within the limits.

Nevertheless it is nerve-racking to know you're living under the scrutiny of an extratemporal Eye. As he walked into the lobby of the V Building a month later, Clay realized that light-vibrations reflected from his own body were driving irretrievably into the polished onyx walls and floor, photographing themselves there, waiting for a machine to unlock them, some day, some time, for some man perhaps in this very city, who as yet didn't know even the name of Sam Clay. Then, sitting in his relaxer in the spiral lift moving swiftly up inside the walls, he knew that those walls were capturing his image, stealing it, like some superstition he remembered . . . ah?

Vanderman's private secretary greeted him. Clay let his gaze wander freely across that young person's neatly-dressed figure and mildly attractive face. She said that Mr. Vanderman was out, and the appointment was for three, not two, wasn't it? Clay referred to a notebook. He snapped his fingers.

"Three—you're right, Miss Wells. I was so sure it was two I didn't even bother to check up. Do you think he might be back sooner? I mean, is he out, or in conference?"

"He's out, all right, Mr. Clay," Miss Wells said. "I don't think he'll be back much sooner than three. I'm sorry."

"Well, may I wait in here?"

She smiled at him efficiently. "Of course. There's a stereo and the magazine spools are in that case."

She went back to her work, and Clay skimmed through an article about the care and handling of lunar filchards.

It gave him an opportunity to start a conversation by asking Miss Wells if she liked filchards. It turned out that she had no opinion whatsoever of filchards but the ice had been broken.

This is the cocktail acquaintance, Clay thought. I may have a broken heart, but, naturally, I'm lonesome.

The trick wasn't to get engaged to Miss Wells so much as to fall in love with her convincingly. The Eye never slept. Clay was beginning to wake at night with a nervous start, and lie there looking up at the ceiling. But darkness was no shield.

"The question is," said the sociologist at this point, "whether or not Clay was acting for an audience."

"You mean us?"

"Exactly. It just occurred to me. Do you think he's been behaving perfectly naturally?"

The engineer pondered.

"I'd say yes. A man doesn't marry a girl only to carry out some other plan, does he? After all, he'd get himself involved in a whole new batch of responsibilities."

"Clay hasn't married Josephine Wells yet, however," the sociologist countered. "Besides, that responsibility angle might have applied a few hundred years ago, but not now." He went off at random. "Imagine a society where, after divorce, a man was forced to support a perfectly healthy, competent woman! It was vestigial, I know—a throwback to the days when only males could earn a living—but imagine the sort of women who were willing to accept such support. That was reversion to infancy if I ever—"

The engineer coughed.

"Oh," the sociologist said. "Oh . . . yes. The question is, would Clay have got himself engaged to a woman unless he really—"

"Engagements can be broken."

"This one hasn't been broken yet, as far as we know. And *we* know."

"A normal man wouldn't plan on marrying a girl he didn't care anything about, unless he had some stronger motive—I'll go along that far."

"But how normal is Clay?" the sociologist wondered. "Did he know in advance we'd check back on his past? Did you notice that he cheated at solitaire?"

"Proving?"

"There are all kinds of trivial things you don't do if you think people are looking. Picking up a penny in the street, drinking soup out of the bowl, posing before a mirror—the sort of foolish or petty things everyone does when alone. Either Clay's innocent, or he's a very clever man—"

He was a very clever man. He never intended the engagement to get as far as marriage, though he knew that in one respect marriage would be a precaution. If a man talks in his sleep, his wife will certainly mention the fact. Clay considered gagging himself at night if the necessity should arise. Then he realized that if he talked in his sleep at all, there was no insurance against talking too much the very first time he had an auditor. He couldn't risk such a break. But there was no necessity, after all. Clay's problem, when he thought it over, was simply: How can I be sure I don't talk in my sleep?

He solved that easily enough by renting a narcohypnotic supplementary course in common trade dialects. This involved studying while awake and getting the information repeated in his ear during slumber. As a necessary preparation for the course, he was instructed to set up a recorder and chart the depth of his sleep, so the narcohypnosis could be keyed to his individual rhythms. He did this several times, rechecked once a month thereafter, and was satisfied. There was no need to gag himself at night.

He was glad to sleep provided he didn't dream. He had to take sedatives after a while. At night, there was relief from the knowledge that an Eye watched him always, an Eye that could bring him to justice, an Eye whose omnipotence he could not challenge in the open. But he dreamed about the Eye.

Vanderman had given him a job in the organization, which was enormous. Clay was merely a cog, which suited him well enough, for the moment. He didn't want any more favors yet. Not till he had found out the extent of Miss Wells' duties—Josephine, her Christian name was. That took several months, but by that time friendship was ripening into affection. So Clay asked Vanderman for another job. He specified. It wasn't obvious, but he was asking for work that would, presently, fit him for Miss Wells' duties.

Vanderman probably still felt guilty about Bea; he'd married her and she was in Antarctica now, at the Casino. Vanderman was due to join her, so he scribbled a memorandum, wished Clay good luck, and went to Antarctica, bothered by no stray pangs of conscience. Clay improved the hour by courting Josephine ardently.

From what he had heard about the new Mrs. Vanderman, he felt secretly relieved. Not long ago, when he had been content to remain passive, the increasing dominance of Bea would have satisfied him, but no more. He was learning self-reliance, and liked it. These days, Bea was behaving rather badly. Given all the money and freedom she could use, she had too much time on her hands. Once in a while Clay heard rumors that made him smile secretly. Vanderman wasn't having an easy time of it. A dominant character, Bea—but Vanderman was no weakling himself.

After a while Clay told his employer he wanted to marry Josephine Wells. "I guess that makes us square," he said. "You took Bea away from me and I'm taking Josie away from you."

"Now wait a minute," Vanderman said. "I hope you don't—"

"My fiancée, your secretary. That's all. The thing is, Josie and I are in love." He poured it on, but carefully.

It was easier to deceive Vanderman than the Eye, with its trained technicians and forensic sociologists looking through it. He thought, sometimes, of those medieval pictures of an immense eye, and that remainded him of something vague and distressing, though he couldn't isolate the memory.

After all, what could Vanderman do? He arranged to have Clay given a raise. Josephine, always conscientious, offered to keep on working for a while, till office routine was straightened out, but it never did get straightened out, somehow. Clay deftly saw to that by keeping Josephine busy. She didn't have to bring work home to her apartment, but she brought it, and Clay gradually began to help her when he dropped by. His job, plus the narco-hypnotic courses, had already trained him for this sort of tricky organizational work. Vanderman's business was highly specialized—planet-wide exports and imports, and what with keeping track of specific groups, seasonal trends, sectarian holidays, and so forth, Josephine, as a sort of animated memorandum book for Vanderman, had a more than full-time job.

She and Clay postponed marriage for a time. Clay—naturally enough—began to appear mildly jealous of Josephine's work, and she said she'd quit soon. But one night she stayed on at the office, and he went out in a pet and got drunk. It just happened to be raining that night. Clay got tight enough to walk unprotected through the drizzle, and to fall asleep at home in his wet clothes. He came down with influenza. As he was recovering, Josephine got it.

Under the circumstances, Clay stepped in—purely a temporary job—and took over his fiancée's duties. Office routine was extremely complicated that week, and only Clay knew the ins and outs of it. The arrangement saved Vanderman a certain amount of inconvenience, and, when the situation resolved itself, Josephine had a subsidiary job and Clay was Vanderman's private secretary.

"I'd better know more about him," Clay said to Josephine. "After all, there must be a lot of habits and foibles he's got that need to be catered to. If he wants lunch ordered up, I don't want to get smoked tongue and find out he's allergic to it. What about his hobbies?"

But he was careful not to pump Josephine too hard, because of the Eye. He still needed sedatives to sleep.

The sociologist rubbed his forehead.

"Let's take a break," he suggested. "Why does a guy want to commit murder anyway?"

"For profit, one sort or another."

"Only partly, I'd say. The other part is an unconscious desire to be punished—usually for something else. That's why you get accident prones. Ever think about what happens to murderers who feel guilty and yet who aren't punished by the law? They must live a rotten sort of life—always accidentally stepping in front of speedsters, cutting themselves with an ax—accidentally; accidentally touching wires full of juice—"

"Conscience, eh?"

"A long time ago, people thought God sat in the sky with a telescope and watched everything they did. They really lived pretty carefully in the Middle Ages—the first Middle Ages, I mean. Then there was the era of disbelief, when people had nothing to believe in very strongly—and finally we get this." He nodded toward the screen. "A universal memory. By extension, it's a universal social conscience, an externalized one. It's exactly the same as the medieval concept of God— omniscience."

"But not omnipotence."

"Mm."

All in all, Clay kept the Eye in mind for a year and a half. Before he said or did anything whatsoever, he reminded himself of the Eye, and made certain that he wasn't revealing his motive to the judging future. Of course, there was—would be—an Ear, too, but that was a little too absurd. One couldn't visualize a large, disembodied Ear decorating the wall like a plate in a plate holder. All the same, whatever he said would be as important evidence—some time—as what he did. So Sam Clay was very careful indeed, and behaved like Caesar's wife. He wasn't exactly defying authority, but he was certainly circumventing it.

Superficially Vanderman was more like Caesar, and his wife was not above reproach, these days. She had too much money to play with. And she was finding her husband too strong-willed a person to be completely satisfactory. There was enough of the matriarch in Bea to make her feel rebellion against Andrew Vanderman, and there was a certain lack of romance. Vanderman had little time for her. He was busy these days, involved with a whole string of deals which demanded much of his time. Clay, of course, had something to do with that. His interest in his new work was most laudable. He stayed up nights plotting and planning as though expecting Vanderman to make him a full partner. In fact, he even suggested this possibility to Josephine. He wanted it on the record. The marriage date had been set, and Clay wanted to move before then; he had no intention of being drawn into a marriage of convenience after the necessity had been removed.

One thing he did, which had to be handled carefully, was to get the whip. Now Vanderman was a fingerer. He liked to have something in his hands while he talked. Usually it was a crystalline paper weight, with a miniature thunderstorm in it, complete with lightning, when it was shaken. Clay put this where Vanderman would be sure to knock it off and break it. Meanwhile, he had plugged one deal with Callisto Ranches for the sole purpose of getting a whip for Vanderman's desk. The natives were proud of their leatherwork and their silver-smithing, and a nominal makeweight always went with every deal they closed.

Thus, presently, a handsome miniature whip, with Vanderman's initials on it, lay on the desk, coiled into a loop, acting as a paper weight except when he picked it up and played with it while he talked.

The other weapon Clay wanted was already there—an antique paper knife, once called a surgical scalpel. He never let his gaze rest on it too long, because of the Eye.

The other whip came. He absentmindedly put it in his desk and pretended to forget it. It was a sample of the whips made by the Alaskan Flagellantes for use in their ceremonies, and was wanted because of some research being made into the pain-neutralizing drugs the Flagellantes used. Clay, of course, had engineered this deal, too. There was nothing suspicious about that; the firm stood to make a sound profit. In fact, Vanderman had promised him a percentage bonus at the end of the year on every deal he triggered. It would be quite a lot. It was December, a year and a half had passed since Clay first recognized that the Eye would seek him out.

He felt fine. He was careful about the sedatives, and his nerves, though jangled, were nowhere near the snapping point. It had been a strain, but he had trained himself so that he would make no slips. He visualized the Eye in the walls, in the ceiling, in the sky, everywhere he went. It was the only way to play completely safe. And very soon now it would pay off. But he would have to do it soon; such a nervous strain could not be continued indefinitely.

A few details remained. He carefully arranged matters —under the Eye's very nose, so to speak—so that he was offered a well-paying position with another firm. He turned it down.

And, one night, an emergency happened to arise so that Clay, very logically, had to go to Vanderman's apartment.

Vanderman wasn't there. Bea was. She had quarreled violently with her husband. Moreover, she had been drinking. (This, too, he had expected.) If the situation had not worked out exactly as he wanted, he would have tried again—and again—but there was no need.

Clay was a little politer than necessary. Perhaps too polite, certainly Bea, that incipient matriarch, was led down the garden path, a direction she was not unwilling to take. After all, she had married Vanderman for his money, found him as dominant as herself, and now saw Clay as an exaggerated symbol of both romance and masculine submissiveness.

The camera eye hidden in the wall, in a decorative bas-relief, was grinding away busily, spooling up its wire-tape in a way that indicated Vanderman was a suspicious as well as a jealous husband. But Clay knew about this gadget, too. At the suitable moment he stumbled against the wall in such a fashion that the device broke. Then, with only that other Eye spying on him, he suddenly became so virtuous that it was a pity Vanderman couldn't witness his *volte* face.

"Listen, Bea," he said, "I'm sorry, but I didn't understand. It's no good. I'm not in love with you any more. I was once, sure, but that was quite a while ago. There's somebody else, and you ought to know it by now."

"You still love me," Bea said with intoxicated firmness. "We belong together."

"Bea. Please. I hate to have to say this, but I'm grateful to Andrew Vanderman for marrying you. I . . . well, you got what you wanted, and I'm getting what I want. Let's leave it at that."

"I'm used to getting what *I* want, Sam. Opposition is something I don't like. Especially when I know you really—"

She said a good deal more, and so did Clay—he was perhaps unnecessarily harsh. But he had to make the point, for the Eye, that he was no longer jealous of Vanderman.

He made the point.

*   *   *

The next morning he got to the office before Vanderman, cleaned up his desk, and discovered the stingaree whip still in its box. "Oops," he said, snapping his fingers—the Eye watched, and this was the crucial period. Perhaps it would all be over within the hour. Every move from now on would have to be specially calculated in advance, and there could be no slightest deviation. The Eye was everywhere—literally everywhere.

He opened the box, took out the whip, and went into the inner sanctum. He tossed the whip on Vanderman's desk, so carelessly that a stylus rack toppled. Clay rearranged everything, leaving the stingaree whip near the edge of the desk, and placing the Callistan silver-leather whip at the back, half concealed behind the interoffice visor-box. He didn't allow himself more than a casual sweeping glance to make sure the paper knife as still there.

Then he went out for coffee.

Half an hour later he got back, picked up a few letters for signature from the rack, and walked into Vanderman's office. Vanderman looked up from behind his desk. He had changed a little in a year and a half; he was looking older, less noble, more like an aging bull-dog. Once, Clay thought coldly, this man stole my fiancée and beat me up.

Careful. Remember the Eye.

There was no need to do anything but follow the plan and let events take their course. Vanderman had seen the spy films, all right, up to the point where they had gone blank, when Clay fell against the wall. Obviously he hadn't really expected Clay to show up this morning. But to see the louse grinning hello, walking across the room, putting some letters down on his desk—!

Clay was counting on Vanderman's short temper, which had not improved over the months. Obviously the man had been simply sitting there, thinking unpleasant thoughts, and just as Clay had known would happen, he'd picked up the whip and begun to finger it. But it was the stingaree whip this time.

"Morning," Clay said cheerfully to his stunned employer. His smile became one-sided. "I've been waiting for you to check this letter to the Kirghiz kovar-breeders. Can we find a market for two thousand of those ornamental horns?"

It was at this point that Vanderman, bellowing, jumped to his feet, swung the whip, and sloshed Clay across the face. There is probably nothing more painful than the bite of a stingaree whip.

Clay staggered back. He had not known it would hurt so much. For an instant the shock of the blow knocked every other consideration out of his head, and blind anger was all that remained.

Remember the Eye!

He remembered it. There were dozens of trained men watching everything he did just now. Literally he stood on an open stage surrounded by intent observers who made notes on every expression of his face, every muscular flection, every breath he drew.

In a moment Vanderman would be dead—but Sam Clay would not be alone. An invisible audience from the future was fixing him with cold, calculating eyes. He had one more thing to do and the job would be over. Do it—carefully, carefully!—while they watched.

Time stopped for him. The *job* would be over.

It was very curious. He had rehearsed this series of actions so often in the privacy of his mind that his body was going through with it now, without further instructions. His body staggered back from the blow, recovered balance, glared at Vanderman in shocked fury, poised for a dive at that paper knife in plain sight on the desk.

That was what the outward and visible Sam Clay was doing. But the inward and spiritual Sam Clay went through quite a different series of actions.

The job would be over.

And what was he going to do after that?

The inward and spiritual murderer stood fixed with dismay and surprise, staring at a perfectly empty future. He had never looked beyond this moment. He had made no plans for his life beyond the death of Vanderman. But now—he had no enemy but Vanderman. When Vanderman was dead, what would he fix upon to orient his life? What would he work at then? His job would be gone, too. And he liked his job.

Suddenly he knew how much he liked it. He was good at it. For the first time in his life, he had found a job he could do really well.

You can't live a year and a half in a new environment without acquiring new goals. The change had come imperceptively. He was a good operator; he'd discovered that he could be successful. He didn't have to kill Vanderman to prove that to himself. He'd proved it already without committing murder.

In that time-stasis which had brought everything to a full stop he looked at Vanderman's red face and he thought of Bea, and of Vanderman as he had come to know him—and he didn't want to be a murderer.

He didn't want Vanderman dead. He didn't want Bea. The thought of her made him feel a little sick. Perhaps that was because he himself had changed from passive to active. He no longer wanted or needed a dominant woman. He could make his own decisions. If he were choosing now, it would be someone more like Josephine—

Josephine. That image before his mind's stilled eye was suddenly very pleasant. Josephine with her mild, calm prettiness, her admiration for Sam Clay the successful business man, the rising young importer in Vanderman, Inc. Josephine whom he was going to marry— Of course he was going to marry her. He loved Josephine. He loved his job. All he wanted was the status quo, exactly as he had achieved it. Everything was perfect right now—as of maybe thirty seconds ago.

But that was a long time ago—thirty seconds. A lot can happen in half a minute. A lot had happened. Vanderman was coming at him again, the whip raised. Clay's nerves crawled at the anticipation of its burning impact across his face a second time. If he could get hold of Vanderman's wrist before he struck again—if he could talk fast enough—

The crooked smile was still on his face. It was part of the pattern, in some dim way he did not quite understand. He was acting in response to conditioned reflexes set up over a period of many months of rigid self-training. His body was already in action. All that had taken place in his mind had happened so fast there was no physical hiatus at all. His body knew its job and it was doing the job. It was lunging forward toward the desk and the knife, and he could not stop it.

All this had happened before. It had happened in his mind, the only place where Sam Clay had known real freedom in the past year and a half. In all that time he had forced himself to realize that the Eye was watching every outward move he made. He had planned each action in advance and schooled himself to carry it through. Scarcely once had he let himself act purely on impulse. Only in following the plan exactly was there safety. He had indoctrinated himself too successfully.

Something was wrong. This wasn't what he'd wanted. He was still afraid, weak, failing—

He lurched against the desk, clawed at the paper knife, and, knowing failure, drove it into Vanderman's heart.

"It's a tricky case," the forensic sociologist said to the engineer. "Very tricky."

"Want me to run it again?"

"No, not right now. I'd like to think it over. Clay . . . that firm that offered him another job. The offer's withdrawn now, isn't it? Yes, I remember—they're fussy about the morals of their employees. It's insurance or something, I don't know. Motive. Motive, now."

The sociologist looked at the engineer.

The engineer said: "A year and a half ago he had a motive. But a week ago he had everything to lose and nothing to gain. He's lost his job and that bonus, he doesn't want Mrs. Vanderman any more, and as for that beating Vanderman once gave him . . . ah?"

"Well, he did try to shoot Vanderman once, and he couldn't, remember? Even though he was full of Dutch courage. But—something's wrong. Clay's been avoiding even the appearance of evil a little too carefully. Only I can't put my finger on anything, blast it."

"What about tracing back his life further? We only got to his fourth year."

"There couldn't be anything useful that long ago. It's obvious he was afraid of his father and hated him, too. Typical stuff, basic psych. The father symbolizes judgment to him. I'm very much afraid Sam Clay is going to get off scot-free."

"But if you think there's something haywire—"

"The burden of proof is up to us," the sociologist said.

The visor sang. A voice spoke softly.

"No, I haven't got the answer yet. Now? All right. I'll drop over."

He stood up.

"The D. A. wants a consultation. I'm not hopeful, though. I'm afraid the State's going to lose this case. That's the trouble with the externalized conscience—"

He didn't amplify. He went out, shaking his head, leaving the engineer staring speculatively at the screen. But within five minutes he was assigned to another job—the bureau was understaffed—and he didn't have a chance to investigate on his own until a week later. Then it didn't matter any more.

*   *   *

For, a week later, Sam Clay was walking out of the court an acquitted man. Bea Vanderman was waiting for him at the foot of the ramp. She wore black, but obviously her heart wasn't in it.

"Sam," she said.

He looked at her.

He felt a little dazed. It was all over. Everything had worked out exactly according to plan. And nobody was watching him now. The Eye had closed. The invisible audience had put on its hats and coats and left the theater of Sam Clay's private life. From now on he could do and say precisely what he liked, with no censoring watcher's omnipresence to check him. He could act on impulse again.

He had outwitted society. He had outwitted the Eye and all its minions in all their technological glory. He, Sam Clay, private citizen. It was a wonderful thing, and he could not understand why it left him feeling so flat.

That had been a nonsensical moment, just before the murder. The moment of relenting. They say you get the same instant frantic rejection on the verge of a good many important decisions—just before you marry, for instance. Or—what was it? Some other common instance he'd often heard of. For a second it eluded him. Then he had it. The hour before marriage—and the instant after suicide. After you've pulled the trigger, or jumped off the bridge. The instant of wild revulsion when you'd give anything to undo the irrevocable. Only, you can't. It's too late. The thing is done.

Well, he'd been a fool, Luckily, it *had* been too late. His body took over and forced him to success he'd trained it for. About the job—it didn't matter. He'd get another. He'd proved himself capable. If he could outwit the Eye itself, what job existed he couldn't lick if he tried? Except—nobody knew exactly how good he was. How could he prove his capabilities? It was infuriating to achieve such phenomenal success after a lifetime of failures, and never to get the credit for it. How many men must have tried and failed where he had tried and succeeded? Rich men, successful men, brilliant men who had yet failed in the final test of all—the contest with the Eye, their own live at stake. Only Sam Clay had passed that most important test in the world—and he could never claim credit for it.

". . . knew they wouldn't convict," Bea's complacent voice was saying.

Clay blinked at her. "What?"

"I said I'm so glad you're free, darling. I knew they wouldn't convict you. I knew that from the very beginning." She smiled at him, and for the first time it occurred to him that Bea looked a little like a bulldog. It was something about her lower jaw. He thought that when her teeth were closed together the lower set probably rested just outside the upper. He had an instant's impulse to ask her about it. Then he decided he had better not.

"You knew, did you?" he said.

She squeezed his arm. What an ugly lower jaw that was. How odd he'd never noticed it before. And behind the heavy lashes, how small her eyes were. How mean.

"Let's go where we can be alone," Bea said, clinging to him. "There's such a lot to talk about."

"We *are* alone," Clay said, diverted for an instant to his original thoughts. "Nobody's watching." He glanced up at the sky and down at the mosaic pavement. He drew a long breath and let it out slowly. "Nobody," he said.

"My speeder's parked right over here. We can—"

"Sorry Bea."

"What do you mean?"

"I've got business to attend to."

"Forget business. Don't you understand that we're free now, both of us?"

He had a horrible feeling he knew what she meant.

"Wait a minute," he said, because this seemed the

quickest way to end it. "I killed your husband, Bea. Don't forget that."

"You were acquitted. It was self-defense. The court said so."

"It—" He paused, glanced up quickly at the high wall of the Justice Building, and began a one-sided, mirthless smile. It was all right; there was no Eye now. There never would be, again. He was unwatched.

"You mustn't feel guilty, even within yourself," Bea said firmly. "It wasn't your fault. It simply wasn't. You've got to remember that. You *couldn't* have killed Andrew except by accident, Sam, so—"

"What? What do you mean by that?"

"Well, after all. I know the prosecution kept trying to prove you'd planned to kill Andrew all along, but you mustn't let what they said put any ideas in your head. I know you, Sam. I knew Andrew. You couldn't have planned a thing like that, and even if you had, it wouldn't have worked."

The half-smile died.

"It wouldn't?"

She looked at him steadily.

"Why, you couldn't have managed it," she said. "Andrew was the better man, and we both know it. He'd have been too clever to fall for anything—"

"Anything a second-rater like me could dream up?" Clay swallowed. His lips tightened. "Even you—What's the idea? What's your angle now—that we second-raters ought to get together?"

"Come on," she said, and slipped her arm through his. Clay hung back for a second. Then he scowled, looked back at the Justice Building, and followed Bea toward her speeder.

The engineer had a free period. He was finally able to investigate Sam Clay's early childhood. It was purely academic now, but he liked to indulge his curiosity. He traced Clay back to the dark closet, when the boy was four, and used ultra-violet. Sam was huddled in a corner, crying silently, staring up with frightened eyes at a top shelf.

What was on that shelf the engineer could not see.

He kept the beam focused on the closet and cast back rapidly through time. The closet often opened and closed, and sometimes Sam Clay was locked in it as punishment, but the upper shelf held its mystery until—

It was in reverse. A woman reached to that shelf, took down an object, walked backward out of the closet to Sam Clay's bedroom, and went to the wall by the door. This was unusual, for generally it was Sam's father who was warden of the closet.

She hung up a framed picture of a single huge staring eye floating in space. There was a legend under it. The letters spelled out: THOU GOD SEEST ME.

The engineer kept on tracing. After awhile it was night. The child was in bed, sitting up wide-eyed, afraid. A man's footsteps sounded on the stair. The scanner told all secrets but those of the inner mind. The man was Sam's father, coming up to punish him for some childish crime committed earlier. Moonlight fell upon the wall beyond which the footsteps approached showing how the wall quivered a little to the vibrations of the feet, and the Eye in its frame quivered, too. The boy seemed to brace himself. A defiant half-smile showed on his mouth, crooked, unsteady.

This time he'd keep that smile, no matter what happened. When it was over he'd still have it, so his father could see it, and the Eye could see it and they'd know he hadn't given in. He hadn't . . . he—

The door opened.

He couldn't help it. The smile faded and was gone.

"Well, what was eating him?" the engineer demanded.

The sociologist shrugged. "You could say he never did really grow up. It's axiomatic that boys go through a phase of rivalry with their fathers. Usually that's sublimated; the child grows up and wins, in one way or another. But Sam Clay didn't. I suspect he developed an externalized conscience very early. Symbolizing partly his father, partly God, an Eye and society—which fulfills the role of protective, punishing parent, you know."

"It still isn't evidence."

"We aren't going to get any evidence on Sam Clay. But that doesn't mean he's got away with anything, you know. He's always been afraid to assume the responsibilities of maturity. He never took on an optimum challenge. He was afraid to succeed at anything because that symbolic Eye of his might smack him down. When he was a kid, he might have solved his entire problem by kicking his old man in the shins. Sure, he'd have got a harder whaling, but he'd have made some move to assert his individuality. As it is, he waited too long. And then he defied the wrong thing, and it wasn't really defiance, basically. Too late now. His formative years are past. The thing that might really solve Clay's problem would be his conviction for murder—but he's been acquitted. If he'd been convicted, then he could prove to the world that he'd hit back. He'd kicked his father in the shins, kept that defiant smile on his face, killed Andrew Vanderman. I think that's what he actually has wanted all along—recognition. Proof of his own ability to assert himself. He had to work hard to cover his tracks—if he made any—but that was part of the game. By winning it he's lost. The normal ways of escape are closed to him. He always had an Eye looking down at him."

"Then the acquittal stands?"

"There's still no evidence. The State's lost its case. But I . . . I don't think Sam Clay has won his. Something will happen." He sighed. "It's inevitable, I'm afraid. Sentence first, you see. Verdict afterward. The sentence was passed on Clay a long time ago."

Sitting across from him in the Paradise Bar, behind a silver decanter of brandy in the center of the table, Bea looked lovely and hateful. It was the lights that made her lovely. They even managed to cast their own shadows over that bulldog chin, and under her thick lashes the small, mean eyes acquired an illusion of beauty. But she still looked hateful. The lights could do nothing about that. They couldn't cast shadows into Sam Clay's private mind or distort the images there.

He thought of Josephine. He hadn't made up his mind fully yet about that. But if he didn't quite know what he wanted, there was no shadow of doubt about what he *didn't* want—no possible doubt whatever.

"You need me, Sam," Bea told him over her brimming glass.

"I can stand on my own feet. I don't need anybody."

It was the indulgent way she looked at him. It was the smile that showed her teeth. He could see as clearly as if he had X-ray vision how the upper teeth would close down inside the lower when she shut her mouth. There would be a lot of strength in a jaw like that. He looked at her neck and saw the thickness of it, and thought how firmly she was getting her grip upon him, how she maneuvered for position and waited to lock her bulldog clamp deep into the fabric of his life again.

"I'm going to marry Josephine, you know," he said.

"No, you're not. You aren't the man for Josephine. I know that girl, Sam. For a while you may have had her convinced you were a go-getter. But she's bound to find out the truth. You'd be miserable together. You need me, Sam darling. You don't know what you want. Look at the mess you got into when you tried to act on your own. Oh, Sam, why don't you stop pretending? You know you never were a planner. You . . . what's the matter, Sam?"

His sudden burst of laughter had startled both of them. He tried to answer her, but the laughter wouldn't let him. He lay back in his chair and shook with it until he almost strangled. He had come so close, so desperately close to bursting out with a boast that would have been confession. Just to convince the woman. Just to shut her up. He must care more about her good opinion than he had realized until now. But that last absurdity was too much. It was only ridiculous now. Sam Clay, not a planner!

How good it was to let himself laugh, now. To let himself go, without having to think ahead. Acting on impulse again, after those long months of rigid repression. No audience from the future was clustering around this table, analyzing the quality of his laughter, observing that it verged on hysteria, measuring it against all possible occasions in the past that could not explain its exact depth and duration.

All right, so it was hysteria. Who cared? He deserved a little blow-off like this, after all he'd been through. He'd risked so much, and achieved so much—and in the end gained nothing, not even glory except in his own mind. He'd gained nothing, really, except the freedom to be hysterical if he felt like it. He laughed and laughed and laughed, hearing the shrill note of lost control in his own voice and not caring.

People were turning to stare. The bartender looked over at him uneasily, getting ready to move if this went on. Bea stood up, leaned across the table, shook him by the shoulder.

"Sam, what's the matter! Sam, do get hold of yourself! You're making a spectacle of me, Sam! What *are* you laughing at?"

With a tremendous effort he forced the laughter back in his throat. His breath still came heavily and little bursts of merriment kept bubbling up so that he could hardly speak, but he got the words out somehow. They were probably the first words he had spoken without rigid censorship since he first put his plan into operation. And the words were these.

"I'm laughing at the way I fooled you. I fooled everybody! You think I didn't know what I was doing every minute of the time? You think I wasn't planning, every step of the way? It took me eighteen months to do it, but I killed Andrew Vanderman with malice aforethought, and nobody can ever prove I did it." He giggled foolishly. "I just wanted you to know," he added in a mild voice.

And it wasn't until he got his breath back and began to experience that feeling of incredible, delightful, incomparable relief that he knew what he had done.

She was looking at him without a flicker of expression on her face. Total blank was all that showed. There was a dead silence for a quarter of a minute. Clay had the feeling that his words must have rung from the roof, that in a moment the police would come in to hale him away. But the words had been quietly spoken. No one had heard but Bea.

And now, at last, Bea moved. She answered him, but not in words. The bulldog face convulsed suddenly and overflowed with laughter.

As he listened, Clay felt all that flood of glorious relief ebbing away. For he saw that she did not believe him. And there was no way he could prove the truth.

"Oh, you silly little man," Bea gasped when words came back to her. "You had me almost convinced for a minute. I almost believed you. I—" Laughter silenced her again, consciously silvery laughter made heads turn. That conscious note in it warned him that she was up to something. Bea had had an idea. His own thoughts outran hers and he knew in an instant before she spoke exactly what the idea was and how she would apply it. He said:

"I *am* going to marry Josephine," in the very instant that Bea spoke.

"You're going to marry me," she said flatly. "You've got to. You don't know your own mind, Sam. I know what's best for you and I'll see you do it. Do you understand me, Sam?

"The police won't realize that was only a silly boast,"

she told him. "They'll believe you. You wouldn't want
me to tell them what you just said, would you, Sam?"

He looked at her in silence, seeing no way out. This
dilemma had sharper horns than anything he could have
imagined. For Bea did not and would not believe him,
no matter how he yearned to convince her, while the
police undoubtedly would believe him, to the undoing
of his whole investment in time, effort, and murder. He
had said it. It was engraved upon the walls and in the
echoing air, waiting that invisible audience in the future to observe. No one was listening now, but a word
from Bea could make them reopen the case.

A word from Bea.

He looked at her, still in silence, but with a certain
cool calculation beginning to dawn in the back of his
mind.

For a moment Sam Clay felt very tired indeed. In
that moment he encompassed a good deal of tentative
future time. In his mind he said yes to Bea, married
her, lived an indefinite period as her husband. And he
saw what that life would be like. He saw the mean
small eyes watching him, the relentlessly gripping jaw
set, the tyranny that would emerge slowly or not slowly,
depending on the degree of his subservience, until he
was utterly at the mercy of the woman who had been
Andrew Vanderman's widow.

Sooner or later, he thought clearly to himself, *I'd
kill her.*

He'd have to kill. That sort of life, with that sort of
woman, wasn't a life Sam Clay could live, indefinitely.
And he'd proved his ability to kill and go free.

But what about Andrew Vanderman's death?

Because they'd have another case against him then.
This time it had been qualitative; the next time, the
balance would shift toward quantitative. If Sam Clay's
wife died, Sam Clay would be investigated no matter
how she died. Once a suspect, always a suspect in the

eyes of the law. The Eye of the law. They'd check back. They'd return to this moment, while he sat here revolving thoughts of death in his mind. And they'd return to five minutes ago, and listen to him boast that he had killed Vanderman.

A good lawyer might get him off. He could claim it wasn't the truth. He could say he had been goaded to an idle boast by the things Bea said. He might get away with that, and he might not. Scop would be the only proof, and he couldn't be compelled to take scop.

But—no. That wasn't the answer. That wasn't the way out. He could tell by the sick, sinking feeling inside him. There had been just one glorious moment of release, after he'd made his confession to Bea, and from then on everything seemed to run downhill again.

But that moment had been the goal he'd worked toward all this time. He didn't know what it was, or why he wanted it. But he recognized the feeling when it came. He wanted it back.

This helpless feeling, this impotence—was this the total sum of what he had achieved? Then he'd failed, after all. Somehow, in some strange way he could only partly understand, he had failed; killing Vanderman hadn't been the answer at all. He wasn't a success. He was a second-rater, a passive, helpless worm whom Bea would manage and control and drive, eventually, to—

"What's the matter, Sam?" Bea asked solicitously.

"You think I'm a second-rater, don't you?" he said. "You'll never believe I'm not. You think I couldn't have killed Vanderman except by accident. You'll never believe I could possibly have defied—"

"What?" she asked, when he did not go on.

There was a new note of surprise in his voice.

"But it wasn't defiance," he said slowly. "I just hid the dodged. Circumvented. I hung dark glasses on an Eye, because I was afraid of it. But—that wasn't defiance. So—what I really was trying to prove—"

She gave him a startled, incredulous stare as he stood up.

"Sam! What are you doing?" Her voice cracked a little.

"Proving something," Clay said, smiling crookedly, and glancing up from Bea to the ceiling. "Take a good look," he said to the Eye as he smashed her skull with the decanter.

This one's a story about ghost hunting, and it's a little different; trust me on it.

Nigel Kneale has written prose excellently, but he makes his living primarily by writing for the screen. In the 1950s he did three chillingly effective six-part teleplays for BBC about a Dr. Quatermass (there was another in the late '70s). The third, reshot as a feature film and released in this country in 1968 as Five Million Years to Earth, *is right up there with (the original version of)* The Thing *and* Alien *as one of the best SF/horror films to date.*

The prose SF field is heavily influenced by the visual media, TV and movies. This isn't unusual for genre fiction —detective dime novels influenced silent movies which influenced pulp writers who influenced film noir . . . *and so on, with a similar chain in the Western genre.*

The connection may be a little more extreme in SF, though, since a picture does a much better job than words in describing objects and events that are wholly imaginary. (Consider Westerns if horses were imaginary creatures; you'd need movies to get a grasp of what was really going on.)

It's also my gut belief that many of the writers in this field watch a lot of movies, which makes the cross-

fertilization especially strong. For example, it's hard to imagine Steve King, a compulsive movie watcher, having written The Tommyknockers *had he not been familiar with* Five Million Years to Earth.

Mr. Kneale has written and seen produced quite a number of other SF and fantasy screenplays in addition to those in the Quatermass series. This is one of them, given here in teleplay form. The fact that the format of the dialogue, settings, and descriptions of action are a little different from those in the other pieces I've included here doesn't make "The Road" any less intelligible or any less of a story.

I've included dozens of stories in this series. This is one of the four which have had the greatest emotional impact on me on rereading.

Trust me.

THE ROAD

Nigel Kneale

CAST OF CHARACTERS
SIR TIMOTHY HASSALL.................James Maxwell
LAVINIA, his wife ....Ann Bell
GIDEON COBB...................................John Phillips
JETHRO, Cobb's servant.....................Clifton Jones
SAM TOWLER...............................Rodney Bewes
TETSY ....Meg Ritchie
LUKEY CHASE....................................Victor Platt
BIG JEFF..David King
   PRODUCER John Elliot
   DIRECTOR Christopher Morahan
Produced on BBC Television, September 29, 1963

The Woods—a Clearing

It is approaching dusk of an autumn day. Leaves are turning brown on the crooked oak branches. A distant owl hoots. The camera tracks slowly forward.
The owl hoots again, closer.

*The camera pans suddenly, to a close shot of a fright-
ened man. He is a young countryman in coarse woollen
shirt and leather jerkin. His eyes search the darkening
trees. His hands are working feverishly to bind two
twigs together with strands of grass, into the rough
shape of a cross.*

*A dog barks somewhere nearby. He turns to look in
that direction, grateful for the familiar sound.*

The Woods—some hundreds of feet away

The dog barks again, close at hand.

*Here a group of men are at work. Four of them are
knotting stout ropes taut between the tree trunks to
form a line that leads away out of sight, a couple of feet
from the ground.*

All are countrymen, roughly dressed.

*And now another comes, his whiskered face topped
by a tricorne hat. He is wearing a cast-off coat of the
squire's, for Lukey Chase is one of the squire's servants
and in charge of the work here.*

*He is followed by a lad with a sack, from which
Lukey is selecting metallic oddments to hang on the
ropes—old bells, jangling bits of harness and chain,
scrap from a rural forge. Lukey tests the effect as he
approaches, tugging at the rope.*

*The ironware clatters and jangles behind him all
along the line. As he reaches the men working on the
ropes, one of them turns to him—a huge fellow with a
broad, beaming, gap-toothed face.*

BIG JEFF: Hey, Lukey—you're gettin' a bit of a tune
    in it now!

*Grunts of laughter from the rest. Lukey dissociates
himself from the scheme.*

LUKEY: I be just doin' what squire showed us.

BIG JEFF: Sort o' tune as spooks'd take to, I'd say. He
    reckon to charm 'em out, hey?

LUKEY: You heard what he said, Jeff. *(To the lad)*
    What you got left there?

He delves in the sack and finds a rusty cowbell.

BIG JEFF: I only heard 'un say he were after spooks.

The mock-solemn faces of the others nod agreement.

LUKEY: Squire reckons to stop anybody comin' through here in the dark without us know.

He attaches the bell to the rope.

BIG JEFF: Ah, spooks'll just pass clean through a rope. Don't he know that? Pass through anythin', a spook can. Don't even tickle him.

LUKEY: 'Taint spooks he's settin' this up for, Jeff, it's jokers. We got plenty o' them hereabouts.

BIG JEFF *(shaking with laughter)*: Oh, ah?

LUKEY: Any tricky lad come boltin' through 'ere tonight—he'll set this lot off an' we'll have him. Now it's time to finish. Just take it as far as that thorn thicket and we'll go. *(As they move)* Hey, where's young Sam?

BIG JEFF *(pointing)*: There, look. Just went off by hisself.

LUKEY: Young devil . . .

BIG JEFF: Reckon he's frikkened?

LUKEY: Frikkened o' squire, more like, for makin' it all up.

He ducks under a branch and makes for where Jeff pointed.

The Clearing

Sam is standing where he was, still listening and watching for something.

A wider shot shows this as a small clearing. In it is a fallen tree, a grotesque lightning-seared ruin with one end torn open. It is covered with flat plates of fungus.

There is a tiny squeal a short distance away in the darkening undergrowth. He starts, with the twig cross clutched to his chest. The thin sound is drowned by a series of sharp screeches that move rapidly away.

Lukey appears through the branches at his side.

LUKEY: Killin' early tonight, that owl.
SAM: Ay.
LUKEY: An old rat squealin' there . . . make some folk frikkened, they dunno what it were.
SAM: I know them noises. 'Tweren't like I heard that other time.
LUKEY (*scrutinising him*): Ay?
SAM: Lukey, I don't want to come back here tonight.
LUKEY: Tell that to the squire. Come on now . . .

The Roped Trees

The lad has strung the last scraps of chain and iron on the completed barrier. Men are picking up their bundles and coils of rope as Lukey and Sam join them.
BIG JEFF: Hey, Lukey . . . reckon we all get a free drink on this?
LUKEY: Squire's promised it.
Grunts of approval as they start to move off.
BIG JEFF: I'll say this for squire. He may be soft in the head, but he's open in the hand . . .
They hurry off along the track. One of them whistles and calls to his dog.

Outside a Tavern

The last glow in the sky picks out an inn sign: "The Three Companions", pictured as a donkey, a dragoon and death, walking arm in arm.
The camera pans down. The windows of the tavern are lit. Outside the front door stands a large four-wheeled handcart with a long shaft. It is loaded with wooden boxes, planks and lanterns.
Beside it are two men.
One of them, in the decent dress of a rural gentleman, is Sir Timothy Hassall, Bt, squire of the district—tall and nervous, his face sensitive and uncertain. He lifts a wooden box from the cart and as he turns with it,

the other man, a servant, makes to relieve him of the burden. But he is not to be trusted with it.

Sir Timothy makes for the tavern door, carrying the box carefully.

Inside the Tavern

The tavern is a crabbed little old place, no more than an occasional halt for passing coaches. Its customers come from the surrounding village, and there are half a dozen of them in the bar now, men in smocks or jerkins exchanging the day's slow gossip over tankards of ale.

They watch Sir Timothy pass through with his box. One man with his back turned is nudged out of the way by a neighbour.

MAN: Oh . . . sorry, squire.

SIR TIMOTHY: No matter, Gibbs. No matter.

He has almost reached the door of the private parlour at the back when it flies open. The landlord, a harrassed, grizzled man, emerges in a hurry.

SIR TIMOTHY: Careful!

LANDLORD: Beg pardon, squire! *(Confusedly)* I'll just get the logs.

SIR TIMOTHY: Logs? Surely I need no logs.

LANDLORD *(nodding at the private room)*: He wants 'em!

A deep-throated roar from the room sends him on his way.

GIDEON COBB *(off-stage)*: And brandy, landlord! Quick, now!

LANDLORD: Yes, sir.

Sir Timothy disappears into the private room, closing the door. The landlord hurries behind the bar and shouts to his daughter, Tetsy, the ugly-pretty girl of 18 who is serving ale there.

LANDLORD: Where's Jack? *(She shrugs)* Devil take him! Brandy then—quick! I must go for logs.

He shuffles out through a dark open doorway behind

the bar and can be heard thumping about there and cursing.

   Tetsy finds the brandy bottle, looks for glasses. There is a ripple of renewed interest among the villagers.

FIRST VILLAGER: Makin' your ol' daddy jump, girl! *(A nod at the private room)* Who is he?

TETSY: Mr Cobb.

FIRST VILLAGER: Who's Mr Cobb, then?

SECOND VILLAGER: Friend o' squire's.

FIRST VILLAGER: I can see that, but . . .

TETSY: He got off the London coach.

   She polishes glasses.

SECOND VILLAGER: I seen 'em—him an' his black man.

FIRST VILLAGER: Black man?

TETSY *(sharply)*: Shhh!

   The door of the private room has opened. A tall negro is standing there. He is impeccably liveried as a gentleman's personal servant. His manner is cool and dignified. He calls in a voice that carries both culture and authority.

JETHRO: Where is the brandy for my master? *(Seeing Tetsy with the bottle and glasses)* Bring it.

   She manages to nod, and he goes back into the room. She is plainly terrified.

TETSY *(whispering)*: My mam says black men come from the Devil.

SECOND VILLAGER *(grinning)*: He comes from London. Same thing, eh, Tetsy?

FIRST VILLAGER: 'Tis the fashion there, they say, to have a black boy in yer house, dressed up like a great dolly. All the rich men got one. An' ladies too!

   Tetsy has brandy and three glasses on a tray. She calls into the dark doorway.

TETSY: Father, I've got the brandy.

LANDLORD *(off-stage)*: Take it in, then.

TETSY: Eh? Me?

LANDLORD *(off-stage)*: Yes, you!

Trembling, Tetsy makes for the private room and knocks. The door opens immediately and there is Jethro's face a foot from her own. She nearly drops the tray.

Inside the Private Room

There are three people in the private room. Sir Timothy is standing by the table, using what part of it is not covered with food to display the apparatus he has brought in—a couple of weirdly-eccentric, lop-sided jars with stubby off-shoots of tubing and stoppers, not unlike alchemists' alembics but with heavy, domed lids added.

He also has a crude electroscope in an ornamented case. Some of its internal parts are made of small bones, and it is topped with a mummified cat's head with whiskers.

Behind sits his wife Lavinia in an elegant riding habit. She is something of a beauty, not much over 20 and ambitious. Her clothes are London fashion. So is her imitated, malicious smile.

But dominating the room is Mr Gideon Cobb. Bulky and ugly, he carries himself with style. His fleshy face is neatly shaved and laced about at the neck. His clothing is plain but characterful in contrast to the absent-minded dullness of the squire's. It seems designed to set off the pugnacious force of his expression. He is a man accustomed to dominate, and takes it for granted that his hearers enjoy the experience.

Many of them do.

He now has a collection of used plates in front of him, the remnant of a steak pie and an empty pudding bowl, with coffee jugs and cups. He is still gobbling spoonsful of pudding from a plate, while Sir Timothy tries to explain his apparatus.

SIR TIMOTHY: . . . and in jars like this I'm hoping to secure samples of the imponderable fluids which, if I am right . . .

Cobb swings round in his chair to shout through a mouthful of pudding.

COBB: Where are those damned logs? Send him in with them! I'm dying of cold.

Tray of brandy in hand, Jethro turns to disclose the girl in the open doorway. Seeing his mistake, Cobb guffaws.

COBB: Ah, my dear! Thought it was your villain of a father.

TETSY: He's getting the logs, sir.

Cobb on his feet and taking the brandy from Jethro.

COBB: Good. What's your name?

Tetsy with a rapid, unskilled curtesy.

TETSY: Tetsy, so please you.

Sir Timothy has swung round to his wife in a cold fury.

SIR TIMOTHY (*whispering*): Why did you ask him here?

Lavinia flicks him a look of faint amusement. Then the door is closing and Cobb is pouring himself brandy.

COBB: Mm, pretty. (*To them*) Will you join me? (*Sir Timothy puts up his hand. Lavinia shakes her head, smiling. Cobb drinks*) . . . You're wise. At least it washes away the coffee. I really doubt that they've ever made coffee here before. I do.

LAVINIA: I must apologise again, Mr Cobb, for having put you to all this . . .

COBB: No, no. The coach was late.

LAVINIA: We had everything ready for you at the Hall. Timothy'd even been to the cellar to choose wines.

COBB: Wines? Not imponderable fluids? I'm honoured. (*He laughs. She laughs. Sir Timothy is tight-lipped, and Cobb is quickly grave again*) Sir, do you keep a chymical chamber at the Hall? A laboratory?

SIR TIMOTHY: Yes.

COBB: You've studied long?

SIR TIMOTHY: A number of years, mostly on my own.

COBB: Rewarding, heh?

SIR TIMOTHY: Yes, indeed.

LAVINIA: Often I scarce see him for a week. He's shut away there with his reports and the whole parish may go rot.

COBB: Most singular—a squire that would sooner hunt a chymical element than a fox.

SIR TIMOTHY (*hand on the jar again*): Shall I go on?

COBB: Please.

SIR TIMOTHY: If tonight there should be a manifestation, I'd expect changes in the air, the release of—of imponderable fluids. Phlogiston caloric, even the electric fluid. Now, for the electric—

He draws forward the electroscope. At the same moment there is a bump on the door, which flies open. It is the landlord, with his arms full of logs.

LANDLORD: Here you are, sir.

SIR TIMOTHY: It's intolerable.

LANDLORD: Logs.

COBB: Throw them all on—I need a great blaze to thaw my vitals. If you'd dragged for ten hours behind those damned lame jades . . .

LAVINIA: I feel so guilty!

Cobb to the landlord as he builds up the fire.

COBB: And then make more coffee (*To the others*) I don't know how he brews it—I've tasted naught like it in London.

LANDLORD (*with modest pride*): We have our ways, sir.

COBB (*heavily*): Ay. (*To Lavinia*) Coffee is the element I float in, madam, be it exquisite or vile. I chart my way through the flavours like the great whale in his sea. Now where did we meet in London —I'd swear it was at Mrs Brook's?

LAVINIA: It was.

COBB: There! I never forget a bean! The aroma . . . nay, the aura . . . of that Mrs Brook's. But you, squire . . . I think you were not there?

SIR TIMOTHY: No.

LAVINIA: I was up in town alone, visiting my cousin.

Cobb gives a faint smile as he glances from wife to husband.

COBB: No, sir, I think you were not.

The landlord turns from the fire and picks up the tray of plates.

LANDLORD: There, sir . . . that'll soon pick up.

COBB: Thank'ee.

Sir Timothy looks at his fob watch. He follows the landlord to the door and looks out.

SIR TIMOTHY: My men not returned?

LANDLORD: Not yet, sir.

SIR TIMOTHY: Be sure to let me know. Send Lukey to me.

LANDLORD: I will, squire.

He goes, shutting the door. Cobb has risen and is warming his back at the fire.

COBB: This witness of yours.

SIR TIMOTHY: Sam Towler

COBB: He's with them?

SIR TIMOTHY: Yes. They've been roping off the area with alarm bells to detect intruders.

COBB: You mean hoaxers?

SIR TIMOTHY (*unhappily*): Yes.

COBB: You admit it could all be an imposture, then?

SIR TIMOTHY: To keep an open mind, I must. But I *think* not. I think there is something here worth probing with all the means we have!

He claps his hands confidently on the alembic-like jars.

LAVINIA: Not forgetting pussy.

COBB: Ah, yes, the cat's head. (*He peers at it*) What does it do?

SIR TIMOTHY: Er—it may provide additional attraction for electrical fluid.

COBB: How?

SIR TIMOTHY: The whiskers.

COBB: Ah. And ornamental, in a way. In a way. Now, sir . . . you've formed your theory already—no, don't protest—I can see you're positively agog with it.

SIR TIMOTHY: In some sense, I . . .

COBB: A new proof of the existence of hobgoblins!

SIR TIMOTHY (*protesting*): No, sir!

COBB: Then confound me, sir!

SIR TIMOTHY: Imagine—imagine that hereabouts in the far past there was some great catastrophic event.

COBB: Was there one?

LAVINIA: So they say.

COBB: What?

LAVINIA: That Queen Boadicea fled through these woods with her army.

COBB: Ah, Queen Boadicea.

SIR TIMOTHY: Wait, wait! An event of such spiritual force that it somehow imprinted itself on the very landscape.
He breaks off, listening.

LAVINIA: What is it?

SIR TIMOTHY: They're back!
He hurries to the door.

Inside the Tavern Bar

The working party is streaming in behind Lukey Chase.
Sir Timothy meets them, calling to the landlord.

SIR TIMOTHY: Ale for these fellows! Two full tankards each, no more. I want cool heads tonight. (*He ignores groans from Big Jeff and one or two others, and draws Lukey aside*) Now, Lukey?

LUKEY: We finished, squire, sir.

SIR TIMOTHY: You'd metal enough?

LUKEY: Ay.

SIR TIMOTHY: Our guest was late, or I'd have come out again myself. Tell me, was anything heard or seen?
Lukey frowns. Then, understanding, he shakes his

head. The camera pans to the bar, where the new arrivals are being served. Tetsy slips from her work quickly round to Sam's side.

TETSY *(whispering)*: Sam . . . they been talking about you. I was frikkened, love.

SAM: Eh? Who?

Inside the Private Room

Cobb is impatient. He pours more brandy, with a glance at Lavinia, who declines.

COBB: Where's this fellow, now?

LAVINIA: Towler?

COBB: Ay. Jethro, find him and we'll proceed.
Jethro goes to the door.

Inside the Tavern Bar

As before, those nearest turn to stare as Jethro appears. Further along there is a more pronounced reaction. Tetsy jerks Sam round to see the negro. So it is to him that Jethro speaks.

JETHRO: Sam Towler? *(Faces turning to Sam confirm his guess. Jethro moves towards him)* My master wishes to speak to you. *Tetsy clings to the young man, whispering in his ear.*

TETSY: Don't go with him! His master ain't yourn . . . he can't make you.

JETHRO: Will you come, please?

Sir Timothy pushes through from where he has been talking to Lukey.

SIR TIMOTHY: Now, now, this is well enough. Come along, lad. Bring your ale if you will. *(Jethro goes before and holds the door for them. The squire calls to the rest:)* Stay close. We leave within the half-hour.

Inside the Private Room

Cobb scrutinises the young man fiercely. Sam faces him, the tankard clutched in his hands.

SIR TIMOTHY: This is Sam.

COBB: Are you honest, Sam?

Sam turns to Sir Timothy indignantly.

SIR TIMOTHY: I can answer for him. He's worked in my stables for . . . how long?

SAM: Since a young lad, sir.

COBB: So . . . you can curry a hunter's coat, Sam? Wax a saddle and shine brasses? All honest things. But are you honest in the mind?

SAM: What's he mean, sir?

SIR TIMOTHY: Indeed, Mr Cobb—

COBB: Honest with yourself. Not many achieve it.

Seeing Sam's jaw set, Lavinia interposes.

LAVINIA: Sam . . . Mr Cobb has come from London to help us tonight. I think you should tell him your story.

COBB *(taking cue)*: Don't fear me, lad. I'm neither a judge nor a High Constable. I'm a philosopher. D'you know what that is?

SAM: Ay, sir, like the squire.

COBB: Not exactly like. As I have none of those remarkable chymical jars I am obliged merely to think. About the truth. *(Lavinia shoots her husband a look as she passes, changing her seat for a better view of the proceedings)* Come now.

Sam turns to Sir Timothy.

SAM: I think he'll mock me.

COBB: I mock nothing but folly and knavery. Let us be two good fellows—heh? . . . helping each other to illumination. Jethro, take notes.

Jethro sits, pulling from his tail pocket a portable inkwell and quill. There is paper on the table.

Inside the Tavern Bar

Tetsy is straining to hear what is going on in the private room. Watching her, the villagers grin.

LANDLORD: Tetsy . . . come away.

She glances at him, but does not move from the door.

BIG JEFF: Hey, Tetsy . . . they're feedin' him to the black man!

Inside the Private Room

Jethro is scribbling with his quill as Sam talks.

SAM: 'Twas last year, a couple of days after Michaelmas.

SIR TIMOTHY: Exactly a year ago tonight, the first day of October 1769. And that night you were out in the woods?

SAM: Yes, sir.

COBB: Why?

SAM: Just . . . just wandering about.

COBB: Alone?

SAM *(after a moment)*: Yes.

COBB: How long?

SAM: Hours. It was full dark when I heard the noises.

COBB: The noises.

SAM: Weren't much at first; like some sort of whistles or squeaks, and I thought . . . birds. But 'tweren't birds.

COBB: What were they, then?

SAM: I dunno. Then they started to burst out more. Very loud. And between whiles there was quiet. And then . . . I was laid on the ground an' I could feel it startin' to shake . . . An' the noises come nearer, a-roarin' and a'rattlin' like naught I ever did hear. I was frikkened, sir.

COBB: Rattling . . . of what? Wheels? Chains?

SAM: Neither one, I don't think.

COBB: Can you imitate any of these sounds for us? With your mouth? *(Sam frowns. He manages a low-pitched hum. He parts his lips and it comes out as a harsh buzzing. He stops abruptly, embarrassed, and clears his throat)* Thank you. How did you set that down, Jethro?

JETHRO: "A kind of buzz or hum".
   Cobb grunts approval.
SAM: There seemed to be voices too.
COBB: Human voices?
SAM: Ay, sir. Yelling and screeching. *(The memory of it catches at him)* And footsteps running . . . under the ground I was lyin' on!
   Lavinia gives a tiny involuntary shiver. Jethro glances up from his notes at Sam.

Inside the Tavern Bar

   Tetsy is pressed against the door listening. She grasps the doorknob.

Inside the Private Room

COBB: You mean they ran in the earth?
SAM: Right under me where I lay. But the queer thing was . . . they sounded like feet on cobbles.
JETHRO *(writing)*: Footsteps on cobbles . . .
SIR TIMOTHY: There's nothing but turf and leafmould throughout the woods.
COBB: And the voices?
SAM: They were all round me. I stopped up my ears like this . . . but . . . oh, I tried, but it made no matter.
COBB: Could you pick out words?
SAM: None I could make sense on.
SIR TIMOTHY: Latin, perhaps.
COBB: Were they in our tongue?
SAM: Some . . . some might have been . . . I can't tell now. *(His voice grows increasingly high and distressed)* But mainly it was all screams and screechings . . . near and far away too, like as if all the dead people was risin' out o' Hell an' coverin' the land! *(Staring in front of him)* An' then—it must have stopped, I don't recall. I run home an' when I seen the houses I

cried. *(He turns to Cobb as if dazed)* The queerest of
all . . . nobody else had heard it!

COBB: No one?

SAM: I couldn't believe that, I couldn't!

*The door is flung open. Tetsy runs to his side, cling-
ing to him and shouting.*

TETSY: Don't torment him!

SIR TIMOTHY: There's no harm, girl.

TETSY: Sir, you must stop them.

LAVINIA: She was listening.

TETSY: I had to! I couldn't help it.

LAVINIA: Get out of here.

COBB: No, wait. Please.

Inside the Tavern Bar

*The landlord comes round from the bar. Big Jeff,
Lukey and others drift towards the open door of the
private room.*

COBB *(off-stage)*: Now, Sam, I want you to tell me . . .

Inside the Private Room

COBB: . . . For whom were you waiting in the woods
that night? For her?

TETSY *(before Sam can answer)*: Oh no, sir . . . we
were not then . . . not . . .

She breaks off, blushing.

COBB: I beg pardon. *(To Sam)* Some former sweetheart?

Sam nods unhappily.

TETSY *(whispering to Sam)*: Was it Meg?

Sam nods again, not looking at her.

SAM: But she didn't come. Not that night.

COBB: Ah. You waited in vain. And there's our picture! An overwrought young man in a lonely place
. . . his fancy hard at work . . .

LAVINIA: You mean he made it up?

SAM: I didn't, sir.

COBB: I'll tell you what you heard. You heard your own heartbeats throbbing against the ground. You heard the small creatures of the undergrowth.

SAM (*positively*): No, sir, no.

COBB: But chief of all, you heard your own memory. I'm told there's a local tale . . . (*He glances at Lavinia*) . . . about that queen of ancient times.

He snaps his fingers, frowning.

SAM: Queen Boadicea.

COBB (*trapping him*): There . . . he knows it!

SAM: They say she come through those woods with her whole army in rout.

Inside the Tavern Bar

The watchers through the open doorway nod to each other. This is familiar ground.

Then they draw back a little, for Cobb is moving about the inner room, eyeing them. But his words are half-addressed to them, as a useful part of his audience.

COBB: All those sad barbarians, sweating the blue woad off their bodies as they fled. Tossing their spears away . . .

Inside the Private Room

COBB: . . . Yelling and screaming in their terror. And behind them . . . the trumpets and the drums, the rolling drums (*he savours the word*) of the Roman Army.

SIR TIMOTHY: It may well have happened.

COBB: Happened or not, it's what he learned at his mother's knee. See how the rascal's eyes shine! Oh, Sam, you'd make a writer, a veritable Grub Street romantic . . . if you'd only learned your A.B.C.! It's been in his mind since childhood, this fustian tale, and when he's in an emotional state it comes back to him and . . . there's your phantom army!

Sam turns, aware that Cobb is playing to some gallery behind him. He walks slowly towards the men in the doorway.

SAM *(quietly)*: That wasn't what I heard.

COBB: What does he say.

Sam turns on him.

SAM: You try to show me as a fool, sir. But I've thought about this many a day, as honestly as you'd wish. *(Jethro looks up from his note-taking, glances at his master. Cobb frowns too, at this returning of his own words)* And I *know*. 'Tweren't that old queen and her people that I heard. *(He turns to Sir Timothy)* If they *had* come by here, they'd have had chariots— that's like carts, ain't it, sir? . . . and horses. *(To Cobb)* I've heard drums, too, and trumpets . . . in town when the soldiers came. *(Finally)* 'Twas none of these. None of 'em. *(He pushes through those in the doorway)* Let me by.

Everyone is staring at him. Even Cobb's complacent mask is disturbed.

Tetsy starts after Sam. Just through the doorway she meets her father's eye and halts.

Inside the Tavern Bar

Sam is walking slowly down the empty bar-room. All his concentration is directed within himself. He turns as the others come straggling after him.

SAM: I heard men running on a great cobbled road through them woods. But there's no road, nor ever has been.

SIR TIMOTHY *(from doorway)*: That's true. It's always been forest land.

A momentary silence. Then Cobb is beside him, breaking the spell.

COBB: Come, sir, come . . . you realise what you're doing? You're adducing this very lack, this nothing . . . as if it *supported* his tale! *(Sharply)* Has no one else ever heard these sounds?

BIG JEFF: Job Mousley.

An amused murmur.

SIR TIMOTHY: An old poacher. Three years ago. He was in the woods on what must have been the same night of the year, but that signified naught until Sam here . . .

COBB: Where is this old man?

SIR TIMOTHY: He died. A week or two later.

COBB *(heavily)*: Of shock, no doubt?

Some nods and mutterings.

LANDLORD: He was took mortal strange.

COBB: How disobliging of him. *(He glances round)* And there's no other witness of this remarkable annual uproar? You must all live within a mile or two. Nobody? *(As heads are shaken, he turns to Sir Timothy)* Yourself, sir? Your lady . . . your servants . . . *(He looks down the bar)* . . . with one exception.

Sam is at the window, peering out through the tiny panes at the darkening village street.

SIR TIMOTHY: It seems you have to be in the woods. *(He looks at his watch again, calls out)* We leave in ten minutes.

BIG JEFF: It'll be a cool night, sir.

SIR TIMOTHY: Very well . . . *(To landlord)* . . . Hot toddy for every man before we go. Small ones, though. *(To Cobb)* I take it, sir, you will not be with us?

LAVINIA: Oh, he must. Who else will stand for common sense?

COBB: Thank'ee, madam.

LAVINIA: It was for that I invited Mr Cobb.

Cobb shows her back into the private room.

COBB: And for that only?

Inside the Private Room

LAVINIA: What do you mean, sir? When Sir Timothy told me he was going to investigate . . . *(She suddenly breaks into a direct, disarming smile)* . . . I thought you might . . . like to come . . . *(He moves towards her. Conscious of Jethro's presence, she moves away. It is a kind of unskilled coquettishness, clumsy for lack of practice. She picks up Jethro's notes and after a glance casts him a look of mild surprise)* . . . a neat hand! *(She is conscious of both men, as just now she was conscious of Cobb and her husband. To Cobb)* What did you think of him?

COBB: Your rustic? A head full of fright and old wives' tales!

Jethro watches him with an irony that is never far below the surface. Resentment at being taken for granted has taught him subtle ways to provoke, and to use them when Cobb is ruffled, as now.

JETHRO: He seemed . . . honest in the mind.

COBB: Did he so!

JETHRO *(to Lavinia)*: When I was a child in Jamaica, Ma'am, the generality of people believed in such things.

COBB: His people were savages . . . slaves!

LAVINIA: That was no fault of theirs.

COBB: Who said it was?

LAVINIA: Without benefit of religion, what else could . . . ?

COBB: They had religion enough! Demons, idols, voodoo.

JETHRO: Obeah, we called it, sir.

COBB: Obeah, then. Every possible consolation. What they lacked was the benefit of *real* . . . *human* . . . *thought*. *(He stabs the words out)* Of philosophy! *(At Jethro)* Which he lacks not!

JETHRO: I am most gratefully aware, sir . . .

COBB *(to Lavinia)*: As you see, he's had more than a flunkey's training. He has a brain. I've made him use it.

JETHRO: I use it.

COBB: Demonstrate. Show the lady some excellence on this topic.

JETHRO (*hesitantly*): I have thought . . . (*To Cobb*)
You may not approve of this . . . it is a matter of
scale: our minds are limited, in a limitless universe.
There may be forces whose nature we can in no way
grasp—inaccessible to our finest philosophy.

COBB (*flatly*): Don't quote.

JETHRO: Did I?

COBB: "More things in heaven and earth, Horatio".
Above all, don't quote a poet, a professional liar. (*His
anger rising*) You have been taught some discipline
of the mind, Jethro. Never, never betray that. I will
not have those about me who would open doors to
confusion and magic! (*Breathing harder, he waves
him away*) Get out. Get out there and help them.
The door opens. It is Sir Timothy.

JETHRO (*stiffly*): Sir . . . can I take these things out
for you? The electroscope?

SIR TIMOTHY: You know what it is?

JETHRO: Yes. In spite of the cat.

SIR TIMOTHY: Er . . . Please take it.
Jethro picks it up deftly.

Inside the Tavern Bar

*The men are crowding round the bar as Jethro passes.
The landlord is serving hot toddy.*
*Sam Towler is standing where he was, near the win-
dow. Tetsy is with him. She shrinks against him as
Jethro passes.*

LANDLORD (*off-stage*): Tetsy. Where are you, girl?

TETSY: Coming, father—
She runs to help him.

Outside the Tavern

*Jethro comes out of the tavern. He glances about,
goes to the handcart. He sets the electroscope into a
pad of sacking, covers it and starts to strap it down.*

Inside the Private Room

The landlord enters with a tray on which are a glass jug of steaming toddy and three glasses. He places it before Sir Timothy, who pours.

COBB: Jethro's an experiment—*(to Sir Timothy)* You see, I make them too. On the whole, he works.

SIR TIMOTHY: He's a man.

COBB: He is now. Almost. He was bought in slavery by an old friend of mine. His mind was a child's. Less, with nothing in it but a little darkness. I emptied it clean, poured in new impressions and the ideas they formed. Nothing old or false, no cant. I set him at all matters, to seek truth. Tested his brain against others in argument. And at last—that savage is the equal of any man in the kingdom.

SIR TIMOTHY: Then why do you not respect him?

COBB *(astonished)*: Respect? Respect, sir, is no part or parcel of the matter. You might as sensibly ask me to respect him for the silver buckles I've put upon him.

SIR TIMOTHY: I can respect him.

Cobb stares at him. The ready guffaw does not come. He is uneasy at the working of something on another level. The way to deal with it is to demolish it.

COBB *(roaring)*: Sir, you have a vice of politeness in you.

LAVINIA *(laughing)*: Politeness a vice?

COBB: Nay, in many it is. Should he succeed this night, he'll beg pardon of the ghosts for raising 'em. *(He laughs with Lavinia, raising his glass to Sir Timothy)* Truth in toddy, sir. Well, here's to your enterprise—

Inside the Tavern Bar

The toddy is going down fast in the bar outside. There is a buzz of drink-warmed argument, at the centre of which are Big Jeff and Sam Towler.

BIG JEFF: And there's not even a gibbet round these parts.

SAM: I know naught about that—

BIG JEFF: A gibbet's where you find 'em. Ay. Over to Palehouse Common, there was that old gibbet there, and the place was alive with 'em. (*A wink at his neighbour on the other side*) Every night, mark you, not just once a year—

The camera pans to Tetsy. She is crossing with a couple of tankards in her hands when something catches her attention. She goes to the door and looks out.

Outside the Tavern

Jethro is crouching beside the handcart. His manner has changed: His face is somehow loosened, the eyes wide and distant. He is crooning to himself a tune of deep and ancient sadness, the words forgotten.

He is oblivious of the girl watching him from the doorway.

Inside the Private Room

Sir Timothy is pulling on his greatcoat. Cobb picks his up and struggles with it.

COBB: Where's that damned cannibal of mine? Never where I need him.

LAVINIA: You speak so, Mr. Cobb—

COBB (*lost in the folds*): And mean it too.

LAVINIA: Yet you fight against slavery—

COBB (*emerging*): Slavery has always existed, madam.

LAVINIA: You have written against it.

COBB: I have said it will come to an end. Not quite the same thing. Good or bad, it must end by being ridiculous. Machines will supplant it.

SIR TIMOTHY: Machines.

COBB: I've no possible doubt of it. The great steam pumps we see now—are going to have a million descendants. In a hundred years— in two, certainly— machines will do all the world's fetching and carrying. They'll be more obedient, loyal and industrious than any slaves in history. They'll carry men through the air and over the seas.

LAVINIA (*disbelievingly*): Mr Cobb—

COBB: They'll sow and reap for us—water the deserts— melt the polar snows—

LAVINIA: All this with steam?

COBB: There'll be far greater forces.

SIR TIMOTHY: The imponderables—

COBB (*losing patience*): No, sir. Powerful, real forces that actually exist—that must exist to bind this universe and to quicken it. The very sources of life. Man will find them in the end.

SIR TIMOTHY: Yes, I suppose so, as each of us contributes his—

COBB: My poor squire. Man will do it by using his mind utterly anew, plumbing the deepest levels of insight and reason—(*He laughs*) not by sniffing at those sorcerors' jars. (*Injured, Sir Timothy snatches up the box of jars*) The nose will not serve, sir, but to find a bad smell. (*Lavinia laughs with him as Sir Timothy kicks the door open and goes*) 'Tis the brain must do it.

Inside the Tavern Bar

Men turn, wiping their mouths, as the squire makes for the outer door. Lukey bobs responsibly forward and signs to the others. They surge towards the door.

Outside the Tavern

Jethro scrambles to his feet as men straggle out of the tavern.

Inside the Tavern Bar

As Cobb and Lavinia follow, he catches her arm.

COBB: Is your carriage here?

LAVINIA: Yes, but we go to the woods on foot—

COBB: The woods. Are we really bound to this buffoonery?

LAVINIA: We?

COBB: You and I. When I think of those wines of yours back at the Hall—

LAVINIA *(seeing the drift)*: Oh, no—

COBB: Lying untasted.

For a moment, Lavinia is torn. Then there is a scuttle of feet as Tetsy runs from the doorway behind the bar, pulling a shawl about her.

LAVINIA: Your world of machines—I think I should like that. *(She watches Tetsy run on out, turns to him quickly)* I can't. Not yet. We must go with the others. Please. *(He nods, humoring her. As They go)* Perhaps there'll even be philosophical machines.

COBB: To do our thinking? *(Pleased by the notion)* Ay. At least they'd not believe in bogeys.

He follows her out.

Outside the Tavern

Big Jeff is brandishing a pitchfork, stabbing ferociously at the air.

BIG JEFF: Take that, you headless old horror, you. *(Laughing to Sir Timothy)* I'll kill 'em dead all over again.

SIR TIMOTHY: Careful with that—

Lukey is issuing stout staffs and rakes and hoe-handles to the men.

BIG JEFF: An' nail 'em up like vermints to frikken their friends. How much'll you gimmee for 'em, squire?

SIR TIMOTHY: A shilling a head.

BIG JEFF: Hey—what about the fellers as got none?

SIR TIMOTHY: Shilling a body. *(Turns to Lukey)* Has each man got a staff now?

Sam is the last to get one. As he turns with his, he finds Tetsy in front of him, the shawl pulled round her head.

TETSY: What's them for?

SAM: Oh—makes the lads feel braver. In case, like.

TETSY: Can I have one? Lukey—

SAM: You ain't comin'.

TETSY: I am then, Lukey—

SIR TIMOTHY: What's this about?

SAM: She wants to come, sir.

TETSY (*pointing to Lavinia*): If Lady Hassall can go, I can. I don't get easy frikkened, sir—

SIR TIMOTHY: Faith, let her come. (*Turning to the rest*) Now remember all what I said—no shouting, no laughing, and keep your ears open. We're like to return no wiser than we are now—but let's be sure. If you do hear anything, come to me at once. Now—two men to light the way. Lukey and another—

Lukey and the lad pick up lighted lanterns while the others apply themselves to the long shaft and pull the cart round. Tetsy stays close to Sam's side.

Lantern in hand, Jethro joins his master, who is watching with Lavinia. As the cart rumbles and jolts on the cobbles:

LAVINIA: You really believe in those machines.

COBB: They can free man from his folly. I believe that, yes.

LAVINIA: How can they? He'll have made them.

Cobb gives her a quick grin of appreciation. Then Sir Timothy is beckoning and they move to join him. Jethro brings up the rear with his lantern.

The camera cranes up a high shot as the heavily laden cart is turned and moves slowly off. Again it takes in, close at hand, the inn sign with its "Three Companions".

The Woods—The Roped Trees

It is dark now in the wood. Two points of light bob in the distance. The creaking of the cart can be heard, then voices in sudden subdued argument, until, above the others:

BIG JEFF (*off-stage*): She's stuck against this root—

SIR TIMOTHY (*off-stage*): Right, pull this way. Heave now, lads—heave. Heave.

A jolting, exclamation of success, and the cart rumbles on again.

LAVINIA (*off-stage*): Oh, it's so muddy.

COBB (*off-stage*): Jethro—help the lady. I'll take the lantern.

The two points of light enlarge into the lanterns carried by Lukey Chase and the lad. They flicker across branches and ropes as Lukey comes running ahead.

LUKEY: This is the place, squire. Through here.

He moves on round the obstruction of a rope that zigzags between the trees. Sir Timothy follows and in the darkness Lukey has left behind him, collides with the rope.

Bells jangle. Bits of harness rattle. He gives a muffled yell.

Lukey and the lad run back. The squire has gone headlong over the rope and is spluttering in the leafmould. Lukey sets his lantern down and helps him.

Sir Timothy wipes the soil from his mouth.

SIR TIMOTHY: I—I didn't see the rope.

Cobb comes up with the third lantern. Just behind is Jethro, carrying Lavinia. She drops to her feet.

LAVINIA: Timothy. You're not hurt?

SIR TIMOTHY (*as Lukey dusts him down*): The bones seem sound, eh, Lukey?

COBB: Well, sir, you sprung your own trap.

SIR TIMOTHY: Yes, I—you see how it works? It sets off the alarm if anyone—(*lamely*) You saw.

The cart is drawing up to them. Men are grinning, some laughing. Big Jeff to the next man, in a stage whisper:

BIG JEFF: Squire was just puttin' it to the test, like—
SIR TIMOTHY: Where's Sam Towler?
SAM (*coming forward*): Here, sir.
SIR TIMOTHY: Now show us the exact spot.
SAM: Yonder. By the fallen tree.

The Clearing

Waving the cart on, Lukey trots up and sets his lantern on the great fallen trunk.
SIR TIMOTHY: That'll serve, lads. (*As the cart halts*) Now to unload.
Straps are whipped asunder, coverings removed, boxes lifted down. Sir Timothy stands by to supervise the handling of the more fragile items.
Cobb looks about, frowning, swinging his lantern to cast light into the dark places of the undergrowth. Lavinia pulls her cloak tight. She looks with revulsion at the fungus on the dead tree.
LAVINIA: Loathsome. What is it?
Cobb tears off a piece. He shows it to Jethro.
JETHRO: Polyporus betulinus.
LAVINIA: He has Latin—
JETHRO: It is a poison plant.
COBB: In Jamaica they used it in their soup, no doubt.
JETHRO: No, only for obeah.
The smile is wiped from Cobb's face. There is a faint suggestion of one on Jethro's.
COBB: Go help there.
He points to the cart. Jethro does as he is bidden. Lavinia watches Cobb, puzzling him out.
Half a dozen planks are being unloaded. Jethro helps Lukey down with one. Other men swing down a big hamper.
Sir Timothy sets a tall, narrow box down by the tree. He opens it and extracts a wooden frame with glass tubing attached. He inspects the fancifully shaped thing briefly, then checks the other one in the box.

SIR TIMOTHY: Both intact. *(To Cobb)* Thermometers. It's said that supernatural events are marked by a great chilling of the air. I am ready to test that.

COBB *(dryly)*: Good.

Sir Timothy turns quickly back to the cart, where Jethro and Lukey are lifting down heavy iron tripods.

SIR TIMOTHY: Now my tripods. Bear them over here—to the planks. *(He hurries past Tetsy, who is busy lighting lanterns, to where the planks are being laid out on different sides of the clearing)* This way— this way—

Behind, Cobb glowers.

COBB: Are you not to help him?

LAVINIA: He's not taught me in these matters.

COBB: Say "either."

LAVINIA: Either. *(Dimpling)* Mr Cobb—

COBB: He'll be out after marsh damps or subjecting copper to the seven heats when he'd do better in bed. *(She laughs)* Why did you marry him? Grew up in the country—a vicar's daughter? I knew it. A match for the young squire, well, younger than some and a baronet—*(She nods, her eyes growing hard)* I've met a score of him—gentlemen amateurs with a nose for idle novelty—*(He stares suddenly)* God a mercy. Look at this. *(Theatrical props are being unloaded. Two fanciful Roman helmets, plumed with feather boas and a cardboard shield. And a large scroll on wooden rollers. And a human skull)* Yorick too. What company of actors had he these from?

LAVINIA: They passed in the spring, playing Julius Caesar.

COBB: And he sets the scene.

He roars with laughter. She glances at him. Her voice is sharp.

LAVINIA: Show him! *(He looks at her)* What he is!

COBB: Ah . . .

LAVINIA: You can!

COBB: A bargain! *(She frowns. He studies her)* I had a

cat once. Her name was Tibb and she was a great
killer. Yes, there was something about her—

LAVINIA: Her eyes?

COBB: The corner of her mouth.

*With a sudden sweep of his arm he clears the fungus
from part of the trunk. He lifts Lavinia by the waist
and seats her upon it. She stares at him. As he turns
away towards her husband, her smile flickers back.*

*Unloading the last things from the cart—two "Ro-
man" swords and a horse's skull—Lukey glances at her.
He catches Big Jeff's eye and grins.*

*The tripods have been set up in four places, strad-
dling planks. They are a couple of feet high and two of
them already contain the alembic-jars they are meant to
take. On the plank below each sits a lighted lantern and
the removed lid of the jar.*

*Sir Timothy is now arranging a third jar in its tri-
pod. Sam stands by with a fourth in its box, while Tetsy
has a lighted lantern. A lantern is already in place
below where Sir Timothy is working, casting a bright
upward glow on him as he moves the lid.*

Cobb comes up.

COBB: Surely you cannot catch imponderables in a jar?
   By their very nature they will escape through the
   very glass—that is, if they exist at all.

SIR TIMOTHY: There may be something else.

COBB: Oh?

SIR TIMOTHY: Something heavier. *(He places the lids
   carefully on the plank below)* An animal-magnetic
   fluid. I should call it that. Something like the mag-
   netic fluid of iron, but exuded instead by living
   creatures?

COBB: Is this your own idea?

Sir Timothy is apparently unaware of any irony.

SIR TIMOTHY: Suppose it had the quality of lingering
   —say, where some violent action of the past had
   riven it into the earth—to issue forth again at certain
   times and under certain conditions. Times like the

130   Nigel Kneale

SIR TIMOTHY: They might help to distill out the—

COBB: To chase her into your bottle! (He calls after the smarting Sir Timothy) But the text, sir! From Caesar!

—Caesar's day—

She was not born in Caesar's day—

surrounded by the other men, Lukey

the squire means some-
thing more—more chemical than souls. Besides, Queen Boadicea may be officially doubted to have had any. She was a pagan. (*He glances across at Lavinia, his wrist round Tetsy's waist for a moment more, till she frees herself and moves towards the scowling Sam*) Your master's going to insist on the old queen, my lad. She fits his theory. So if she shows herself tonight, he'll bottle her up!

Sir Timothy rises from his work, scowling.

SIR TIMOTHY: If anything happens—(*seeing the mockery in Cobb's face*) Oh, leave me be!

He turns away, but Cobb keeps with him, enjoying it now.

COBB: But you'll make it happen, sir—try at least. Or why all this?

He points to the "Roman" props. The skull is wearing one of the plumed helmets and has been stuck bizarrely on a post. The other helmet is fixed nearby, empty. The horse's skull is hung below the human one, while the swords and shields have been hooked on branches.

The scroll is suspended open to reveal a Latin text. The effect is amateurishly occult.

COBB (*continuing*): Ancient Rome! The centurion and his horse!

By the cart, Chase has some bizarre instruments—*two long toasting* forks, each soldered at the blunt end to a large coil of bright wire. The lad has a similar pair of forks and is handily putting the coils over his arm.

BIG JEFF: Lukey goin' to fight th' old devils with their own weapons!

Sir Timothy, sharply over the laughter:

SIR TIMOTHY: Come now! Who's your helper?

LUKEY (*struggling with the coils*): Him. I told him what to do.

SIR TIMOTHY: Right. (*Glancing up*) Let him take that tree. And you, Lukey, this one.

The lad is the nimbler. He is up among the branches in a moment. Lukey fumbles for footholds, gasping.

BIG JEFF: Get after them devils, Lukey! (*Feinting at him with the pitchfork*) Like this!

LUKEY (*scrambling up*): Hey, hey!

Sir Timothy turns to find Cobb taking another of the forks from the cart. He relieves him of it.

SIR TIMOTHY: Yes, an ordinary toasting fork. Another of—my own ideas. (*He passes it to Jethro—and the transfer is not lost on either master or man. Then a second fork-and-coil from the box*) Wedge them there in the thorn bush. (*Turns to call up into the trees*) Are you ready?

A high shot of Lukey in the tree, holding both forks away from him while he shakes the coils free. He peers across at the other tree.

LUKEY: Right, lad? Chuck 'em down!

He throws his coils down, unwinding as they fall.

Below, they watch the four coils come rustling down and Sir Timothy darts forward to grab them. He pays out the wire as he makes for a plank where six primitive

*Leyden Jars, and the cat-headed electroscope, have been
set out in the light of a lantern. They are only a yard or
so from the "Roman" oddities.*

*Jethro meets him, unwinding the wires from the thorn
bush.*

JETHRO: Join to the electroscope?

SIR TIMOTHY: No, those to a Leyden Jar— *(Realising
he is taking the negro's knowledge for granted)* Can
you do that?

JETHRO: Yes, sir.

They work quickly, fixing the connections.

SIR TIMOTHY *(joining a wire to the electroscope)*: I've
made trial before with electrical discharges. During
thunderstorms.

JETHRO: With kites, like Benjamin Franklin?

SIR TIMOTHY *(pleased)*: That's right! Flying forks up
into the storm—the fluid comes down the wet line. I
got a bad burn once.

JETHRO: Shall we get burns tonight?

SIR TIMOTHY: I'd be glad to. *(Suddenly confidential)*
With so many people here, it may excite the forces.
And should these things, in a sense, focus them—
*(He indicates the "Roman" items. Jethro looks at
them, unsure)* You understand, don't you?

COBB'S VOICE: Well, Jethro? Do you?

He is standing a yard away.

*Jethro rises. Standing by the skull with its theatrical
helmet, he looks at one man to the other as if aware of
having to make a judgment between them. Then Sir
Timothy scrambles up, calling.*

SIR TIMOTHY: Get the cart away now. I want it down
there—

*He points. Big Jeff and others seize the shaft to pull it
round. Cobb takes a pinch from a heavy silver snuff
box.*

COBB: Sir, a word. Before this addled attempt goes too
far—

SIR TIMOTHY *(waving at the cart)*: By the rope!

COBB: —and you're the laughing stock of the entire county. Think of your lady there. (*This brings Sir Timothy round to face him*) You're a singular fellow, sir—but do not set up to be an eccentric!

SIR TIMOTHY: Sir!

COBB (*waving a hand round the clearing*): Where did you get all this rubbish? From a bankrupt sorcerer? You don't know what half of it is!

SIR TIMOTHY (*indignantly*): I make serious observations.

COBB: The best of them are so crude you can prove whatever you fancy! That mice are generated by sour cheese—that sneezing endangers the monarchy—

SIR TIMOTHY (*controlling himself*): I'm not a fool, sir!

COBB: Then throw away the toys.

SIR TIMOTHY: I have an open mind.

COBB: Close it, sir. Close it to nonsense!

SIR TIMOTHY: Keep your voice down.

They move closer, towards Lavinia, who is drinking in every word.

COBB: If you want proof, I can tell you how to find it.

SIR TIMOTHY: Pray do.

COBB: You need not seek it with quaint instruments. You have only to open your eyes—if you can—and see what is before you.

SIR TIMOTHY: That is too easy.

COBB (*fiercely*): It is not easy! It is so hard that only a handful in the land—or any land—have yet achieved it! They must scour their minds clean, ready for a new usage. Then turn their whole imagination right round—away from all the romantic fancies that delight it and then blur and deaden it. And bring that imagination to bear instead on the real world it has taken for granted, and see *into* it. And seek its deepest sense. The truth is all round us, but it is hard. (*He looks from one to the other*) And ordinary. And supreme.

Lavinia is enchanted simply with the sound of the words. Sam and the girl are listening nearby. Jethro

*sits on a box with his eyes to the ground. He has heard
it before.*

SIR TIMOTHY: Have *you* achieved this—cleansing of
the brain?

COBB (*confidently*): Not wholly. But I shall.

SIR TIMOTHY: And how many others?

COBB: In time, a world-full. Man will change himself!

SIR TIMOTHY: I could not.

COBB: Then you will be left behind, sir. A mere bone
in the rocks like a creature of the Great Flood. And
all like you. The men of the future will be those who
see things as they are.

LAVINIA (*with a laugh of exhilaration*): Go on, Timothy
—argue! Refute him!

SIR TIMOTHY: How can I? He denounces fantasy,
only to set up another one.

COBB: I give good sense for nonsense, new lamps for
old!

LAVINIA: Bravo!

COBB: Come, sir—try the exchange? He will not.

LAVINIA: Let's leave poor Timothy in his rock and go
on. I want to feel history sweeping me away like a
great warm tide!

COBB: It will be the world of men—and women—with
opened eyes. They'll be strong. They'll need no
crutches of petty, trammelling morality—

LAVINIA: Faith, is there morality *now*?

COBB (*quickly*): No, but they'll be spared the pre-
tence. (*She laughs, sensing how all this relates to the
three of them*) They'll see each other as they truly
exist, and count each other's needs and accept them.
Even joyfully. But above all honestly. They may count
our virtues vice and our vices natural wisdom. They'll
judge all things afresh, by their own enlightenment.

SIR TIMOTHY: God will judge.

COBB: *They* will judge! They won't go in dread seeking
heavenly marks for good behavior, like tots in dame-
school. They'll have grown up!

SIR TIMOTHY (*shaking his head*): There must be God, and justice—

COBB (*roaring*): Justice, sir, *is* a god—the god of misers! It defines the way we may snatch from each other and then guard our grabbings! *You* say justice and you exalt a golden blindfold lady. *I* see a gibbet and a thing hanging with eyes pecked out!

He snatches out his snuffbox and takes a great pinch.

LAVINIA: Oh, you're right!

COBB: Law is for cowards and blockheads. For today's foul little world, not for theirs. They'll have no filth and cholera and killing for theft—who will steal in a world where every man's a prince? There'll be neither squire nor servant then.

JETHRO: Nor slave?

COBB: Nor—slave. They'll have such riches that our great King George would look like a pauper. It's in the earth for the asking—and they'll have learned to ask, that's all. They'll build a world that's clean and ordered and swift. It'll come. It must.

LAVINIA: The world of machines.

COBB: Ay, great engines that could build you a pavilion of shining metal and keep your beauty perfect for a hundred years.

The directness of it, in Timothy's presence, is too much for her. She takes refuge in coquetry.

LAVINIA: Is this the new realism?

COBB: No disease, no cruelty, no want. All that man gains, man will give.

LAVINIA: Love, too?

COBB: Ay, that too. That most of all.

While his wife remains staring at Cobb, Sir Timothy turns away. Big Jeff and the other men have settled down on the ground or are leaning against trees. He looks at his watch and snaps it shut.

SIR TIMOTHY: You're not bound to stay. For those who do, there'll be food in an hour. (*No one offers to leave. He turns)* You blind us with your Golden Age, Mr Cobb. Tell me, do you have no doubts?

COBB: Few.

SIR TIMOTHY: I have doubts. I doubt everything I do.

COBB *(with a grunt of amusement)*: With reason! You're a fool to go on.

SIR TIMOTHY: I know that, but I must. I go slowly. I get knowledge grain by grain, as I come upon it. I go without direction, feeling my way. I test the ground and move aside if it won't bear me, and go on again.

COBB: Like a beetle.

SIR TIMOTHY: No, a man. *(Cobb grunts. Sir Timothy regards him with a thin smile)* It's the only discovery I've made, Mr Cobb. Hassall's Law: Man can never move back.

For a moment a quick retort hovers on Cobb's lips. Then he frowns. He looks at Sir Timothy seriously for the first time, watching him as he goes to search among the ropes and boxes.

Sir Timothy rises with a gun in his hands, a wide-muzzled blunderbuss. Men turn idly to watch him. He sits on a box and prepares to load the weapon. Surprisingly, he is expert with it, his fingers deft with the powder-horn and ram-rod, caressing the gun.

He glances at Cobb, who has his eyes fixed on him. Sir Timothy's expression has altered. All the uncertainty and gentleness seem to have gone, as if the touch of the weapon despatched them.

SIR TIMOTHY *(almost whispering)*: You will talk. And I will do.

The Roped Trees

It is a couple of hours later.

A low shot through the wheels of the cart. Men are moving about in the lighted area beyond. Two figures move into shot in the foreground, walking along just

*inside the rope barrier; Big Jeff and another man. Jeff
has the pitchfork over his shoulder, and has an ale-mug
in his hand.*

BIG JEFF (*peering outwards*): Not even the owl now.
He's gone to his bed. (*He finishes his ale and shakes
the last drops out into the darkness, calling*) Come
along, my dears—show y'selves! There's gentry here
awaitin' for yer!

*After a moment of silence, he giggles. He claps the
other man on the shoulder, shaking with increasingly
convulsive laughter.*

The Clearing

*Sir Timothy is looking towards the cart. Lukey Chase
comes trotting back from that direction. He, too, has a
mug in his hand, and a piece of bread in the other.*

LUKEY: Ay, 'tis only Big Jeff foolin' about.

SIR TIMOTHY (*calling*): Quiet down there! (*He turns*)
Now, Lukey, back to your place.

LUKEY: Squire, what's the use?

SIR TIMOTHY: Back, I said.

LUKEY: But already? I'm still stiff—

SIR TIMOTHY: And you, lad. (*Lukey and the lad finish
their ale and start for their places in the trees. Sir
Timothy catches Lukey as he climbs*) Lukey, can you
see through the branches up there?

LUKEY: Only a little.

SIR TIMOTHY: Keep an eye on Big Jeff—I don't trust
him.

*Lukey nods and climbs. Sir Timothy turns, pulling an
elegant little notebook from his pocket.*

*The meal has been eaten. Sam closes the lid on the
hamper and straps it. Tetsy is drawing the last ale from
a small cask. Men are wiping their mouths, putting
knives back in their pockets, stretching. The air of
vague expectation has thinned to boredom.*

At Sir Timothy's signal, two of them pick up their

*staffs and make for another part of the rope barrier.
Two more go to another section.*

*In the tree, Lukey settles and adjusts his toasting
forks. He glances across at the other tree, catches the
lad's eye and grimaces as he points down.*

*Below, Tetsy brings a refilled tankard to Cobb. He is
sitting on the ground by the ruined tree. Lavinia is a
yard away, balanced on a trailing branch, pouring
herself another small glass from a brandy flask.*

COBB: Thank you, my dear.

LAVINIA (*as Tetsy goes*): Would you share her?

COBB: She's got a man. She's satisfied. (*He takes a
gulp of ale*) For the present.

*She looks from him to her husband. Sir Timothy is
going from plank to plank inspecting his apparatus.
Thermometers and barometers have been set up alongside the jars. He is noting readings with a crayon in his
book.*

*She looks at Cobb again. There is a compact between
them now, as if he has filled his part in humiliating her
husband, and has earned her promise.*

LAVINIA: You were saying just now—

COBB: Mm?

LAVINIA (*puzzling it out*): That immorality—is what
gives us pain. (*Cobb nods*) Then—the London wives
and their lovers must suffer a great deal?

COBB (*grinning*): Not a bit.

LAVINIA: But surely—

COBB: They're not immoral. They're enjoying a natural
virtue. What morality is there in being tied to—a
dotard, for instance?

LAVINIA (*softly*): Or a dullard. (*She laughs prettily*) I
begin to understand.

COBB: You've much to learn. You must learn it.

LAVINIA: Yes. I must.

*For a sudden, split second there is a disturbance in
the air, a mere blink of sound, shrill and gone in a
moment.*

Tetsy, who is filling a mug at the cask, drops it. She gives a wail of terror.

Sam runs to her. Her cry dies into sharp sobbing. She seems unaware even of his arms around her.

Men are scrambling to their feet. Sir Timothy comes running. Lavinia springs from her seat and starts towards the spot.

SIR TIMOTHY: That noise frightened her.

She shakes her head, unable to speak.

LAVINIA: What was it?

SIR TIMOTHY: Sounded like—a shot somewhere across the valley.

SAM: No, it was here. *(Pulling the girl round)* All right, love. 'Tis gone now.

TETSY *(looking into his face and whispering)*: I seen the road!

SAM: Eh!

SIR TIMOTHY: What does she say?

Tetsy turns to him, her voice gaining strength as she speaks.

TETSY: Like a lightnin' flash, I seen it! There wasn' no trees, but a huge, wide road—an' things movin'— *(Clutching at Sam)* Didn' you see it? *(Sam shakes his head. She looks again at Sir Timothy and from him to the other men. Heads shake)* Nobody?

She looks even to Lavinia, whose white face shows only distaste. But beyond her is a surprising sight. Cobb sits with his face buried in his hands. His spilled tankard lies on the grass beside him.

SIR TIMOTHY: Cobb—

He kneels by him. After a moment the heavy face is uncovered, chalk-white. The eyes look warily, slowly about.

COBB: A touch of dyspepsia. I must have eaten too quickly. Rather distressful.

TETSY: Did you see it, sir?

COBB: I—heard a curious sound.

SIR TIMOTHY: That might have been the echo of a fowling piece. A poacher somewhere.

TETSY: It was real—it was real to me! Oh, Sam—
She clings to him, shivering.
SIR TIMOTHY *(to Cobb)*: Nothing else?
Cobb shakes his head. Sir Timothy goes briskly back to his observations.
Cobb meets Lavinia's curious eyes and manages a smile.
COBB *(putting a hand to his stomach)*: Greed. Clear example of vice, it's so painful.
His hand stops rubbing his belly and his smile fades as he looks past her to Jethro.
The negro is regarding him with total disbelief.
A yard away, Tetsy senses the silence and turns from sheltering in Sam's arms.
TETSY *(whispering)*: He was lyin'.
Cobb looks up at the ring of doubting faces.
JETHRO: Were you?
COBB: Jethro!
JETHRO: Were you?
COBB *(pulling himself up on one knee)*: I will not have you speak so—
JETHRO: Here in this place, I can! I am not real to you, am I? I'm something you made, not a man. But the man is speaking to you now! Mr Cobb, you have a great mind, but there are too many things it won't admit—troubling, odd, hid-away, mean things—even in yourself. Yes, listen to me! They'll rise up and spoil your grand design—you can't talk them away and make a new world just with words—not even all *your* words, Mr Cobb—
There is a wild jangling and clashing from the rope barrier.

The Roped Trees

Near the cart, bells and coils of rusty iron are jumping and clanking on the rope. Sam and one or two other men come running. They can see no cause.

The Clearing

Sir Timothy pauses only to grab the loaded blunderbuss before running after Sam and the others. Jethro glances at Cobb, picks up a lantern and goes too.

Lavinia looks at Cobb. He is breathing fast, all complacency gone.

The Roped Trees

A long shot across a different section of the rope barrier. Sir Timothy and Jethro join the other searchers. The rope in the foreground is undisturbed. But now something creeps towards it from outside. A pitchfork.

It tweaks the rope deftly and sharply, then whips out of sight. The cowbell and scraps of harness on the rope are set jangling.

JETHRO *(pointing)*: There!

The men come running, Sir Timothy in the lead with his blunderbuss. The others have their staffs and rakes at the ready. As they peer about, there is growing alarm in their faces.

From the silhouetted shape of a tree in the foreground outside the rope—something projects. The end of a pitchfork. A man's head follows it, watching them go.

Jethro suddenly turns, flashing the lantern round. Before the head can withdraw, he has seen it.

JETHRO *(shouting)*: It's Jeff! Behind that tree.

They turn quickly back. The big man springs out into the lamplight, roaring with laughter.

BIG JEFF: How's that for a spook? You should'a seen your faces!

His wild laughter is cut off by a thunderous boom from the blunderbuss.

Sir Timothy has fired over his head. Jeff cringes,

He crouches over the Leyden Jars. Cobb stares at him, momentarily baffled.

COBB: That—humility again. *(As the implications begin to reach him, he draws back, suddenly and strangely appalled)* Selfless. Aimless. Mindless. Why do I suddenly find danger in it? *(He starts back towards the middle of the clearing)* Yes, danger—danger!

The camera pans from him to a couple of men on watch by the rope. They turn back to look out into the darkness.

COBB *(joining Lavinia)*: Make sure you despise him for the right reasons. *(She frowns)* He is ruthless in his way.

LAVINIA: Timothy!

COBB *(seized with insight)*: One of a blind, mad pack! They will do things!

LAVINIA: What do you mean?

COBB *(coming to himself)*: Let us leave this place. *(She shakes her head, watching him)* Why not? *(She says nothing)* I'm afraid now. You know that.

LAVINIA: Yes.

COBB: And you want to watch it.

She says nothing. The camera pans from them to where Sam is wiping down the reloaded blunderbuss with a greasy rag. Tetsy is at his side. Jethro sits without expression. In the tree above, Lukey is cramped and watchful. He stretches.

At the rope barrier, a man joins two of the others and they crouch, listening.

The camera pans to Sir Timothy. He is just rising from his observations when he freezes at a small, sharp sound. It lasts perhaps two seconds, distant and uncanny, a fragment of a shrill wail.

Sam is instantly on his feet, the gun raised.

Above in the tree, Lukey stares about in alarm, grabbing at the trunk.

Lavinia is looking to Cobb when her husband hurries across and grabs Sam by the arm.

SIR TIMOTHY: Was that like the sounds you heard?

SAM: Yes, I—think so—

*Cobb steps forward, fighting to maintain his compo-
sure. His voice has a shake in it.*

COBB: This is where we must take a grip on our
senses. Whatever this be, it is of the world we in-
habit. We *can* understand it if we seek a profoundly
natural—

*This time the distant wail lasts a fraction longer,
three or four seconds. And there are other, more staccato, sounds superimposed on it.*

SAM (*pointing*): Far away yonder! That's where it started
before—

COBB: Quiet, lad.

*There is a blast of sound in the very clearing. Again
it cuts in sharply, but this is a terrible medley of noises,
of deafening loudness. It lasts only a second or so.
Then it cuts again.*

*Lavinia clings to Cobb in terror. All round the clear-
ing the men are shouting out their alarm. The lad
comes tumbling down from his tree almost at Sir Timothy's feet.*

*The squire brushes aside the shuddering lad and
crouches by his precious apparatus on the nearest plank.
Sweat is streaming down his face.*

*Cobb looks jerkily about, his heavy face loose. Sam
has dropped the gun. One arm is round Tetsy, his other
hand creeps to the hidden talisman within his jerkin.*

In the tree, Lukey has stuck to his post.

LUKEY (*shouting down*): Squire! Squire!

*Below, Sir Timothy is at the electrical apparatus. He
yells back.*

SIR TIMOTHY: Stay where you are!

*The tiny gold leaves of the electroscope are moving,
opening and closing as a charge reaches them through
the wire. Sparks flicker between two brass knobs.*

*The distant sounds come again—and again—in short,
irregular bursts. From now on they do not cease.*

Sir Timothy sits back on his haunches, watched by fearful men nearby. He wipes his sleeve across his streaming face and turns again to his notes.

Lavinia looks to Cobb with a desperate trustfulness.

LAVINIA: Say what this is! I know you can! You must.

But he has no comfort for her. He shakes his head, looking vaguely about—and encounters Tetsy's eyes fixed on him across Sam's shoulder. He frees himself from Lavinia and calls to her.

COBB: Do you see anything?

TETSY: No—not now.

COBB: Nor I.

Sam turns.

SAM: Now you believe me!

Cobb looks round the clearing in a wave of demoralisation. The distant sounds go on—and for the first time it is possible to read some meaning into them.

Nothing that Cobb can understand, as his expression shows—but to listeners of two centuries later, the sounds would be hideously significant.

As they blend more and more it is just possible to discern the rising and falling of numerous air-attack sirens at a considerable distance. Unsynchronised, they tend to merge into a single wavering throb, but even that is unmistakably evocative. Superimposed on it are small, sharper sounds—distant car horns in frantic chorus.

Two men on watch suddenly throw down their staffs and run across the clearing past Cobb. One ducks under the ropes and is away. The other gets tangled. Bells ring and clatter.

SIR TIMOTHY: Stop them! You there—come back! I need you—

But the men are gone, and the others are on the brink of doing the same.

The second, far louder, type of sound breaks out again—at first in half a dozen rapid, fragmentary blips, then slowing to irregular bursts that last three or four seconds each. The sheer volume of sound is terrifying. It shatters those in the clearing. More men run off.

Glass jars are kicked aside, smashed by running feet. The rope itself is trampled down. A man stumbles through Sir Timothy's electrical apparatus, dragging wires, scattering Leyden Jars.

Lukey Chase lets go his toasting forks and slithers down through the branches.

Below, Sir Timothy runs from hopelessly trampled apparatus to the next position. There is dread in his face, but he manages to concentrate enough to get the lids on to the jars.

Lukey tumbles to the ground behind him and is about to run after the other men when he sees the squire. He rushes across and grabs him by the shoulder.

LUKEY: Quick, sir—get out of this!

But Sir Timothy shakes him off wildly. Lukey shrinks as another clap of sound strikes, and runs for his life.

He bolts past Sam, on his knees now and still holding on to the terrified Tetsy.

SAM: Hear the road now! Hear them running there!

The intermittent bursts of the louder sound are blending into a single roar. And picked out in it, as if close at hand, is the particular sound of running feet on concrete, of many feet, moving fast.

Sam suddenly makes a plunge for the gun and stands up facing the unseen runners.

SAM: Stop, you—devils or whatever you be! Hold or I'll shoot! Hold, will ye!

But the noises crash on, and in another moment Sam's gesture is over. He drops to the ground in abandonment to mortal terror. Tetsy crawls over to him, looking to the others in desperate appeal.

Lavinia is crouching by the fallen tree. Her cloak has slipped off and she is shaking with cold and terror, her arms crossed across her breasts. Cobb is on his feet but seems to be supporting himself against the shattered trunk as if he has lost the power to move.

Suddenly Lavinia starts forward, hands over her ears to keep the battering noises out until she reaches safety. She runs only a few paces before tumbling, tripped by a root. As if the fall frees some paralysed mechanism in her, she starts to scream.

She finds herself lifted, turned about, and looks into the face of the negro.

LAVINIA: Save me! Oh, save me!

But he glances round at the others who are equally helpless. He tugs off his livery coat and throws it over the shuddering woman—

Cobb stands rigid, hypnotised by the experience.

The running footsteps seem to have passed. And the huge formless roaring that lay behind them has sharpened in its turn—to the engines of innumerable cars. It is as if they are roaring through this very clearing in hundreds. A burst of angry hooting in the distance is echoed by horns close at hand as they scream by.

Jethro is tugging at Cobb's arm.

COBB (*resisting*): No—

JETHRO: Come quick, sir—

COBB: Listen! It's machines!

JETHRO: Please—

COBB: Machines, Jethro, great machines! This can be nothing of the past!

JETHRO: Master—

COBB: I must hear! Leave me!

He shakes off the servant's grip, clings again to the trunk for support as Jethro goes.

The noises are almost continuous now, and changing their nature. Brakes scream, horns blare close at hand. A rending crash is followed by a rapid series of metallic crunches, as if cars have piled together. Women scream, men shout. There is a brutal revving of engines as if in the worst, most frantic traffic jam of all time. More and more voices are shouting, at first unintelligibly. Car doors are slammed. There are more footsteps ringing out on the concrete.

Sir Timothy totters to the middle of the clearing with his notebook still in his hand. Cobb has not moved.

Sam, flat on the ground with Tetsy at his side, draws the twig cross out of his jerkin and holds it before the shaking girl.

Lavinia is lying where she fell, hiding under the negro's discarded livery with her hands clamped on her ears. Jethro is nearby. He is bare to the waist, on his knees facing the direction from which the noises first came. He has drawn two spindly saplings together across the track and is fumbling to tie them with a strip of livery braid. He mumbles to himself, half-remembered words from the past. His eyes are squeezed shut as if he is trying to close his mind against the noise.

The camera pans to the ground, to the raw, trodden leafmould.

The strangely blurred voices of the unseen people are clearer, sharp with fear.

VOICES: Get out of it! Get back there! Where's the police? Get out of the way! Get back! Back up there! Drive into them! Go on, that'll shift 'em! It's a pile-up, can't you see! It's hopeless! They're all shunted up! Dozens of 'em . . .

WOMAN ONE: Oh God, oh God, oh God!

MAN ONE *(almost sobbing)*: Clear it, make them clear it!

MAN TWO: All lanes blocked—it's hopeless!

WOMAN TWO: More to the side there, quick! On to the hard shoulder—

MAN TWO: It's no use!

WOMAN TWO: They're all doing it!

MAN TWO: No bloody use—

WOMAN TWO: Quick, before he does!

MAN TWO: It's all blocked solid.

MAN ONE: That crash did it. If it hadn't been for that—

WOMAN ONE: Oh God, oh God, oh God—

MAN ONE *(bellowing)*: Let us through! For Christ's sake let us through!

MAN THREE: Out of the car—quick!

WOMAN THREE: What's the use? It must be time—

MAN THREE: Come on, kids! All out, quick!

WOMAN THREE: They said four minutes! It must be about that—

MAN THREE: Quick, I said!

WOMAN THREE: Oh, Charlie—

MAN THREE: Now we're going for a run—first to reach the signboard gets a shilling—

WOMAN ONE: Oh God, oh God, oh God—

MAN ONE: We can crawl across the bonnets!

MAN THREE: Run like hell! Run, damn you, run!

WOMAN ONE: Oh God, oh God!

She slurs into helpless sobbing.

MAN TWO: Four minutes, it's far more than that now—

MAN ONE: What's the time, then?

MAN TWO: Far more than four minutes—

WOMAN TWO: P'raps it's not going to—p'raps it won't—p'raps it's all a mistake—

She goes off into hysterical laughter.

The voices blur again, yelling, arguing and simply gibbering with helpless fright.

Close shot of Cobb. He gives a sudden moan, a curious formless cry at the impact of a sensation too great to bear:

COBB: Oh, there—

Tetsy, on the ground, covers her eyes even from the rough cross. As Sir Timothy drags himself towards the fallen tree:

COBB: I can see them! I can see the road!

Appalled, he stares along the leafy space of the clearing.

SIR TIMOTHY: What are they?

COBB (*vaguely*): People—

The voices sharpen again.

WOMAN TWO: Why don't they come! I want them to come! I want the rockets!

CHILD: What rockets! Daddy, what rockets?

MAN FOUR: Shut up!

WOMAN TWO: Send them quick! Send the rockets quick! Get it over—get it over!

Cobb rubs a hand hard across his eyes.

COBB: I can't see—it's gone again—

SIR TIMOTHY: They said—"rockets"—

A wide shot of the clearing with its few crouching figures, as the sounds and voices go on. The traffic roar has died away. Instead, there is a huge, murmurous lull. A few voices, far off, are singing a hymn.

Car doors slam in increasing numbers and the walking feet move rapidly, between the unseen halted vehicles.

Close shot of the ground, all grass and earth, with Sam's shaking hand in frame clutching his twig cross. The footsteps clatter only a few feet away, and voices are clear and close.

MAN FOUR: Quicker! Quicker, darling—gimme the baby!

WOMAN FOUR: Can you manage?

MAN FOUR: I can manage another! Now then— *(Roars)* Ronnie!

WOMAN FOUR: Ronnie, hold on to Sue's hand! Keep together among the cars!

CHILD: We're walking on the motorway!

WOMAN FOUR *(with dreadful, anguished firmness)*: That's right. Walking on the motorway. Isn't that a funny thing? Because you're not supposed ever—

Wide shot of clearing.

The individual voices are lost in an extraordinary human sound. A vast anguish that seems to start far off along the motorway and sweep it along, growing. A multitude in total desolation.

The camera cranes slowly towards Cobb.

COBB *(crying out)*: I see them! All!

The wail dies slowly. Only a few tiny, sporadic sounds—a dog barking, babies crying, a bell—break the relative quiet.

The camera reaches close shot of Cobb and halts as a

thunderous nuclear roar crashes out from an explosion perhaps twenty miles away.

Cobb convulses at what he sees. The camera cranes in closer and closer as—

Demoralised, random cries break out again, close at hand. A woman screams in short, sharp barks. A man's voice is shouting in hysterical relief:

MAN: They missed us! We're all right, we're all right—

The camera is tight on Cobb's staring eyes.

All sound cuts dead.

Cobb's eyes squeeze shut. He claps his fingers upon them, as if to crush the eyeballs and destroy the sight in them. And the colossal sound of a thermonuclear blast wave, sweeping outwards from the point of impact, thunders out and spreads and fades.

A low, wide shot of the clearing. For some seconds there is hardly a movement. Jethro, his bare torso glistening with sweat, looks fearfully round from the crossed Obeah branches. Lavinia lies there with one fragile hand extended to clutch the charm like a drowning creature. Her eyes flutter open.

Cobb is on his feet, shuffling forward in tiny steps. He takes his hands from his eyes at first fearfully. His face has curiously collapsed. He stares straight before him.

SIR TIMOTHY (*at his side*): What did you see? Who were they? You *did* see—tell me! Tell me!

Cobb nods almost imperceptibly.

SIR TIMOTHY: I must know!

Cobb nods on. There is a sound at their feet like an animal worrying. It is Sam, his face distorted as he rocks the limp shape of the girl.

SAM: She's dead! I felt her heart burst!

LAVINIA: Dead—

JETHRO (*whispering*): She saw too—

They move towards Sam and the body he holds. Sir Timothy is crouching there, opening the girl's eyelids for a sign of life.

Cobb hardly notices one more after so many.

His face is vacant, gentle, vulnerable. He drops to his knees and remains there without moving. Jethro looks round and comes to him in concern. He puts a hand on Cobb's shoulder.

JETHRO: Master.

Cobb hardly turns. But it is as if the familiar voice restores some habit of thinking. And consciousness returns to his eyes. He puts a hand to the ground and brings it up full of leafmould. He shows this to Jethro, scattering it through his fingers.

COBB: Yet some day men will come here and make a
    great road through these very woods—a road—

His face shakes into a grotesque mask. His body is racked with great tearing sobs that trail slowly into a low howl of utter despair.

The camera cranes away to a wide, high shot of the clearing.

I think it's pretty well known that Harlan Ellison was auctioneer of the charity auction at the 1986 Worldcon to raise money for the widow of Manly Wade Wellman. Some of the items put up for auction were quite amazing, and the generosity of the many hundreds of bidders was remarkable testimony to the essential goodness of ordinary people when they're given an opportunity to demonstrate it.

But the fact the auction raised over $27,000 for Frances Wellman (and ended any fear that she might lose her house in trying to pay Manly's heavy medical expenses) is due in large measure to the energy with which Harlan threw himself into the business of auctioneering. A lot of people made a difference that day; but Harlan made a lot of difference.

That was public; some could claim that Harlan did it for personal publicity (they would be wrong). Therefore, let me tell you what happened the afternoon of April 5, 1986.

Harlan was in Chapel Hill to speak at the university the night before, and to do a book signing that morning. He'd arranged to come out and see Manly after the signing.

Manly had been bed-ridden since a fall ten months

before. He died while Harlan was on his way to the house.

Instead of mumbling regrets and leaving, Harlan spent the rest of the afternoon with Manly's widow, doing as much or more to comfort her as any of Manly's closest friends. It was at Harlan's suggestion that we reinstated the planned party that had been hastily cancelled, getting Frances out of the house and into the company of a large number of sympathetic people.

When all's said and done, I think that afternoon was more important to Frances than the money gathered over Labor Day weekend.

Harlan Ellison isn't in this collection because he's a nice guy. He's in here because he's one of the top handful of writers in the field, and because he's written some stories which fit the theme of these anthologies perfectly.

But he is a nice guy.

FINAL TROPHY

Harlan Ellison

It was the grisliest trophy of them all. Hanging there
in the main club room of the Trottersmen, it was a grim
reminder that not all the members were idle playboys
who had bought their memberships with animals shot
from ambush in the interdicted kraals of Africa or the
blue mist-jungles of Todopus III.

It was a strange trophy, plaque-mounted between the
head of a Coke's hartebeest and the fanged jaws of a
szlygor. There was the damndest watchfulness in the
eyes.

It had been Nathaniel Derr's final grant to his club.
A visitor to the Trottersmen's gallery (invited down
from the weekly open cocktail party) could walk through
room after room filled with the bloody booty of two
hundred hunting expeditions Derr had commissioned.
A visitor (whether hip-booted spacer or effete digni-
tary) would surely marvel at the quantity and diversity
of wildlife Derr had mastered. Photoblox showed him
proudly resting one foot on the blasted carcasses of

*Mountain Gorilla and Cape Lion, butchered Hook-lipped
Rhino and puma. Hides with the Derr emblem branded
on them festooned every wall: cheetah and javelina,
Huanaco and Sika Deer, deeler and ferrl-cat. The
mounted heads were awesome: bull elephant and prestosaur, king cobra and desert wolf. The word* hunter
*seemed weightless when applied to Nathaniel Derr; per-
haps agent of destruction might have approached the
reality.*

Even among the Trottersmen he had been sui gene-
ris. *His fellow clubmen had called him a fanatic. Some
even called him butcher—but not publicly. Nathaniel
Derr had left the Trottersmen almost thirteen million
dollars.*

And the final trophy.

*But if the visitor was particularly trustworthy, and if
they had all taken several stingarees too many, and if
the visitor wheedled properly, the Trottersmen might
just tell him the story behind that gruesome trophy.*

*The story of Nathaniel Derr's last kill. And of his
visit to the planet Ristable.*

The day, like all the days since he had arrived at
Ristable, was too placid for Derr. Had the planet sported
thirty-two kilometer an hour gales, or freezing snow-
storms, or unbearable heat as in the veldt . . . then he
would have gladly suffered, and even reveled in it.
Discomfort was the hunter's environment.

But this baby-bath of a world was serene, and calm,
and unflurried.

Nathaniel Derr did not care to have his hunter status
challenged, even by the climate.

He stared out of the slowly-moving half-track truck,
watching the waist-high, unbroken plain of dull russet
grass whisper past. He felt the faint stirring of the winds
as they ruffled his thick, gray hair.

Derr was a big man: big of chest, big of hand. Big
even in the way he watched, and the way he fondled

the stet-rifle. As though he had been born with the gun grafted to him.

His eyes had the tell-tale wrinkles around them that labeled him a watcher. In a stand of grass, in the bush, or waiting for a flight of mallards to honk overhead, he was a watcher. Again, there was something else, less simple, in his face.

A hunter's face . . .

. . . but something else, too.

"Hey, you!" he yelled over the noise of the truck's antique water-piston engine. The nut-brown native who drove the half-track paid no attention. The truck made too much noise. Derr yelled again, louder: "Hey, you! Dummy!" The native's oblong head turned slightly; he inclined an ear; Derr yelled, "What is this we're going to?"

The native's voice was deep and throaty, a typical Ristabite tone. "Ristable, *shasir* Derr." Nothing more. He turned back to the driving.

Derr let his heavy features settle down into a frown. The word "ristable" seemed to mean many things on this planet. First, it meant "home," the name of the world; and now it was the name of a ceremony or something he was about to attend. He had heard it used several other ways during the past week.

Nathaniel Derr turned his thoughts inward as the half-track rolled over the grassland. The past week; he dwelled on it sequentially.

When he had applied to the Mercantile System for super-cargo passage on a liner out to the stars, he had hoped for bigger hunts, better kills, finer trophies. But though it had cost him more for this one trip than all the safaris he had staged on Earth—and they were many, many—so far his appetite had only been whetted. The szlygor he had bagged on Haggadore was a puny thing . . . even though it had gutted three of his bearers before he'd gotten the 50.50 charge into the beast's brain. The prestosaur was big, but too cumbersome to have been any real threat. The ferrl-cat and the deeler had been the roughest. The deeler was more an asp than a spider, but had exhibited the deadliest traits of both before he had slit its hood with his vibroblade. The ferrl-cat had dropped from a feathery-leafed tree on Yawmac; and it was proof indeed that Derr's age had not diminished his strength, for he had strangled the fearsome yellow feline. Even so, the vibrant surge of the *maximum kill* had been absent. Perhaps he had expected too much.

But Ristable was just *too* dead, *too* boring, *too* unexciting.

The planet was old; so ancient; all mountains had long since flattened away; undisturbed grassland swayed from one end of the single great continent to the other. The natives were simple, uncomplicated agrarian folk, who just happened to thresh from their grasses a sweet flour much enjoyed by gourmets on a hundred worlds, and worth all the plasteel hoes and rakes the merc-ships could trade.

So here he was on Ristable, where the rubble of the glorious ancient cities lay at the edges of the grasslands, slowly dissolving into the land from which they had come.

The past week had been one of utter boredom, while the natives went about their haggling, the merc-ship's crew stretched and mildly leched, and the big red sun, Sayto, burned its way across the sky.

No hunting, too much sleeping, and a growing disgust of the slothful natives. It was true they were anxious to learn about civilization—take the driver of this half-track—but though they mimicked the Earthmen's ways, still they were farmers, slow and dull. He had watched them all week, tending their farms, having community feasts, and taking care of the animals that lives out on the plains.

In fact, today had been the first break in the monotony. Nerrows, the captain of the merc-ship, had come to him that morning, and offered him a chance to see a "ristable."

"I thought that was the name of the planet?" Derr had said, pulling on his bush-boots.

Nerrows had thumbed his cap back on his crewcut head, and his slim face had broken lightly in a smile. "When these people come up with a good word, they don't let it go easily. Yeah, that's right. The planet *is* Ristable, but so are the animals out there." He jerked a thumb at the grasslands lying beyond the hut. "And so is the ceremony they have once a week . . . ristable, that is."

Derr had perked up sharply. "What ceremony?"

Nerrows smiled again, and said, "You know what the word 'ristable' means in this usage? I didn't think so; it means, literally, 'Kill day.' Want to take it in? The ship won't be unsaddled here more than a couple days, so you'd better take in all you can."

Derr stood up, smoothing out his hunt-jacket, slipping into it, sealing it shut. "Is it safe? They won't try to lynch me for observing the secret ceremony, or anything?"

Nerrows waved away the worried comment. "Safest planet on our route. These people haven't had wars since before man was born. You're completely safe, Derr."

The hunter clapped the captain on his thin shoulders, wondering inwardly how such a scrawny sample could get to be a merc-ship officer . . . he'd *never* make it where it counted . . . as a hunter. "Okay, Captain, thanks a lot. Got someone who can direct me out there?"

Derr tapped the native again. "How much farther?"

The native's horny shoulders bobbed. "Ten, 'leven k'lometer, *shasir* Derr. Big ristable today."

Derr pulled a black cigar from the cartridge ring, one of ten in a broken row across his jacket. He lit it. Drew deeply. He never kept extra cartridges in the rings; if he hadn't bagged his quarry by the time the stet-rifle was empty, Derr felt he deserved to die. That was his philosophy. He drew down on the black cigar, let a heavy cloud of smoke billow up over his head.

The ancient water-piston half-track rolled steadily out into the grasslands.

They passed a pile of rubble; Derr recognized it as another of the lost cities. The faintly pink columns rose spiraling, then broke with ragged abruptness. Strangely-pyramidal structures split down the middle. Carved figures with smashed noses, broken arms, shattered forms . . . forms which could not be understood . . . humanoid or something else?

As they came abreast of the ruined city with huge clumps of grass growing up in its middle, Derr crossed his legs in the back seat, and he said, "Those cities, who made them?"

The native shrugged. "Don't know. Ristable."

Ristable again.

The half-track passed walking natives, heading toward a plume of gray smoke that twisted out of the grasslands ahead. Eventually, they drew up on the edge of a widely-cleared dirt area. Surrounded by the waist-high russet grass on all sides, it was like a bald spot on someone's head. The dirt was packed solid and hard with the footprints of a hundred thousand bare feet. The smoke rose from a large bonfire used to summon the natives. Even as Derr watched, the crowd that had already gathered swelled at the edges.

Strangely enough, a path quite wide and straight leading out to the grasslands was left in the circle of natives.

"What's that?" Derr asked the driver, motioning to the circle, to the path, to the Ristabites watching at nothing. The native motioned him to silence and Derr realized, for the first time, that there wasn't a sound in the crowd. The natives, male and female, children and old dark-brown crones, stood silently, shifting their feet, watching, but not speaking.

"Come on, boy, open up!" Derr prodded the native angrily. "What's this whole thing . . . what's that path there . . . ?"

The native spun around, looked at Derr for a moment in annoyance and open anger, and then vaulted out of the half-track. In a moment he was lost in the crowd.

Derr had no other choice: he slung the stet-rifle over his shoulder, and slid up onto the rollbar between the driver's cab and the back seat, getting a better view of what was happening.

What was happening, as he settled himself, was that a medium-sized animal—the ones taken care of by the natives, and labeled, inevitably, ristables—was loping in from the grasslands; on six double-jointed legs.

It was the size of a large horse, or a small black bear. It was dull gray in color, mottled with whitish spots along the underbelly. Its chest was massive. It was built as an allosaurus might have been. Smooth front that rose straight up to a triangular skull with huge, pocketed eyes set forward on each side of the head. The back sloped sharply at forty-five degrees, ending in a horny tail. The head was darker gray, and had one gigantic unicorn-like horn protruding from a space midway between the eyes. No . . . as Derr watched it coming closer, he saw that the horn was not single; there was a smaller, less apparent horn stuck down near the base of the larger one.

The beast also had two groups of vestigial tentacles, appearing to be six or eight to a cluster; one on either side of its body, halfway up the massive neck.

This was a ristable. As everything was ristable.

The beast charged down the path between the natives, much like a bull entering the *Plaza de Toros*, and stopped in the center, its little red eyes glaring, the two front paws clopping at the dirt, leaving furrows.

Abruptly, a native stepped out of the crowd, and removed all his clothing—little enough to begin with—

and called to the animal (Derr continued to think of it as a bull, for no good reason, except this seemed to be a bullfight), clapping his hands, stamping his feet.

Bullfight, Derr thought. *This is more like it*. Then he thought, *Ristable. Kill Day*.

The native moved slowly, letting the beast edge in on him. It pawed the ground, and snorted through a pair of breather holes below the horns. Then the native leaped in the air, and chanted something unintelligible. As he came down in the dirt, the animal moved sharply, and charged across the cleared space. People in its line of attack stepped back quickly; and the native leaped agilely out of the way.

It went that way for over an hour.

The ristable charged, and the native leaped out of its path.

Then, when Derr was convinced it would go on this way till darkness . . . the dance changed. Radically.

The native settled down cross-legged in the dirt, and clasped his hands to his chest. He settled down, and the bull charged. He settled down . . . and . . .

Great God! thought Derr in horror, *he's sitting there, letting it gore him. He's* . . .

Then it was over, and they carried the native away, as the ristable loped back down the path to the grassland.

There was no reaction from the crowd: no dismay, no applause, no notice taken.

Derr slipped back into the half-track, bewildered; and sometime later, though Derr was unaware of it, the driver came back to the truck, stared at him silently for a few seconds, then vaulted over the low door, and started the engine.

Derr stirred slightly as the half-track rolled away from the cleared space. His tracker's mind registered that the dirt was of a darker hue than when they had arrived; and that the rest of the natives were walking swiftly back toward the village . . . carrying something sodden; but he seemed to be far lost in thought.

The half-track passed the natives, and arrived in town an hour before the sodden cargo was brought in and laid to rest alongside hundreds of previous loads filling identical graves.

"I'm not going on with you, Nerrows," Derr said.

"You know we'll be heading out—Artemis, Shoista, Lalook, Coastal II—and we won't be able to pick you up for almost three months." He stared at Derr with annoyance.

"I know that."

"Then why do you want to stay?"

"There's a trophy here I want."

Nerrows' eyes slitted down. "Watch that stuff, Derr."

"No, no, nothing like that. The ristable."

"You mean the animal out there in the fields, the one they go fight every week?"

Derr nodded, checked the stet-rifle, though he was not going hunting for a while yet. "That's it. But there's something important these natives don't know about that creature."

"Yeah? What?"

"How to kill it."

"What are you talking about?"

Derr settled back on the cot, looked at Nerrows carefully. "I talked to some of the natives when I got back yesterday from that ceremony. They go out every week to fight the ristable."

"So?"

"They always lose."

"Always?"

"Every damned time. They haven't won a bout with those beasts for as long as they can remember. Do you know that they plant their dead in rows of two hundred?"

The captain nodded. "Yes, I've noticed that."

Derr pulled a cigar loose, lit it, smiled grimly. "But there's something you *didn't* know . . . namely, they plant rows on *top* of the rows. What's out there now," he waved at the native cemetery, "is the five-hundredth generation, or something like that. They've been fighting the ristables, dying regularly, and being planted for time beyond memory."

The captain looked bemused. "The best fertilizer, they tell me."

"Ah, that's just it!" Derr waved the cigar melodramatically. "They've been winding up like that for centuries . . . without once winning."

"Don't they *want* to win?"

Derr looked perplexed for a moment, spread his hands. "From what I can tell, from what I was able to get out of the Headsman, they just don't know any other way. They've been doing it that way, *just* that way, since before they can remember, and they don't know why. I asked the Headsman, and he stared at me as if I'd asked him why he breathed.

"Then he answered that it was just the way things were; that's all."

Nerrows scuffed his feet at the hard-packed floor of the hut. He looked up at Derr finally. "What's that got to do with you?"

"I got the permission of the Headsman to go into the cleared space, in place of a native some week soon. He thought I was nuts, but he'll soon see how an Earthman fights!"

For ten weeks Derr had watched them get mauled and bloodied and ripped and killed. Now, stripped to the waist, clad only in a breechclout, the ornately-carved bush-knife in his thick, square hand, Nathaniel Derr moved into the cleared space to face his first ristable.

The beast loped in from the grassland almost immediately, passing between the natives lining the path without touching anyone. *Strange how it seems to know what it's to fight, and not bother any others*, he thought, hefting the razor-bladed weapon. Sweat had begun to

stand out on his face, and the smooth handle of the
knife felt slippery in his grip. He dried his hand on the
breechclout, and took the knife again.

The ristable lumbered into the clearing, and Derr
made note that it was not the one he had seen the week
before last, nor the week before that, nor last week.
Each week seemed to bring another beast—at some
unknown, unbidden signal—ready to gore a nut-brown
native with that deadly, alabaster horn.

Derr circled around the edge of the clearing, feeling
the heat-sink of the natives behind him. The beast
pawed and circled, too, as though uncertain.

Then it charged. It shot forward on six double-jointed
legs, its tentacle clusters flailing, its head lowered, the
breath snorting from its breather holes.

Derr spun out of the way. The beast pulled up short
before it rammed the crowd.

It turned on him, staring with little red eyes.

Derr stared back, breath coming hot and fast. He felt
good; he felt fine; he felt the kill coming. It was always
like this.

The ristable lurched forward again, this time seeming
to make a short, sharp, sidestepping movement; Derr
had to be quick. He managed to twirl himself past the
beast with only a scant millimeter between his flesh and
that bone-white horn.

The ristable brought up sharply, stopped, turned,
and glared at Derr.

This was the *pojar*, as the natives called it. The time
to stop, the moment to sit down and be killed. So Derr
sat down, in the manner he had seen the natives do it
. . . and oddly, the crowd exhaled with relief.

The ristable pawed, snorted, charged.

It came for him . . . and suddenly Derr was up,
thrusting himself from the dirt with the strength of his
legs, and the ristable could not stop its movement, and
it was past the spot where Derr had sat cross-legged, its

horn tearing the air viciously where Derr's chest had
been a moment before.

But Derr was not there to die.

He was whirling, clutching, and in a stride and a breath
he was on the ristable's back; and the knife hand came
up with a slash and the blood, and down with a thud and
the blood, and back again with a rip and more blood, and
three times more, till the ristable convulsed and tried to
bellow, and tipped over, the legs failing in precision step.

Derr leaped free as the ristable collapsed to the dirt.
He watched in silence and power, the awe and fury of
the triumphant hunter flowing in him like red, rich
wine; watched as his trophy bled to death on the sand.

It died soon enough.

Then the natives seized him.

"Hold it! Stop! What are you doing? I won, I killed
the thing . . . I showed you how to do it . . . let me
go!" But they had him tightly by the arms and the
waist, without word and without expression. They started
to take him away, back to the village.

He struggled and screamed, and had they not taken
the blade from him he would no doubt had slashed
them. But he was powerless, and screamed that he had
done them a favor, showed them how to kill the ristable.

Then when they had him tied in the hut at the edge
of the village, the Headsman told him . . .

"You have killed the ristable. You will die."

As simply as that. No question, no comment, no
appeal, he was to die. The night came all too soon.

When the moons were high overhead he called for
the Headsman. He called, and the Headsman thought
it was for a final wish, a boon. But it was not, for this
was not a Ristabite: this was the Earthman who had not
known the way of it, who had killed the god ristable.

"Look," Derr tried to be calm and logical, "tell me
why I'm to die. I don't know. Can't you see, if I'm to
die, I have a right to know *why*!"

So the Headsman drew from the tribal legend, from memories buried so deeply they were feelings in the blood without literal word or meaning, but were simply "the way of it."

And this was it . . . this was the secret behind it, that wasn't really a secret at all, but just the way of it:

Who rules who? [the Headsman said.] Take the blood in your veins. How do you know that at one time the blood might not have been the dominant life form of Earth, ruling its physical bodies, using them as tools. Then, as time and eons passed, the blood turned its thought to other things, maintaining the bodies merely as habitations.

It *could* be so . . . if the blood ruled you, and not you the blood, it could be so [the Headsman said.] The last thing you would do, under any circumstances, is spill your blood. Don't you wince when you bleed, when you cut yourself, and you rush to bandage yourself? What if it were so, and you had lost the racial memory that said I am ruled by my blood . . . but still you would know the way of it.

That was how it was on Ristable. At one time the bulls, the ristable beasts, ruled the natives. They built the cities with what were now atrophied tentacles. Then as the eons passed, they turned to higher things; and allowed their bodies to graze in the fields; and let the natives feed them; and let the cities rot into themselves.

As time passed, the memories passed—oh, it was a long time; long enough for the mountains of Ristable to sink into grasslands—and eventually the natives had no recollection of what they had been, not even considering themselves ruled, so long and so buried was it. Then they took care of the ristables, and one last vestige of caste remained, for the bulls accepted sacrifices. The natives went to die . . . and one a week was put beneath the sod . . . and that was the way of it.

So deep and so inbred, that there was not even a conscious thought of it; that was simply the way of it.

But here was a stupid Earthman who had not known the way of it. He had won. He had killed a god, a ruler, deeper than any rule that ever existed . . .

That was the secret that Derr learned; the secret that was not even a secret really: just the way of it.

"So if there is anything I can grant," said the Headsman in true sorrow, for he bore this Earthman no malice, "just tell it."

And Nathaniel Derr, the great white hunter from Earth, thought about it.

Finally, as they untied him, taking him to the cleared area outside the village where he had killed the god ruler, the final twist came to him. Then he made his request, knowing the Mercantile Ship would come months too late, and there was nothing to be done.

He made his request, and they tied him between the posts, and finally the new ristable came, with its snow-white horn lowered, and fire in its eyes.

He watched the ristable pawing and snorting and charging, and he knew his request would be carried out.

How strange, he thought, as the tip of the horn plunged deep to the softness that lies within all hard men. *Of all the trophies I've gathered . . .*

Then there was no thought of trophies.

So there it is, hanging between the hartebeest and the szlygor in the Trottersmen's trophy room. There was no choice about hanging it; after all, thirteen million dollars *is* thirteen million dollars. But it does give the members a chill from hell.

Still, there it hangs, and usually the room is closed off. But occasionally, if drinks are too many, and wit is abundant, the tale will be told. Perhaps not always with accuracy, but always with wonder.

Because it *is* a marvelous job of taxidermy.

There are even members who are willing to pay to find out how the Ristabite natives who did the job were able to retain the clean white color of the hair.

. . . and that damned *watchfulness* in the eyes.

The notion of a vessel traveling on a lengthy voyage of discovery is as old as SF (and a great deal older than the English language). I'm tempted to call it the most successful SF format ever, because if a writer can tell a good story in any context, he can tell it in this one (but then, I'm a sucker for travelers' tales, going back to John de Mandeville and Onesicratos before him). The format has been widely used, and its popularity will almost certainly continue even in the unlikely event that something disastrous happens to the starship Enterprise.

Poul here (and in the other story in series with this one "Kith") adds a dimension to the voyage format which I believe is unique.

Perhaps the most frightening of the medieval legends (and there are some doozies, believe me) is that of the Wild Hunt: the band of men who, for their sins, are condemned to hunt on the stormwinds throughout eternity. Poul has used the legend directly in fantasies, which proves he has a good ear for a story; but more remarkably, he has a number of times transmuted that concept into true SF.

"The Horn of Time the Hunter" is, for me, a particularly telling example of this. By blending the Wild Hunt with the voyage of discovery, Poul has created some-

thing literally hellish. Imagine Odysseus if he knew he would never be permitted to reach Ithaka. Imagine Alexander the Great doomed to march eastward forever, until he and everyone who started with him had died. Imagine the Space Beagle *sailing outward, star by star, with no prayer of ever seeing Earth again. . . .*

Imagine the Golden Flyer *here . . . and remember that the Wild Hunt was a special form of damnation.*

THE HORN OF TIME THE HUNTER

Poul Anderson

Now and then, on that planet, Jong Errifrans thought he heard the distant blowing of a horn. It would begin low, with a pulse that quickened as the notes waxed, until the snarl broke in a brazen scream and sank sobbing away. The first time he started and asked the others if they heard. But the sound was on the bare edge of audibility for him, whose ears were young and sharp, and the men said no. "Some trick of the wind, off in the cliffs yonder," Mons Rainart suggested. He shivered. "The damned wind is always hunting here." Jong did not mention it again, but when he heard the noise thereafter a jag of cold went through him.

There was no reason for that. Nothing laired in the city but seabirds, whose wings made a white storm over the tower tops and whose flutings mingled with wind skirl and drum roll of surf; nothing more sinister had appeared than a great tiger-striped fish, which patrolled near the outer reefs. And perhaps that was why Jong feared the horn: it gave the emptiness a voice.

171

At night, rather than set up their glower, the four would gather wood and give themselves the primitive comfort of a fire. Their camping place was in what might once have been a forum. Blocks of polished stone thrust out of the sand and wiry grass that had occupied all streets; toppled colonnades demarked a square. More shelter was offered by the towers clustered in the city's heart, still piercing the sky, the glasit windows still unbroken. But no, those windows were too much like a dead man's eyes, the rooms within were too hushed, now that the machines that had been the city's life lay corroded beneath the dunes. It was better to raise a tent under the stars. Those, at least, were much the same, after twenty thousand years.

The men would eat, and then Regor Lannis, the leader, would lift his communicator bracelet near his mouth and report their day's ransacking. The spaceboat's radio caught the message and relayed it to the *Golden Flyer*, which orbited with the same period as the planet's twenty-one-hour rotation, so that she was always above this island. "Very little news," Regor typically said. "Remnants of tools and so on. We haven't found any bones yet for a radioactivity dating. I don't think we will, either. They probably cremated their dead, to the very end. Mons has estimated that engine block we found began rusting some ten thousand years ago. He's only guessing, though. It wouldn't have lasted at all if the sand hadn't buried it, and we don't know when that happened."

"But you say the furnishings inside the towers are mostly intact, age-proof alloys and synthetics," answered Captain Ilmaray's voice. "Can't you deduce anything from their, well, their arrangement or disarrangement? If the city was plundered—"

"No, sir, the signs are too hard to read. A lot of rooms have obviously been stripped. But we don't know whether that was done in one day or over a period maybe of centuries, as the last colonists mined their homes for stuff they could no longer make. We can only be sure, from the dust, that no one's been inside for longer than I like to think about."

When Regor had signed off, Jong would usually take out his guitar and chord the songs they sang, the immemorial songs of the Kith, many translated from languages spoken before ever men left Earth. It helped drown out the wind and the surf, booming down on the beach where once a harbor had stood. The fire flared high, picking their faces out of night, tinging plain work clothes with unrestful red, and then guttering down so that shadows swallowed the bodies. They looked much alike, those four men, small, lithe, with sharp, dark features; for the Kith were a folk apart, marrying between their own ships, which carried nearly all traffic among the stars. Since a vessel might be gone from Earth for a century or more, the planetbound civilizations, flaring and dying and reborn like the flames that warmed them now, could not be theirs. The men differed chiefly in age, from the sixty years that furrowed Regor Lannis's skin to the twenty that Jong Errifrans had marked not long ago.

Ship's years, mostly, Jong remembered, and looked up to the Milky Way with a shudder. When you fled at almost the speed of light, time shrank for you, and in his own life he had seen the flower and the fall of an empire. He had not thought much about it then—it was the way of things, that the Kith should be quasi-immortal and the planetarians alien, transitory, not quite real. But a voyage of ten thousand light-years toward galactic center, and back, was more than anyone had ventured before; more than anyone would ever have done, save to expiate the crime of crimes. Did the Kith still exist? Did Earth?

After some days, Regor decided: "We'd better take a look at the hinterland. We may improve our luck."

"Nothing in the interior but forest and savannah," Neri Avelair objected. "We saw that from above."

"On foot, though, you see items you miss from a boat," Regor said. "The colonists can't have lived exclusively in places like this. They'd need farms, mines, extractor plants, outlying settlements. If we could examine one of those, we might find clearer indications than in this damned huge warren."

"How much chance would we have, hacking our way through the brush?" Neri argued. "I say let's investigate some of those other towns we spotted."

"They're more ruined yet," Mons Rainart reminded him. "Largely submerged." He need not have spoken; how could they forget? Land does not sink fast. The fact that the sea was eating the cites gave some idea of how long they had been abandoned.

"Just so," Regor nodded. "I don't suppose plunging into the woods, either. That'd need more men and more time than we can spare. But there's an outsize beach about a hundred kilometers north of here, fronting on a narrow-mouthed bay, with fertile hills right behind—hills that look as if they ought to contain ores. I'd be surprised if the colonists did not exploit the area."

Neri's mouth twitched downward. His voice was not quite steady. "How long do we have to stay on this ghost planet before we admit we'll never know what happened?"

"Not too much longer," Regor said. "But we've got to try our best before we do leave."

He jerked a thumb at the city. Its towers soared above fallen walls and marching dunes into a sky full of birds. The bright yellow sun had bleached out their pastel colors, leaving them bone-white. And yet the view on their far side was beautiful, forest that stretched inland a hundred shades of shadow-rippled green, while in the opposite direction the land sloped down to a sea that glittered like emerald strewn with diamond dust, moving and shouting and hurling itself in foam against the reefs. The first generations here must have been very happy, Jong thought.

"Something destroyed them, and it wasn't simply a war," Regor said. "We need to know what. It may not have affected any other world. But maybe it did."

Maybe Earth lay as empty, Jong thought, not for the first time.

The *Golden Flyer* had paused here to refit before venturing back into man's old domain. Captain Ilmaray had chosen an F9 star arbitrarily, three hundred light-years from Sol's calculated present position. They detected no whisper of the energies used by civilized races, who might have posed a threat. The third planet seemed a paradise, Earth-mass but with its land scattered in islands around a global ocean, warm from pole to pole. Mons Rainart was surprised that the carbon dioxide equilibrium was maintained with so little exposed rock. Then he observed weed mats everywhere on the waters, many of them hundreds of square kilometers in area, and decided that their photosynthesis was active enough to produce a Terrestrial-type atmosphere.

The shock had been to observe from orbit the ruined cities. Not that colonization could not have reached this far, and beyond, during twenty thousand years. But the venture had been terminated; why?

That evening it was Jong's turn to hold a personal conversation with those in the mother ship. He got his parents, via intercom, to tell them how he fared. The heart jumped in his breast when Sorya Rainart's voice joined theirs. "Oh yes," the girl said, with an uneven little laugh, "I'm right here in the apartment. Dropped in for a visit, by chance."

Her brother chuckled at Jong's back. The young man flushed and wished hotly for privacy. But of course Sorya would have known he'd call tonight. . . . If the Kith still lived, there could be nothing between him and her. You brought your wife home from another ship. It was spaceman's law, exogamy aiding a survival that was precarious at best. If, though, the last Kith ship but theirs drifted dead among the stars; or the few hundred aboard the *Golden Flyer* and the four on this world whose name was lost were the final remnants of the human race—she was bright and gentle and swayed sweetly when she walked.

"I—" he untangled his tongue. "I'm glad you did. How are you?"

"Lonely and frightened," she confided. Cosmic interference seethed around her words. The fire spat sparks loudly into the darkness overhead. "If you don't learn what went wrong here . . . . I don't know if I can stand wondering the rest of my life."

"Cut that!" he said sharply. The rusting of morale had destroyed more than one ship in the past. Although— "No, I'm sorry." He knew she did not lack courage. The fear was alive in him too that he would be haunted forever by what he had seen here. Death in itself was an old familiar of the Kith. But this time they were returning from a past more ancient than the glaciers and the mammoths had been on Earth when they left. They needed knowledge as much as they needed air, to make sense of the universe. And their first stop in that spiral arm of the Galaxy which had once been home had confronted them with a riddle that looked unanswerable. So deep in history were the roots of the Kith that Jong could recall the symbol of the Sphinx; and suddenly he saw how gruesome it was.

"We'll find out," he promised Sorya. "If not here, then when we arrive at Earth." Inwardly he was unsure. He made small talk and even achieved a joke or two. But afterward, laid out in his sleeping bag, he thought he heard the horn winding in the north.

The expedition rose at dawn, bolted breakfast, and stowed their gear in the spaceboat. It purred from the city on aerodynamic drive, leveled off, flew at low speed not far above ground. The sea tumbled and flashed on the right, the land climbed steeply on the left. No herds of large animals could be seen there. Probably none existed, with such scant room to develop in. But the ocean swarmed. From above Jong could look down into transparent waters, see shadows that were schools of fish numbering in the hundreds of thousands. Further off he observed a herd of grazers, piscine but big as whales, plowing slowly through a weed mat. The colonists must have gotten most of their living from the sea.

Regor set the boat down on a cliff overlooking the bay he had described. The escarpment ringed a curved beach of enormous length and breadth, its sands strewn with rocks and boulders. Kilometers away, the arc closed in on itself, leaving only a strait passage to the ocean. The bay was placid, clear bluish-green beneath the early sun, but not stagnant. The tides of the one big moon must raise and lower it two or three meters in a day, and a river ran in from the southern highlands. Afar Jong could see how shells littered the sand below high-water mark, proof of abundant life. It seemed bitterly unfair to him that the colonists had had to trade so much beauty for darkness.

Regor's lean face turned from one man to the next. "Equipment check," he said, and went down the list: fulgurator, communication bracelet, energy compass, medikit— "My God," said Neri, "you'd think we were off on a year's trek, and separately at that."

"We'll disperse, looking for traces," Regor said, "and those rocks will often hide us from each other." He left the rest unspoken: that that which had been the death of the colony might still exist.

They emerged into cool, flowing air with the salt and iodine and clean decay smell of coasts on every Earth-like world, and made their way down the scrap. "Let's radiate from this point," Regor said, "and if nobody has found anything, we'll meet back here in four hours for lunch."

Jong's path slanted farthest north. He walked briskly at first, enjoying the motion of his muscles, the scrunch of sand and rattle of pebbles beneath his boots, the whistle of the many birds overhead. But presently he must pick his way across drifts of stone and among dark boulders, some as big as houses, which cut him off from the wind and his fellows; and he remembered Sorya's aloneness.

Oh no, not that. Haven't we paid enough? he thought. And, for a moment's defiance: *We didn't do the thing. We condemned the traitors ourselves, and threw them into space, as soon as we learned. Why should we be punished?*

But the Kith had been too long isolated, themselves against the universe, not to hold that the sin and sorrow of one belonged to all. And Tomakan and his coconspirators had done what they did unselfishly, to save the ship. In those last vicious years of the Star Empire, when Earthmen made the Kithfolk scapegoats for their wretchedness until every crew fled to await better times, the *Golden Flyer's* captured people would have died horribly—had Tomakan not bought their freedom by betraying to the persecutors that asteroid where two other Kith vessels lay, readying to leave the Solar System. How could they afterward meet the eyes of their kindred, in the Council that met at Tau Ceti?

The sentence was just: to go exploring to the fringes of the galactic nucleus. Perhaps they would find the Elder Races that must dwell somewhere; perhaps they would bring back the knowledge and wisdom that could heal man's inborn lunacies. Well, they hadn't; but the voyage was something in itself, sufficient to give the *Golden Flyer* back her honor. No doubt everyone who had sat in Council was now dust. Still, their descendants—

Jong stopped in midstride. His shout went ringing among the rocks.

"What is it? Who called? Anything wrong?" The questions flew from his bracelet like anxious bees.

He stooped over a little heap and touched it with fingers that wouldn't hold steady. "Worked flints," he breathed. "Flakes, broken spearheads . . . shaped wood . . . something—" He scrabbled in the sand. Sunlight struck off a piece of metal, rudely hammered into a dagger. It had been, it must have been fashioned from some of the ageless alloy in the city—long ago, for the blade was worn so thin that it had snapped across. He crouched over the shards and babbled.

And shortly Mons' deep tones cut through: "Here's another site! An animal skull, could only have been split with a sharp stone, a thong— Wait, wait, I see something carved in this block, maybe a symbol—"

Then suddenly he roared, and made a queer choked gurgle, and his voice came to an end.

Jong leaped erect. The communicator jabbered with calls from Neri and Regor. He ignored them. There was no time for dismay. He tuned his energy compass. Each bracelet emitted a characteristic frequency besides its carrier wave, for location purposes, and— The needle swung about. His free hand unholstered his fulgurator, and he went bounding over the rocks.

As he broke out into the open stretch of sand the wind hit him full in the face. Momentarily through its shrillness he heard the horn, louder than before, off beyond the cliffs. A part of him remembered fleetingly how one day on a frontier world he had seen a band of huntsmen gallop in pursuit of a wounded animal that wept as it ran, and how the chief had raised a crooked bugle to his lips and blown just such a call.

The note died away. Jong's glance swept the beach. Far down its length he saw several figures emerge from a huddle of boulders. Two of them carried a human shape. He yelled and sprinted to intercept them. The compass dropped from his grasp.

They saw him and paused. When he neared, Jong made out that the form they bore was Mons Rainart's.

He swung ghastly limp between his carriers. Blood dripped from his back and over his breast.

Jong's stare went to the six murderers. They were chillingly manlike, half a meter taller than him, magnificently thewed beneath the naked white skin, but altogether hairless, with long webbed feet and fingers, a high dorsal fin, and smaller fins at heels and elbows and on the domed heads. The features were bony, with great sunken eyes and no external ears. A flap of skin drooped from pinched nose to wide mouth. Two carried flint-tipped wooden spears, two had tridents forged from metal—the tines of one were red and wet—and those who bore the body had knives slung at their waists.

"Stop!" Jong shrieked. "Let him go!"

He plowed to a halt not far off, and menaced them with his gun. The biggest uttered a gruff bark and advanced, trident poised. Jong retreated a step. Whatever they had done, he hated to—

An energy beam winked, followed by its thunderclap. The one who carried Mons' shoulders crumpled, first at the knees, then down into the sand. The blood from the hole burned through him mingled with the spaceman's, equally crimson.

They whirled. Neri Avelair pounded down the beach from the opposite side. His fulgurator spoke again. The shimmering wet sand reflected the blast. It missed, but quartz fused where it struck near the feet of the creatures, and hot droplets spattered them.

The leader waved his trident and shouted. They lumbered toward the water. The one who had Mons' ankles did not let go. The body flapped arms and head as it dragged. Neri shot a third time. Jolted by his own speed, he missed anew. Jong's finger remained frozen on the trigger.

The five giants entered the bay. Its floor shelved rapidly. In a minute they were able to dive below the surface. Neri reached Jong's side and fired, bolt after bolt, till a steam cloud rose into the wind. Tears whipped down his cheeks. "Why didn't you kill them, you bastard?" he screamed. "You could have gunned them down where you were!"

"I don't know." Jong stared at his weapon. It felt oddly heavy.

"They drowned Mons!"

"No . . . he was dead already. I could see. Must have been pierced through the heart. I suppose they ambushed him in those rocks—"

"M-m-maybe. But his body, God damn you, we could'a saved that at least!" Senselessly, Neri put a blast through the finned corpse.

"Stop that," commanded Regor. He threw himself down, gasping for breath. Dimly, Jong noticed gray streaks in the leader's hair. It seemed a matter of pity and terror that Regor Lannis the unbendable should be whittled away by the years.

What am I thinking? Mons is killed. Sorya's brother.

Neri holstered his fulgurator, covered his face with both hands, and sobbed.

After a long while Regor shook himself, rose, knelt again to examine the dead swimmer. "So there were natives here," he muttered. "The colonists must not have known. Or maybe they underestimated what savages could do."

His hands ran over the glabrous hide. "Still warm," he said, almost to himself. "Air-breathing; a true mammal, no doubt, though this male lacks vestigial nipples; real nails on the digits, even if they have grown as thick and sharp as claws." He peeled back the lips and examined the teeth. "Omnivore evolving toward carnivore, I'd guess. The molars are still pretty flat, but the rest are bigger than ours, and rather pointed." He peered into the dimmed eyes. "Human-type vision, probably less acute. You can't see so far underwater. We'll need extensive study to determine the color-sensitivity curve, if any. Not to mention the other adaptations. I daresay they can stay below for many minutes at a stretch.

Doubtless not as long as cetaceans, however. They haven't evolved that far from their land ancestors. You can tell by the fins. Of some use in swimming, but not really an efficient size or shape as yet."

"You can speculate about that while Mons is being carried away?" Neri choked.

Regor got up and tried in a bemused fashion to brush the sand off his clothes. "Oh no," he said. His face worked, and he blinked several times. "We've got to do something about him, of course." He looked skyward. The air was full of wings, as the sea birds sensed meat and wheeled insolently close. Their piping overrode the wind. "Let's get back to the boat. We'll take this carcass along for the scientists."

Neri cursed at the delay, but took one end of the object. Jong had the other. The weight felt monstrous, and seemed to grow while they stumbled toward the cliffs. Breath rasped in their mouths. Their shirts clung to the sweat on them, which they could smell through every sea odor.

Jong looked down at the ugly countenance beneath his hands. In spite of everything, in spite of Mons being dead—oh, never to hear his big laugh again, never to move a chessman or hoist a glass or stand on the thrumming decks with him!—he wondered if a female dwelt somewhere out in the ocean who had thought this face was beautiful.

"We weren't doing them any harm," said Neri between wheezes.

"You can't . . . blame a poison snake . . . or a carnivore . . . if you come too near," Jong said.

"But these aren't dumb animals! Look at that braincase. At that knife." Neri needed a little time before he had the lungful to continue his fury: "We've dealt with nonhumans often enough. Fought them once in a while. But they had a reason to fight . . . mistaken or not, they did. I never saw or heard of anyone striking down utter strangers at first sight."

"We may not have been strangers," Regor said.

"What?" Neri's head twisted around to stare at the older man.

Regor shrugged. "A human colony was planted here. The natives seem to have wiped it out. I imagine they had reasons then. And the tradition may have survived."

For ten thousand years or more? Jong thought, shocked. *What horror did our race visit on theirs, that they haven't been able to forget in so many millennia?*

He tried to picture what might have happened, but found no reality in it, only a dry and somehow thin logic. Presumably this colony was established by a successor civilization to the Star Empire. Presumably that civilization had crumbled in its turn. The settlers had most likely possessed no spaceships of their own; outpost worlds found it easiest to rely on the Kith for what few trade goods they wanted. Often their libraries did not even include the technical data for building a ship, and they lacked the economic surplus necessary to do that research over again.

So—the colony was orphaned. Later, if a period of especially virulent anti-Kithism had occurred here, the traders might have stopped coming; might actually have lost any record of this world's existence. *Or the Kith might have become extinct, but that is not a possibility we will admit.* The planet was left isolated.

Without much land surface it couldn't support a very big population, even if most of the food and industrial resources had been drawn from the sea. However, the people should have been able to maintain a machine culture. No doubt their society would ossify, but static civilizations can last indefinitely.

Unless they are confronted by vigorous barbarians, organized into million-man hordes under the lash of outrage. . . . But was that the answer? Given atomic energy, how could a single city be overrun by any number of neolithic hunters?

Attack from within? A simultaneous revolt of every

autochthonous slave? Jong looked back to the dead face. The teeth glinted at him. *Maybe I'm softheaded. Maybe these beings simply take a weasel's pleasure in killing.*

They struggled up the scarp and into the boat. Jong was relieved to get the thing hidden in a cold-storage locker. But then came the moment when they called the *Golden Flyer* to report.

"I'll tell his family," said Captain Ilmaray, most quietly.

But I'll still have to tell Sorya how he looked, Jong thought. The resolution stiffened in him: *We're going to recover the body. Mons is going to have a Kithman's funeral; hands that loved him will start him on his orbit into the sun.*

He had no reason to voice it, even to himself. The oneness of the Kith reached beyond death. Ilmaray asked only if Regor believed there was a chance.

"Yes, provided we start soon," the leader replied. "The bottom slopes quickly here, but gets no deeper than about thirty meters. Then it's almost flat to some distance beyond the gate, farther than our sonoprobes reached when we flew over. I doubt the swimmers go so fast they can evade us till they reach a depth too great for a nucleoscope to detect Mons' electronic gear."

"Good. Don't take risks, though." Grimly: "We're too short on future heredity as is." After a pause, Ilmaray added, "I'll order a boat with a high-powered magna-screen to the stratosphere, to keep your general area under observation. Luck ride with you."

"And with every ship of ours," Regor finished the formula.

As his fingers moved across the pilot board, raising the vessel, he said over his shoulder, "One of you two get into a spacesuit and be prepared to go down. The other watch the 'scope, and lower him when we find what we're after."

"I'll go," said Jong and Neri into each other's mouths. They exchanged a look. Neri's glared.

"Please," Jong begged. "Maybe I ought to have shot

them down, when I saw what they'd done to Mons. I don't know. But anyhow, I didn't. So let me bring him back, will you?"

Neri regarded him for nearly a minute more before he nodded.

The boat cruised in slow zigzags out across the bay while Jong climbed into his spacesuit. It would serve as well underwater as in the void. He knotted a line about his waist and adjusted the other end to the little winch by the personnel lock. The metallic strand woven into its plastic would conduct phone messages. He draped a sack over one arm for the, well, the search object, and hoped he would not need the slugthrower at his hip.

"There!"

Jong jerked at Neri's shout. Regor brought the craft to hoverhalt, a couple of meters above the surface and three kilometers from shore. "You certain?" he asked.

"Absolutely. Not moving, either. I suppose they abandoned him so as to make a faster escape when they saw us coming through the air."

Jong clamped his helmet shut. External noises ceased. The stillness made him aware of his own breath and pulse and—some inner sound, a stray nerve current or mere imagination—the hunter's horn, remote and triumphant.

The lock opened, filling with sky. Jong walked to the rim and was nearly blinded by the sunlight off the wavelets. Radiance ran to the horizon. He eased himself over the lip. The rope payed out and the surface shut above him. He sank.

A cool green roofed with sunblaze enclosed him. Even through the armor he felt multitudinous vibrations; the sea lived and moved, everywhere around. A pair of fish streaked by, unbelievably graceful. For a heretical instant he wondered if Mons would not rather stay here, lulled to the end of the world.

Cut that! he told himself, and peered downward.

Darkness lurked below. He switched on the powerful flash at his belt.

Particles in the water scattered the light, so that he fell as if through an illuminated cave. More fish passed near. Their scales reflected like jewels. He thought he could make out the bottom now, white sand and up-lifted ranges of rock on which clustered many-colored coraloids, growing toward the sun. And the swimmer appeared.

He moved slowly to the fringe of light and poised. In his left hand he bore a trident, perhaps the one which had killed Mons. At first he squinted against the dazzle, then looked steadily at the radiant metal man. As Jong continued to descend he followed, propelling himself with easy gestures of feet and free hand, a motion as lovely as a snake's.

Jong gasped and yanked out his slugthrower.

"What's the matter?" Neri's voice rattled in his earplugs.

He gulped. "Nothing," he said, without knowing why. "Lower away."

The swimmer came a little closer. His muscles were tense, mouth open as if to bite; but the deep-set eyes remained unwavering. Jong returned the gaze. They went down together.

He's not afraid of me, Jong thought, *or else he's mastered his fear, though he saw on the beach what we can do*.

Impact jarred through his soles. "I'm here," he called mechanically. "Give me some slack and—Oh!"

The blood drained from his head as if an ax had split it. He swayed, supported only by the water. Thunders and winds went through him, and the roar of the horn.

"Jong!" Neri called, infinitely distant. "Something's wrong, I know it is, gimme an answer, for the love of Kith!"

The swimmer touched bottom too. He stood across

from what had belonged to Mons Rainart, the trident upright in his hand.

Jong lifted the gun. "I can fill you with metal," he heard himself groan. "I can cut you to pieces, the way you—you—"

The swimmer shuddered (was the voice conducted to him?) but stayed where he was. Slowly, he raised the trident toward the unseen sun. With a single gesture, he reversed it, thrust it into the sand, let go, and turned his back. A shove of the great legs sent him arrowing off.

The knowledge exploded in Jong. For a century of seconds he stood alone with it.

Regor's words pierced through: "Get my suit. I'm going after him."

"I'm all right," he managed to say. "I found Mons."

He gathered what he could. There wasn't much. "Bring me up," he said.

When he was lifted from the bay and climbed through the air lock, he felt how heavy was the weight upon him. He let fall the sack and trident and crouched beside them. Water ran off his armor.

The doors closed. The boat climbed. A kilometer high, Regor locked the controls and came aft to join the others. Jong removed his helmet just as Neri opened the sack.

Mons' head rolled out and bounced dreadfully across the deck. Neri strangled a yell.

Regor lurched back. "They ate him," he croaked. "They cut him to pieces for food. Didn't they?"

He gathered his will, strode to the port, and squinted out. "I saw one of them break the surface, a short while before you came up," he said between his teeth. Sweat—or was it tears?—coursed down the gullies in his cheeks. "We can catch him. The boat has a gun turret."

"No—" Jong tried to rise, but hadn't the strength.

The radio buzzed. Regor ran to the pilot's chair forward, threw himself into it, and slapped the receiver switch. Neri set lips together, picked up the head, and laid in on the sack. "Mons, Mons, but they'll pay," he said.

Captain Ilmaray's tones filled the hull: "We just got word from the observer boat. It isn't on station yet, but the magnascreen's already spotted a horde of swimmers . . . no, several different flocks, huge, must total thousands . . . converging on the island where you are. At the rate they're going, they should arrive in a couple of days."

Regor shook his head in a stunned fashion. "How did they know?"

"They didn't," Jong mumbled.

Neri leaped to his feet, a tiger movement. "That's exactly the chance we want. A couple of bombs dropped in the middle of 'em."

"You mustn't!" Jong cried. He became able to rise too. The trident was gripped in his hand. "He gave me this."

"What?" Regor swiveled around. Neri stiffened where he stood. Silence poured through the boat.

"Down below," Jong told them. "He saw me and followed me to the bottom. Realized what I was doing. Gave me this. His weapon."

"Whatever *for?*"

"A peace offering. What else?"

Neri spat on the deck. "Peace, with those filthy cannibals?"

Jong squared his shoulders. The armor enclosing him no longer seemed an insupportable burden. "You wouldn't be a cannibal if you ate a monkey, would you?"

Neri said an obscene word, but Regor suppressed him with a gesture. "Well, different species," the pilot admitted coldly. "By the dictionary you're right. But these killers are sentient. You don't eat another thinking being."

"It's been done," Jong said. "By humans too. More often than not as an act of respect or love, taking some of the person's mana into yourself. Anyway, how could they know what we were? When he saw I'd come to gather our dead, he gave me his weapon. How else could he say he was sorry, and that we're brothers? Maybe he even realized that's literally true, after he'd had a little while to think the matter over. But I don't imagine their traditions are that old. It's enough, it's better, actually, that he confessed we were his kin simply because we also care for our dead."

"What are you getting at?" Neri snapped.

"Yes, what the destruction's going on down there?" Ilmaray demanded through the radio.

"Wait." Regor gripped the arms of his chair. His voice fell low. "You don't mean they're—"

"Yes, I do," Jong said. "What else could they be? How could a mammal that big, with hands and brain, evolve on these few islands? How could any natives have wiped out a colony that had atomic arms? I thought about a slave revolt, but that doesn't make sense either. Who'd bother with so many slaves when they had cybernetic machines? No, the swimmers are the colonists. They can't be anything else."

"Huh?" grunted Neri.

Ilmaray said across hollow space: "It could be. If I remember rightly, Homo Sapiens is supposed to have developed from the, uh, Neandertaloid type, in something like ten or twenty thousand years. Given a small population, genetic drift, yes, a group might need less time than that to degenerate."

"Who says they're degenerate?" Jong retorted.

Neri pointed to the staring-eyed head on the deck. "That does."

"Was an accident, I tell you, a misunderstanding," Jong said. "We had it coming, blundering in blind the way we did. They aren't degenerate, they're just adapted. As the colony got more and more dependent on the sea, and mutations occurred, those who could best take this sort of environment had the most children. A static civilization wouldn't notice what was happening till too late, and wouldn't be able to do anything about it if they did. Because the new people had the freedom of the whole planet. The future was theirs."

"Yeah, a future of being savages."

"They couldn't use our kind of civilization. It's wrong for this world. If you're going to spend most of your life in salt water you can't very well keep your electric machines; and flint you can gather almost anywhere is an improvement over metal that has to be mined and smelted.

"Oh, maybe they have lost some intelligence. I doubt that, but if they have, what of it? We never did find the Elder Races. Maybe intelligence really isn't the goal of the universe. I believe, myself, these people are coming back up the ladder in their own way. But that's none of our business." Jong knelt and closed Mons' eyes. "We were allowed to atone for our crime," he said softly. "The least we can do is forgive them in our turn. Isn't it? And . . . we don't know if any other humans are left, anywhere in all the worlds, except us and these. No, we can't kill them."

"Then why did they kill Mons?"

"They're air breathers," Jong said, "and doubtless they have to learn swimming, like pinnipeds, instead of having an instinct. So they need breeding grounds. That beach, yes, that must be where the tribes are headed. A party of males went in advance to make sure the place was in order. They saw something strange and terrible walking on the ground where their children were to be born, and they had the courage to attack it. I'm sorry, Mons," he finished in a whisper.

Neri slumped down on a bench. The silence came back.

Until Ilmaray said: "I think you have the answer. We

can't stay here. Return immediately, and we'll get under weigh."

Regor nodded and touched the controls. The engine hummed into life. Jong got up, walked to a port, and watched the sea, molten silver beneath him, dwindle as the sky darkened and the stars trod forth.

I wonder what that sound was, he thought vaguely. *A wind noise, no doubt, as Mons said. But I'll never be sure.* For a moment it seemed to him that he heard it again, in the thrum of energy and metal, in the beat of his own blood, the horn of a hunter pursuing a quarry that wept as it ran.

There are a two carefully-contrived Briticisms in the name 'Brigadier Donald Ffellowes' which I'll try to explain here.

First, the title Brigadier ('Not Brigadier General.') In British parlance, a brigadier was (rather than is; but the present usage dates back to the original meaning) the officer who commanded a brigade. A brigade was an organization of infantry, cavalry, or artillery.

A unit which included infantry, cavalry, and artillery under a single officer, was a 'general command.' (The modern terminology for such an organization is a combined-arms command.)

The smallest combined-arms command was the division. Divisions were commanded by general officers, because those officers had, in the old terminology, general commands.

America didn't follow British terminology precisely. In part, this resulted from a hatred of rank and privilege in 19th century America; the rank of admiral wasn't reinstated in the Federal navy until well after the start of the Civil War. The army officer directly above colonel was of very high rank indeed (the commander of the *entire Army of the Potomac at the First Battle of Bull Run was Brigadier General McDowell), so the addition of 'general' was reasonable even by British standards.*

Next, to the spelling 'Ffellowes'; which is incorrect, but a comment on American copyeditors rather than on Sterling's ignorance. The spelling goes back to changes in British orthography in the 13th century (two centuries before Gutenburg and movable type, in other words).

Throughout the century, text hands (the form of letters used by scribes to copy books) were moving closer to charter hands (the exceedingly ornate forms of letters used to beautify important documents—and make them difficult for non-specialists to read). Capital letters were of course particularly fancy, but until 1260 the capital F was a thin and boring letter. Then some scribe had the bright idea of looping and doubling the vertical stroke of the letter.

This wasn't quite a double small f, but it was very close to it (because the capital and small fs hadn't been very different to begin with). The practice of doubling the stroke caught on, but it was quickly corrupted to ff—double small f. (You will be pleased to know that double small k and some other similar attempts failed immediately.) A few British family names still preserve the 13th century orthography; that of 'ffellowes' apparently among them.

Ah, but American copyeditors—and particularly magazine copyeditors twenty years ago. If it wasn't in the Tarabian, it was out—history, common sense, and the author's intent be damned. (Come to think, copyeditors haven't changed a heck of a lot in the past two decades.) A proper name was going to start with a capital; and they didn't care that ff was a form of capital. The author wasn't going to see the results of their butchery until the story was in print anyway.

So Sterling gave up the fight, and I've preserved the

previously published (stupid American copyeditor) spelling here.

But sometimes I whisper 'ffellowes, ffellowes,' to myself as I reread these excellent stories.

SOLDIER KEY

Sterling Lanier

Everyone in the club, even those who disliked him, agreed that Brigadier ("not Brigadier General, please") Donald Ffellowes, R.A., ret., could tell a good yarn when he chose. He seemed to have been in the British Army, the Colonial Police and M.I.-5 as well at one time or another, and to have served all over the globe.

People who loathed him and the English generally, said all his tales were lies, that he was a remittance man, and that his gift for incredible stories was a direct inheritance from Sir John Mandeville, the medieval rumormonger. Still, even those who denounced his stories the most loudly never left once he started one of them. If Ffellowes was a liar, he was an awfully good one.

Mason Williams, who was one of those who resented Ffellowes as both British and overbearing, had instantly ordered stone crab when he saw it on the club's lunch menu. Of the eight others present at the big table that day, only one besides Williams had ever had stone

197

crab, but we all decided to try it; all, that is, except Ffellowes.

"No, thank you," he repeated coldly, "I'll have the sweetbreads. I don't eat crab or any crustacean, for that matter. I used to love it," he went on, "in fact I ate crab, lobster, langouste, crawfish and shrimp with the best of you at one time. Until 1934 to be exact. An unpleasant and perhaps peculiar set of circumstances caused me to stop. Perhaps you would care to hear why?

"Now, I couldn't get it past my mouth, and if I did I couldn't swallow it. You see, something happened. . . ."

His voice trailed away into silence, and we could all see that his thoughts were elsewhere. He stared at the snowy tablecloth for a moment and then looked up with an apologetic smile. We waited, and not even Williams seemed anxious to interrupt.

"I've never told anyone about this, but I suppose I ought, really. It's a quite unbelievable story, and not a very nice one. Yet, if you'd like to hear it?" he queried again.

An instant chorus of affirmation rose from around the table. We were all men who had traveled and seen at least something of life, but none of our tales ever matched what we extracted from Ffellowes at long intervals.

"Wait until after dinner," was all he would say. "I need a good meal under my belt and some coffee and a cigar before this one."

The rest of us looked at one another rather like boys who have been promised a treat, as indeed we had. Williams grunted something, but made no objection. His denunciations of the British always came *after* Ffellowes' stories, I noticed.

When we were settled in our leather chairs in an alcove of the huge library, with cigars drawing and coffee and brandy beside us, Ffellowes began.

"Did any of you ever sail the Caribbean in the pre-War period? I don't mean on a cruise ship, although that's fun. I mean actually sailed, in a small boat or yacht, touching here and there, calling at ports when you felt like it and then moving on? If not, you've missed something.

"The dawns were fantastic and the sunsets better. The food from the galley, fresh fish we'd caught ourselves usually, was superb, and the salt got into our skin, baked there by the sun.

"Islands rose up out of the sea, sometimes green and mountainous like Jamaica, sometimes low and hidden by mangroves and reefs like the Caymans or Inagua.

"We called at funny little ports and gave drinks to local officials who came aboard and got tight and friendly and told us astonishing scandals and implausible state secrets, and finally staggered off, swearing eternal friendship.

"And then at dawn, we hoisted anchor, set sail and checked our charts, and off we went to see what was over the next horizon, because there was always another island."

He paused and sipped his coffee, while we waited in silence.

"I had three months leave on half pay at the time due to a mixup; so Joe Chapin and I (he's dead a long time, poor fellow, killed at Kohima) chartered an island schooner at Nassau and hired two colored men to help us work her and cook. They were from Barbados and wanted to get back there, and that suited us. Badians are good seamen and good men, too. One, the older, was called Maxton, the other, Oswald, and I've forgotten their last names. We told them to call us Joe and Don, but it was always 'Mistah Don, Sah' to me, and 'Cap'n' to Joe, because he was officially captain on the papers.

"Well, we sailed along south for a month or so, calling here and there, picking up news and having fun at this port or that, until we got to Basse-Terre on Gualdeloupe. We were ashore having a few rums in the bar with the port officials when we first heard of Soldier Key.

"Any of you ever hear of it? Well, you won't now because it's gone. The people are anyway. The big hurricane of 1935 smashed it more than flat, and I'm told the few people left were moved by the British government. I checked up later on and found they went first to Dominica and then elsewhere, but there weren't many left.

"At any rate, the French customs officer we were drinking with suggested we look in at Soldier Key if we wanted an unusual, what you call 'offbeat,' place to visit.

" 'Messieurs,' he told us, 'this is a very strange place. You will not, I think, call twice, because few do, but I do not think you will be bored. These people are British like yourselves, and yet the island has no British official in residence, which is odd. They have an agreement with the government of Dominica that they govern themselves. Twice a year comes an inspection, but otherwise they are alone, with none to disturb them. Curious, is it not?'

"We agreed it sounded mildly strange, but asked why we should bother going at all?

" 'As to that,' he said, 'you must suit yourselves. But you English always seek new things, and this place is a strange one. The people are, how you say it, *forgot* by everyone. They trade little, selling only *langouste* (the spiny lobster) and the meat of green turtle. They are good seamen, but they call at few ports and avoid other fishing boats. For some reason, they never sell the turtle shell, although they could catch all the shell turtles they wish. I cannot tell you more, except I once called there for water when on a cruise and the place made me feel discomfortable.' He paused and tried to convey what he meant. 'Look, these Key of the Soldier people all belong to one church, not mine or yours either. To them, all who are not of this communion are damned eternally, and when they look at you, you feel they wish to speed the process. A funny place, Messieurs, but interesting.'

"He finished his rum and stood up to go. 'And another thing, Messieurs,' he said, 'all people of color dislike this place, and there are none of them who live there. Again, interesting, eh? Why not try it? You may be amused.'

"Well, after we got back to the boat, we hauled out our charts and looked for Soldier Key. It was there all right, but it was quite easy to see how one could miss it. It lay about two days sail west by northwest of Dominica, and it looked like a pretty small place indeed. The copy of the *Mariner's Guide* we had wasn't really new, and it gave the population as five hundred (approximately) with exports limited to lobster and imports nil. A footnote said it was settled in 1881 by the Church of the New Revelation. This, of course, must be the church to which our little customs official had been referring, but I'd never heard of it, nor had Joe. Still, there are millions of sects all over the place; so that meant nothing, really.

"Finally, before we turned in, Joe had an idea. 'I'm certain someone has some reference books in town,' he said. 'I'll have a dekko tomorrow morning, first thing, shall I?'

"Well, he did, and about noon, when I was considering the day's first drink in the same waterfront bar as the night before, he came in with a small volume, very worn-looking, in his hand.

" 'Look at this,' he said, 'I found it in the local library; been there forever, I should think.'

"What he had in his hand was a slim, black book, written in English, cheaply bound and very tattered, with brown pages crumbling at the edges. It was dated London, 1864, and was written by someone who called himself the Opener of the Gate. Brother A. Poole. The title of the book was *The New Revelation Revealed to the Elect*.

" 'One of those island people must have left it here on their way through,' I said, 'or perhaps some fisherman lost it. Have you looked at it?'

"We read it aloud in turn, as much as we could stand, that is, because it was heavy going, and it was really a very boring book. A good bit of it came from Revelation and also the nastier bits of the Old Testament, and practically all of it was aimed at warning Those Who Transgressed.

"But there were stranger parts of it, based apparently on Darwin, of all people, and even some Jeremy Bentham. All in all, a weirder hodgepodge was never assembled, even by your Aimee Semple McPherson or our own Muggletonians.

"The final summing up of the hundred pages or so was a caution, or rather summons, to the Faithful, to withdraw from the world to a Secluded Spot at the first opportunity. Judging from what we had heard, Soldier Key was the Secluded Spot.

" 'It would be fascinating to find out what a gang like this has done in seventy years of isolation, don't you think?' said Joe. I agreed. It sounded like giving a new twist to our trip.

"Well, we weighed anchor that afternoon, after a farewell drink with our customs friend, and his last words intrigued us still more.

" 'Have you any weapons on board?'

"I answered that we had a shark rifle, a .30-30 Winchester carbine, and a Colt's .45 automatic pistol.

" 'Good. I think less well today than I did last night of having directed you to this place. There are strange rumors among les Noirs of Soldier Key. Send me a card from your next port, as a favor, eh?'

"We promised and then said goodbye. Once clear of the harbor, we plotted a course and then told the two crewmen where we were going. The reaction was intriguing.

"Maxton, the older, looked rather glum, but Oswald, who was a six-foot black Hercules, actually forgot his usual respectful terms of address.

" 'Mon, what you go theah fo'? They not good people theah; wery bad people on Soljah Cay, Mon!'

"When Joe and I pressed them to say why exactly they disliked the place, they could not, or would not, give us any answers, except that no one went there from other islands and that the folk were unfriendly, especially to colored people.

" 'Come, come, Oswald,' said Joe finally, 'there surely must be something you are not telling us.'

"The man stared at the deck and finally mumbled something about 'Duppies.'

"Well, you know, this made us laugh and that was an error. Duppies are West Indian ghosts, evil spirits, and are objects of fear among all British West Indian Negroes from Jamaica to Trinidad. When we joshed these two men about them, they shut up like oysters! Not one further word could we get out of them about Soldier Key. No, that's not right. I got one more thing a day later.

"Oswald was fishing with a hand line from the stern at a time when I had the helm. I had asked him idly what he was using for bait.

"He reached into a metal pail beside him and pulled out a huge black and grey snail's shell about six inches across. "Soljah, Mistah Don, Sah.' I noticed he held it gingerly, and I suddenly saw why. The owner of the shell was not the original snail at all, but a weird-looking crab, with great orange and purple claws, too large for its size, beady eyes on stalks and a mass of red spiky legs. In fact, it was the northern hermit crab, simply grown huge and aggressive in the tropics. Its claws snapped and clicked as it tried to reach his fingers, and then he dropped it back into the pail.

" 'They are many of them where we go, Mistah Don, Sah, wery many of the Soljahs.'

"So here was the reason for the name of the island! I had been speculating to myself as to whether the British had ever had a fort there, but the explanation was much simpler. Hermit Crab Island! Under this new name, it made all the vague warnings of our French friend seem quite silly, and when I told Joe about it later when we changed watch, he rather agreed.

"We made our landfall in a trifle under three days, due mostly to light airs, you know. The island was flat, only about seven miles long and two wide; so it would not have been a hard place to miss, actually. We came steadily in from the East, took down sail and started the auxiliary engine, because there was a circular reef marked on the charts as extending almost completely around the island and it only had a few navigable openings.

"It was evening, and the sun was on the horizon when we saw the first lights of the island's only town. There was a hundred-yard passage through the reef, marked clearly as showing seven fathoms opposite the town; so we brought the schooner in until we were no more than fifty or so yards off-shore.

"The town lay in a semicircle about a shallow bay. There was a broken beach, with bits of low cliff about five feet above the water, which we could just dimly make out. I say dimly because it was now completely dark and there was no moon, only Caribbean starlight, although that's pretty bright.

"We switched off the engine, anchored and watched the town, because it was the oddest-appearing port we had ever seen. There wasn't a sound. A few dimmish lights, perhaps half a dozen, burned in windows at wide intervals, but no dogs barked, no rooster crowed, no noise of voices came over the water. There was a gentle breeze in our rigging and the lapping of wavelets on the hull, and that was all.

"Against the sky at one point to the left, we could see

the loom of some tall building, and we thought that this might be a church, but what we were to make of this silence baffled us. Night, especially the evening, is a lively time in the tropics, in fact the liveliest. Where were the people?

"We debated going ashore and decided against it. I say 'we,' but I assure you our crew wasn't debating. They had made it quite plain earlier that they were not going even if ordered, not even in daylight.

" 'This is a bod place, Cap'n,' said Oswald to Joe. 'We do not wish to discommode you, Sah, but we don't go on thot land, at all, Sah, no!'

"And that was that. So, we set anchor watch and turned in. A few mosquitoes came out from shore but not many, and we fell asleep with no trouble at all, determined to solve the mystery of the quiet in the morning.

"I was awakened by a hand on my arm. I blinked because it was still pitch-black out, and I looked at my watch. It was two in the morning. Against the stars I could see Joe's head as he stooped over me.

" 'Come on deck, Don,' he said, 'and listen.' Even as he spoke, I was conscious that the night was no longer completely quiet.

"On deck, the four of us, for the two crewmen were up too, crouched in the cockpit, and we all strained our ears.

"The sound we were hearing was quite far off, a mile at the very least from the volume, but it was unmistakably the sound of many human voices singing. To us, it sounded like a hymn, but the tune was not a familiar one.

"After what seemed about twenty-three stanzas, it stopped, and we listened in the silent night again. Then, there came a distant shout, somewhat sustained and again silence for a moment. Then the rhythmic mass cry again, but longer this time and seeming to go up and down. It went on this way for about ten minutes, first the silence and then the noise of human voices, and I tried without success to make out what was going on. Joe got the clue first.

" 'Responses,' he said, and of course, that was it. We were listening to something very like a psalm, chanted by a lot of people, a long way off, and naturally we couldn't hear the minister at all, but only the antiphony.

"After a bit, it stopped, and after fifteen minutes or so we turned in again. Now we knew why the town was quiet. All the people, apparently including the babies, were celebrating a church service somewhere inland. The Church of the New Revelation seemed to go in for midnight services.

"Well, we woke at six to a typical blazing Caribbean morning and also to a visitor. Standing on the edge of the deck coaming was the hatless figure of a man, staring down at Joe and myself out of pale blue eyes.

"He was about sixty from his looks, clean-shaven and sallow, with thick white hair and a gaunt, peaked face. Not especially impressive until you studied the eyes. Ice blue they were, and so cold they gave me a chill even in the ninety-plus heat on deck.

" 'What do you want here?' he said, with no other introduction at all. 'We seek no visitors. This island is dedicated to the Lord.'

"I introduced Joe and myself, but he paid no attention. I noticed his shabby but clean white suit, shirt and tieless stiff collar, as he stepped down into the cockpit. Behind him, I saw a little skiff tied to the stern in which he had rowed himself out.

" 'Look!' he said suddenly, an expression of disgust crossing his features. 'You are bringing pollution with you. You slay the helpless creatures of the Lord!' With that he reached down and seized the bait bucket and emptied Oswald's bait, three of the big purple hermit crabs, over the side in one convulsive heave.

" 'Now, I say, just a moment, now,' said Joe, letting annoyance show through. 'Exactly who are you, and what's this all about? We've tried to be polite, but there are limited. . . .'

"The cold eyes swept over us again, and their nasty glint deepened. 'I am Brother Poole, son of the Founder. You would call me the Pastor, I suppose. The government of this blessed place is in my keeping. Once again, I say, who are you and what do you want?'

"Joe answered peaceably enough and re-introduced us, but he had obviously been doing some thinking while he listened to Poole.

" 'We just wanted to get some water and a little food,' said Joe, 'and some fresh fruit, before we go to Dominica. No law against going ashore on your island, is there?' He added, 'Isn't this British territory? Doesn't the Dominican governor ever allow people ashore here?'

"It was quite obvious that he had given Brother Poole something to chew on, you know. Whatever Poole's powers were on the island, he wasn't used to having them challenged. And it was evident from his hesitation that he didn't care for the remarks about the British or Crown government. You could see his bony face working as he grappled with the problem. Finally, something he must have thought was a smile struggled to get through. Frankly, I preferred his previous expression. A sanctimonious whine also crept into his hard voice.

" 'I regret my sharpness, gentlemen. We have so few visitors, mostly fishermen of loose morals. I am the guardian of our little Eden here, and I have to think of my flock. Of course, you may come ashore, and buy what you need. I only ask that you kill nothing, do no fishing while here, out of respect to our law.'

"We stated we had no intention of killing anything and said we'd come ashore after we cleaned up and had breakfast. He climbed back into his boat, but before he cast off, turned back to us.

" 'Please see that those two black heathen stay on

your schooner. Their presence is not wanted on our island, where they might corrupt our people.' A good share of the original venom had come back in his speech.

"As he pulled away, I turned to Maxton and Oswald to apologize, but it was unnecessary. Their faces were immobile, but also, it seemed to me, a shade paler under their natural darkness. Before I could say anything, Maxton spoke.

" 'Don't worry about us, Sah. We hov no desiah to enter in thot place. It is of the utmost dislike to us, I ossuah you, Sah.'

"Well, Joe and I shaved, and put on clean clothes, and then rowed our dinghy into the empty dock. There was only one, and that one small. A lot of fishing boats, all under twenty feet, were moored to buoys and also pulled up on the sloping beach—where it existed, that is.

"The town lay before me to observe, as Joe was doing the rowing, and I had a full view from the stern. It looked pretty small, perhaps fifty houses all told, plus the one church we had spotted the night before, a steepled white thing with something metallic, not a cross, on the steeple, which caught the sunlight and reflected it blindingly.

"The houses were all white stucco, mostly palm-thatch roofed, but a few with rusting tin instead, and all set on short stilts a foot or so off the ground. You could have duplicated them on any other island in the Caribbean.

"A few coco palms grew here and there and some shortish trees, mostly in the yards of the houses. Behind the town, a low green scrub rolled away, the monotonous outline broken only by a few of the taller thatch palms. The whole place lay shimmering in the heat, because not a breath of air moved.

"And neither did anything else. A white figure on the end of the dock was Brother Poole, identifiable at long range as waiting for us. But behind him the town lay silent and still. Not so much as a dog or chicken crossed a yard or disturbed the dust of the white roads. It was, if anything, more eerie than the night before.

"We nosed into the dock, and Poole leaned down to catch the painter Joe flung up to him. We climbed up as he was securing it to a post. Then he stood up and faced us.

" 'Welcome to Soldier Key, gentlemen,' he said. 'I hope I did not appear too unfriendly earlier, but I have a precious duty here, guarding my flock. Although you are not of the Elect, I know you would not wish to bring disturbance to a pious community, which has cut itself off from the dross and vanity of the world.' He turned to lead us down the dock without waiting for an answer and threw another remark over his shoulder. 'The Governor of Dominica has given me magistrate's powers.'

"The carrot and the stick, eh! Joe and I exchanged glances behind his back.

"At the foot of the dock, Poole turned again, the cold eyes gleaming in the sunlight. 'I presume you wish to see our little town? You will find it quiet. This is a festival of our church, and all of our people rest during the day to prepare for the evening service, by fasting and by prayer. I would be doing so too, but for the duties of hospitality, which are paramount.'

"I had been trying to analyze his very odd accent since I'd first heard it. It was not West Indian, but a curiously altered Cockney, flat and nasal, something like the worst sort of Australian, what they call 'Stryne.' I thought then, and still think, that I know exactly how Uriah Heep must have sounded.

"As we walked up the silent main street, which lay dreaming in the white heat, our feet kicking up tiny clouds of coral dust, I suddenly saw something move in the shadow of a house. At first I thought it was a cat, then a large rat, but as it moved, it came momentarily into a patch of sunlight, and I stopped to stare.

"It was a soldier, a hermit crab, but enormous in size, at least a foot long, its naked body hidden in and carrying a huge conch shell as it scuttled clumsily along. As we came abreast of it, its stalked eyes seemed to notice us, and to my surprise, instead of retreating, it ran toward us and stopped only a foot away. Its great orange and purple claws looked capable of severing one's wrist, or a finger, at any rate.

"Poole had stopped too, and then, reaching into his pocket, he pulled out a linen bag from which he extracted a strip of dried meat. He leaned down, do you know, and placed it in front of the crab. It seized it and began to shred it in the huge claws, passing bits back to its mouth, where other smaller appendages chewed busily. It was as thoroughly nasty a sight as I'd ever glimpsed. Also, I wondered at the meat.

" 'That's a monster,' I said. 'How on earth do you tame them? I had no idea they grew so big. And I thought you ate no meat?'

" 'They are not *tame*, as you in the gross world think of it,' said Poole sharply. 'They are our little brothers, our friends, as much a part of life as we, and all units of the great chain live here in peace, some higher, some lower, but all striving to close the great circle which holds us to the material earth, at peace, yet in competition, the lower sinking, failing, the higher mastering the lower, then aiding. It is all a part of—' His whining voice rose as he spoke, but then suddenly stopped as he realized that our expressions were baffled, unmoved by the exposition of his extraordinary creed. 'You would not understand,' he finished lamely, and pocketing the still unexplained meat, he turned to lead us on. We followed, glancing at one another. Behind us, the huge crab still crunched on its dainty, clicking and mumbling.

"Wrapped in thought about Poole and his religion, I really didn't notice that we had come to the town square, until I almost ran into Joe, who had stopped in front of me.

"Before us now stood the church we had glimpsed earlier, a massive, white-stuccoed structure with a pointed spire. As I looked up, I could see by squinting that the shiny object on the steeple was, indeed, not a cross. It was a huge crab claw, gilded and gleaming in the sunlight!

"My jaw must have dropped, because Poole felt it incumbent on himself to explain. 'We have abandoned the more obvious Christian symbols,' he said. 'And since our friends, the soldiers, are the commonest local inhabitants, we choose to symbolize the unity of all life by placing their limb on our little place of worship.'

" 'Rather! I can see it's their church,' said Joe pointing. 'Look there, Donald.'

"As he spoke, I saw what he had seen first, that the shadows around the base of the church were moving and alive—alive with the great hermit crabs.

"Large, small, and a few immense, they rustled and clanked in and around the coral blocks which formed the base, and the scrubby bushes which flanked the blocks, a sea of shells, claws, spiny legs and stalked eyes.

"Poole must have seen that we were revolted, because he moved on abruptly, leaving us no choice except to follow him. As we moved, I heard a distant human sound break the hot silence for the first time that morning, the sound of hammering. It came from our right, toward the edge of town, and peering down a sandy street in that direction, I thought I could identify the source as a long shed-like structure, about a third of a mile away.

" 'I thought everyone had retired to pray?' said Joe at the same moment. 'What's that hammering?'

"Poole looked annoyed. I never met a man less good at disguising his feelings, but since he normally never had to while on his island, it must have been quite hard to learn. Finally, his face cleared and the spurious benevolence gained control.

" 'A few of the men are working on religious instru-ments,' he said. 'We have a festival coming: we call it the Time of the Change, so there is a dispensation for them. Would you like to see them at work?'

"Since the silent town had so far yielded nothing of interest except the soldiers, which we loathed, we said yes.

"We came at length to one end of the long build-ing, and Poole held aside a rattan screen door so that we could go in first. A blast of frightful heat hit us in the face as we entered.

"Inside, the building was one long open shed, lit by vents in the walls, and by a fire which blazed in a trench running half the length of the structure. Several giant metal cauldrons bubbled over the fire, with huge pieces of some horn-like material sticking out of them.

"Over against one wall were several long benches, and at these, a number of bronzed white men, stripped to tattered shorts, were furiously hammering at more pieces of the horny substance, flattening it and bending it, forcing it into huge wooden clamps and vises and pegging it together.

"As we watched, several of them stopped work and seized a huge piece of the stuff and dragging it to the fire, dumped it into one of the giant pots. No one paid us the slightest attention, but simply kept working as though driven by some frantic need, some internal pressure. The whole affair was most mysterious.

"I stepped close to one of the pots to see if I could learn what it was they were working on, and as I looked I saw, to my amazement, it was tortoise shell.

"Now, a hawksbill sea turtle, the only known source of shell, seldom grows one much over a yard long, you know. The pieces these men were working on must have been made with many dozens of them at least. What on earth were they doing?

"Poole, who had been surveying our bewilderment with a sardonic smile, decided to mystify us further.

Tapping Joe on the shoulder and pointing, he started walking down the length of the long shed, skirting the fires and the workmen, but ignoring them.

"His goal was the far left-hand corner, which we now saw had a palm-thatch curtain extending from floor to ceiling, masking what lay behind.

"With the air of a second-rate showman on his un-pleasant face, he pulled on a rope and drew the high brown curtain aside. 'Behold our aim, gentlemen. Here is a fitting offering that we make for the altar of the Most High!'

"What we saw was certainly worth more than a little showmanship. Before us, poised on seven or eight large sawhorses, was a giant, gleaming shell, as if some colos-sal and quite improbable snail had washed up from the deeps of the sea. Golden, mottled and semi-translucent, it towered over our heads, and must have been at least twelve feet in diameter from the great opening in the base to the peak of the spiral tip. As we drew closer we saw that the whole marvelous object was artificial, being made of plates of overlapping tortoise shell pegged so cunningly that it was hard to see any joint. At one place on the side, a large gap showed where the work was not yet complete. Obviously, this was why the silent, half-naked workers were toiling so industriously. It was a very beautiful and awe-inspiring sight, if still a mysteri-ous one.

"Poole drew the curtain closed and stood with his arms in his coat pockets smiling at our amazement. 'That's one of the most beautiful things I've ever seen,' I said, quite honestly. 'May I ask what you do with it when it's finished?'

"Some strong emotion flashed for a second across his face, to be replaced by a bland expression of benignity. 'We set it afloat on a large raft, surrounded by offerings of fruit and flowers,' he said. 'An offering to God, to be swept where He wills by the waves and winds.'

"Seeing our incomprehension at the idea of so much

hard work going to waste, he elaborated, still smiling in his sneering way. 'You see, it takes a long time to make the shell. The whole community, our whole little island, participates. Men must catch turtles. Then they must be killed, as mercifully as possible, the shell cured in a special manner and so on, right up until the final work. Then, when we gather at the ceremony of departure, all our people share in the delight of speeding it forth. We feel that we send our sins with it and that our long labor and offering to God may help our souls to Paradise. A naive idea to you, cultivated men of the great, outside world, no doubt, but very dear to us. My father, of blessed memory, the Founder, devised the whole idea.'

"Actually, you know, the idea was a lovely and reverent one. It reminded me of the Doge of Venice marrying the Sea, and other ceremonies of a similar nature. Brother Poole must have spent some time indeed on the composition of his tale, for it was quite the pleasantest thing we had heard about the island.

"While he had been speaking, we had passed out of the shed into the glaring sunlight, which seemed cool after the inferno we had left behind us.

"As we stood blinking in the sun, Poole turned to us with the false benignity now vanished from his face. 'So, gentlemen, you have seen all there is to see of our little town. There is an important religious festival tonight, the launching of our offering. I must ask you to purchase such supplies as you need and leave before this evening, since non-believers are not permitted here during our holy night and day, which is tomorrow. I can sell you any supplies you may need.'

"Well, we had no reason to linger. Personally, as I said earlier, I had taken a profound dislike to the whole town and particularly to Brother Poole, who seemed to embody it, as well as actually to direct it. We walked to the wharf, discussing what we needed on the way. Poole seemed ready to sell fruit, bananas, mangoes and papayas, as well as bread, at perfectly honest prices, and offered us fresh water free of any charge at all.

"Only once did any hardness come back into his voice, and that was when I asked if any spiny lobsters, *langouste*, were for sale.

" 'We do not take life here,' he said. 'I told you earlier of our rule.'

"Joe could not help breaking in with an obvious point, although he should have known better when dealing with a fanatic.

" 'What about the turtles. You kill them for their shells and presumably eat the meat? And what about the fish you catch?'

"Poole looked murderous. 'We do not eat meat,' he snapped. 'You would not understand, being heretics, unaware of the Divine Revelation, but the turtles' deaths are allowable, since we beautify our offering to God with their shells. The greater cause is served through a smaller fault. Also, the fish are set aside to us as our portion, although a sinful one. But what is the use of explaining these holy things to you, since you have not seen the Light?'

"After this, he declined to say anything else at all, except to wish us a good journey in a furious voice and to add that our purchases and water would be on the dock in an hour. With that, he stalked off and disappeared around a corner of the street. Upon his departure, all movement ceased, and the town dreamed on, neither sound nor movement breaking the noon silence. Yet we both had the feeling that eyes watched us from behind every closed shutter and each blank, sealed window.

"We rowed back to the schooner in silence. Only when we climbed aboard, to be greeted by Maxton and Oswald, did our voices break out together, as if pent up.

" 'Appalling character, he was! What a perfectly hellish place! Did you feel the eyes on your back?' et cetera.

"Only after settling down and disposing of lunch, which the men had thoughtfully made in our absence, did we seriously talk. The conclusion we reached was that the British government and the local administration in Dominica needed a good jolt about this place, and that it ought to be thoroughly investigated to find out just how happy the locals really were about Brother Poole and his hermit crab church. Other than that, we decided the sooner we left, the better.

"During lunch we had seen some of the locals, all whites, manhandling a cart down on the dock, and unloading it. We now rowed ashore and found two large, covered baskets of fruit, half a dozen loaves of new bread, and an old oil drum of water, which looked and tasted clean and fresh. We also found Poole, who seemed to appear out of the air and accepted the previously agreed-upon payment for the food. When that was over and we promised to return the water drum after putting the water in our tank, he came to his official business again.

" 'Now that you have water, you can leave, I suppose,' he said. 'There is no further reason for interrupting our holy festivities?' His arrogant whine, half command and half cringe, was on the upsurge. It annoyed Joe as well as me, and his answer to the order, on the face of it, was quite natural, really.

" 'We'll probably use the land breeze this evening,' said Joe. 'Of course, we may decide not to. Your bay is so pretty. We like to look at it.'

" 'Yes,' I added, picking up his cue. 'You know how we yachtsmen are, passionate lovers of scenery. Why, we may decide to stay a week.'

"Of course we were only trying to get a rise out of the Reverend Poole, but he had absolutely no sense of humor. Yet he realized that we disliked him quite as much as he did us. His eyes blazed with sudden rage, and he half-lifted one hand, as though to curse us. But another expression crossed his face first, and the mask dropped again. He must have suddenly realized that he didn't have a pair of his co-religionists to deal with.

"Without another word, he turned on his heel and left, leaving us sitting in our rowboat staring at one another.

"We got the water, bread and fruit out, and I rowed back and left the empty oil drum on the dock. The town still lay as quiet as ever in the sun, and no breeze disturbed the few coco palms. From the pier, I could see no sign of any movement further in, and the harbor was like a mirror, reflecting our schooner and the small, anchored fishing boats suspended motionless in the heat.

"Back aboard again, I conferred with Joe, and then we told the two crewmen we would leave on the evening land breeze. The harbor was deep enough so that tide made no difference. We could have used our engine, of course, but we hated to do so when sails would do the work. Aside from disliking engines, as all who sail for pleasure do, we always thought of emergencies, when the fuel might be desperately needed.

"Oswald and Maxton brightened up when we said we were going, and had we left right then, I'm sure they would have offered to row, or swim, for that matter. Their dislike of Soldier Key had never been plainer.

"The afternoon drifted on, and again the tropical night came quickly, with no real evening. But there was no wind. The expected land breeze simply didn't appear. When this happens, one can usually expect it to come around midnight or a little after in these waters, although I have no idea why. We'd had it happen before, however, so we waited. Since we had anchor lights on, we were perfectly visible from shore, but tonight no lights at all showed there. There was no moon, but brilliant starlight, and we could see the outline of the shore and the loom of the buildings behind, as silent as ever.

"We decided to leave one man awake to look for wind, and the rest would turn in all standing, that is, dressed, not that we wore much but shorts. We could raise sail in no time. Oswald said he was not sleepy, and so he got the job.

"I don't know why I should have wakened at midnight. There was still no wind, and we had all been sleeping on deck. I looked at my watch, cast my eye along the deck to Maxton's and Joe's sleeping forms and then went aft to find Oswald. He wasn't there, so I looked forward again. No sign of him, and the starlight was clear enough to see from bow to stern. There was no use waking the others on a false alarm. I got up and dropped into the cabin, gave it a quick once over, and then came out of the forward hatch and went quickly aft to the stern. No Oswald.

"I woke the others quietly, and explained the situation in a few words. From the moment I spoke, none of us had any doubt as to what had happened. Oswald had never left voluntarily. Someone, or something, with human motivation, had plucked him off the schooner as easily as you gaff a fish and even more quietly, and the purpose and the strength had come from the silent town, from Soldier Key.

"We discovered afterwards that it had been easy for them. Several swimmers approached as silently as sharks and one of them had clipped Oswald over the head with a club as he sat with his **back** to the rail. Then, without a sound, he had been lowered into the bay and towed back to shore. Why they left the rest of us I shall never know, but I suspect that they simply had gotten cold feet. Or perhaps Poole thought we'd be reluctant to report our loss. By the time we got back with help, he could always plead ignorance and say that we had done the poor chap in ourselves. He of course would have his whole island to back him up. As a second purpose, I think he wanted us out of there and that this was perhaps a last warning. Well, if that were so, he had made a mistake.

"Without anyone's having to speak, all three of us went below and began to gather weapons. I took the big Colt automatic pistol, because it was my own, Joe the .30-30 carbine, and Maxton simply tucked his cane knife, a big machete, without which most West Indians feel undressed, in his belt. Then we collected ammunition and went aft to our dinghy. I hauled the painter in without even looking until the cut end came into my hand! I had not noticed its absence on my earlier check, but the Key men had cut it adrift.

"However, this actually didn't put us back a bit. Still without speaking, but all three purposeful, we began to rig a float for the weapons out of small line and four life preservers. We had it done and ready to move in less than ten minutes and were about to slip over the side when Maxton suddenly caught us by the arms and put a hand to his ear.

"As we listened in the quiet dark, a noise, almost a vibration began to come over the water. It was a sound we couldn't identify, a strange sort of muffled rustling or shuffling sound, and Joe and I looked at each other in the starlight, absolutely baffled. Maxton whispered in our ears.

" 'Dot is feet. Dey move somewheah.'

"Of course he was quite right. We were listening to the whole town on the move, the rustle of hundreds of feet scuffing through the coral dust of the streets. Where they were going we didn't know, but we began to drop into the water, because this silent march almost certainly meant no good to Oswald. We all three knew *that*, somehow. I took the lead, carrying the pistol out of the water, so that we should be armed upon landing. Behind me, Joe and Maxton swam, pushing the little raft with the rifle, the spare ammo, our shoes, and two canteens. Joe had added something else, but I didn't find that out until later.

"I swam for the edge of town way over on the left, well away from the dock or the boats, since I had to assume that if they had posted a sentry, he would be placed at that point. It apparently was quite unnecessary, but we had to try to outguess them at every point, and we still thought these people rational. I tried not to think of sharks, which I dislike.

"As we swam, I listened for the sound of the footsteps, but it had died away, and this lent new urgency to our efforts. In a very short time, my feet grated on the coral beach, and keeping the pistol poised, I waded ashore, the other two behind me. Joe had the rifle at ready now, and Maxton had drawn his machete.

"There was no sign of movement. We had landed just on the outer edge of town, the last house looming about two hundred feet to our right. Not a sound broke the silence but faint insect humming and the splash of ripples breaking on the narrow beach.

"After listening a minute, we put on our shoes, then divided the ammunition and the canteens. I saw Joe stick something else in his belt, but I was concentrating so hard on listening that it really didn't register.

"We placed the life preservers above the high water mark under a bush and moved into the town, guns at ready. If the town were quiet by day, it was dead that night. This was a town presumably inhabited by living people, but not a murmur of life came from any of the shuttered houses. At each corner, we stopped and listened, but we could hear nothing. Nothing human, that is. Twice I almost fired at rustling shadows and faint clanking noises, only to realize that it was only the hideous crabs from which the island took its name.

"The church was our goal, by unspoken agreement, but when we reached the square, it loomed silent and unlit in front of us. The central door was wide open, and we could hear no movement from the black interior. Wherever the people were, it was not there.

"Moving on, we struck a broader street, one which

led away from the water inland. As we paused in the shadow of a tamarind tree, Maxton suddenly held up a hand and dropped to his knees. I couldn't make out what he was doing, but he stood up in a second.

" 'This dust has been kicked up wery recent. I think the people come this way, many people.'

"I couldn't smell anything, but Joe and I knew we didn't have his perceptions, and we had no other clues anyway. Besides, we had heard the marching feet, and they had gone somewhere, and then there was the singing of the previous night, too.

"Keeping to the edge of the road, we went inland, walking quickly, but very much on the alert. The road left the town, which wasn't too big, remember, after about two hundred yards and cut straight into the scrub, in the direction of the center of the island, as near as we could make out. At about fifteen minutes walk from the town, we learned that Maxton was right. We were deep in the shadowy scrub now, not a jungle, but the thick, low thorn bush of most West Indian islands. The road still ran straight and smooth ahead of us, a dim, white ribbon under the stars. Only insect noises broke the silence.

"Suddenly, we all halted. Not far off, a half mile at a guess, a sound had erupted into the night. We had heard it before, not so loud, on the previous night and recognized it at once for the mass chorus of human voices in a chant. It came from ahead of us and to one side, the left.

"Our pace quickened to a trot, and as we ran we listened, trying to pinpoint the noise. It was some sort of service, because we could hear the sound die into silence and then start again. As we drew closer to the source, we began to hear the single voice which led the chant, high and faint, and then the muffled roar that followed from the congregation.

"It was only the voices that saved us from missing the path. The trees had increased in height, and shadowed the road a good deal, so that we should have over-shot the left fork if we hadn't been watching for it. Even then, Maxton was the only one to spot it, and he suddenly signaled us to turn into what looked like a dense bush. Following him, we broke through a screen of vegetation, which gave way so easily that we realized that it must have been dragged there after cutting. And there was a road again, narrower but still plain and well-trodden. Some old habit of caution must have led them so to mask their path. We now moved at an increased speed.

"Ahead of us, the voices swelled in another chant, but we could not as yet distinguish words. The single voice was silent. As the noise increased, so did our caution, and we slowed our pace, since we had no wish to burst unexpectedly into the middle of some gathering of goodness knows what.

"All at once, we could see light ahead through the trees, a flickering, reddish glow which lit the path far better than the dim starlight. We eased down to a slow walk and advanced cautiously.

"The light grew continually stronger as we went on, reflected back from our faces and the boles and leaves of the thorn bushes and palmettoes. The sound of voices was almost deafening now, but we were searching so hard for a sight of a guard or sentry, we paid no attention to the words, which were blurred in any case.

"The trees suddenly thinned before us, and stooping low, the three of us crawled abreast of their edge and peered into the open, keeping well behind the screening branches, and off the road, which suddenly appeared to vanish. When we reached the last line of bushes, it was easy to see why. We were gazing down into an immense pit.

"We were on one edge of an enormous hole in the ground, quite round and perhaps seventy feet deep. It was rimmed with greyish limestone rock, level at the edges, to which point the bushes grew all around.

"At our feet, the path, now very narrow, wound down a steep slope to the smooth floor of white sand below. One side of the natural amphitheatre, for such it was, was banked up into lines of crude seats, sloping to the open floor of packed sand. The width of the whole place must have been at least two hundred yards in diameter, if not more.

"The entire population of Soldier Key, now silent, was sitting on the banked seats of this private arena, gazing at the scene before them with rapt attention. We had an excellent view of them, which made up in completeness for what we had missed earlier. Every man, woman and child, perhaps two hundred or more, was stark naked, clothed only in garlands of flowers and flower necklaces. Every single living soul on the island must have been there, and not a sound came from even the smallest baby at its mother's breast, or the oldest crone. I could see no colored people, but only whites. Apparently the creed of the New Revelation was not valid for any but Caucasians.

"Inching forward to get a better look, we were able to see what held their attention. Two great bonfires burned on the floor of the pit, and between them Brother Poole, the Shepherd of his people, was moving about. As naked as his flock, his scrawny white body gleaming as if oiled, he was capering in a strange way around three objects on the sand, between the fires.

"In the center, golden in the firelight, lay the immense shell we had seen earlier in the workshed in town. No holes now marred its perfection, and it lay gleaming and wonderful on one of its sides, the opening facing us as we watched.

"On either side of the shell, dwarfed by its bulk, were two bound human bodies! One was Oswald. He was not only bound but gagged. As far away as we were, we could see his eyes roll and the muscles under his dark skin strain as he tried to break his bonds. The other figure was that of a white girl, perhaps fifteen or so from her build. She lay silent and unmoving, but I could see that her eyes were open. Around the three, the shell and the bodies, Brother Poole danced and waved his hands, as if in some maniac's parody of a benediction. Although he was otherwise quite nude, he wore a strange necklace, of some hard, purplish objects, which bounced and shook as he moved. So silent were the people that even as high as we were lying, I could hear the click and rattle of them. The sound jogged my memory, until I suddenly realized why it was familiar. He was wearing a necklace of hermit crab claws and the noise was just as if some of them were scuttling about.

"I stated that the pit was circular. The floor was level, sloping up on one side to the packed earth seats of the people, and on the other side to the limestone walls. Nothing grew on these smooth walls, excepting only in one place, directly opposite the seats, where dense canopies of some creeper hung down, half obscuring a great triangular opening or cleft in the rock, about twenty feet in height and at least that wide near the base. Pressed against the cliff to one side of this hole was a massive, now open door or gate, made of bulky timbers in a heavy frame. It was hung on great iron hinges driven into the rock. Could this be the Gate of which Poole claimed to be the Opener, I wondered? In front of the hole, and a little to one side, there was a still pool of water, probably a spring. Directly across from us, a path similar to that below us wound up the cliff face and vanished into the dark fringe of foliage at the top.

"Brother Poole suddenly ceased his capering and raised both hands. He was now facing the dark opening across the arena, and to this he addressed his invocation. I cannot at this date give it word for word, but roughly it went rather like this:

*   *   *

'Oh, Lord of Majesty, Incarnation of Survival, Manifestation of Nature and its struggle. Devourer of Sin
and the Flesh, have mercy upon us.'

"Behind him a roar arose as the crowd repeated the
last line, 'have mercy upon us.' He continued:

'Have mercy, Oh Thou, Shelled in Adamant. Of Thy
mercy, accept our offerings, a new home for Thy
greatness, new life for Thy limbs, new viands for Thy
table. Enter now upon Thy new home and partake of
Thine offerings.'

"This rather unpleasant parody of a communion service seemed extraordinarily unreal, it was so fantastic.

"In the red light, Poole's gaunt face, now drooling
slightly, assumed an air of repellent majesty. Much as
he disgusted me, the creature did have a certain hyp-
notic power at that moment. He believed in what he
was doing. Behind his back, his audience sat rapt and
expectant, all of them, old and young, leaning forward
in the same tense pause of anticipation. As he ceased to
speak, time almost seemed to stop, and he held his
hands out, facing the opening in the rock wall.

"Joe broke the spell, pushing the rifle at me and
snatching the Colt from my limp hand.

" 'Stay here and cover us,' he hissed. 'Maxton and I
are going down.'

"The two of them moved like cats, breaking from the
scrub and racing down the path below me with driving
steps. My brain cleared and I aimed the loaded rifle at
Poole. If anybody went, he certainly would be the first.

"Maxton and Joe were on the sandy floor of the pit
before anyone even noticed them. Joe had a clasp knife
in one hand and the pistol in the other, and he flashed
behind Poole's back and stopped to cut the girl's bonds.
Behind him, Maxton was doing the same for Oswald
with the edge of his machete.

"A chorus of screams from the crowd announced that not all of them were in a trance, but none of them moved. I refocussed on Poole, but he still faced the cave, apparently lost to the actual world, entranced in an ecstasy of religion.

"Then, I caught a flicker of movement from the corner of my right eye and risked a glance in that direction. What I saw made my rifle fall with a thud to the earth.

"Framed in the entrance to the cleft was Horror incarnate. Poised on giant, stalked legs, monstrous, incredible gleaming in the firelight, stood the Soldier of Soldier Key, the Living God of Brother Poole and his awful church.

"The giant purple and orange claws, the larger of the two at least six feet long, were held in front of the mass of clicking, grinding mouth parts. From the stalked eyes held out ten feet above the ground, to the great, red-pointed legs, jointed and barbed with three-inch spines, there stood complete and perfect a hermit crab that must have weighed not less than a thousand pounds.

"As it moved slowly forward from the mouth of its private cave, the dragging shell which covered its soft body and rear end became visible, and I saw the true reason for the labor of the whole island. It, the shell, was made of tortoise shell, still recognizable though dirty and scarred, and although enormous, it was obviously too small. The soft body bulging from the opening must have desperately needed more room. The purpose of the new and larger shell, which still lay sparkling on the sand, was now clear. The god was to have a new house.

"As all this flashed through my mind, I recovered my wits and snatched up the rifle again. It was as well I did, because now things were starting to break down on the pit floor.

"Emerging from his trance, Poole had turned around and had seen before his dumbfounded eyes his sacrifices no longer neatly tied up but actually escaping. Joe had the limp body of the girl over one shoulder, and Maxton was aiding Oswald to follow in the direction of the foot of the nearer path, just beneath my own position.

"With a shriek, Poole summoned his nude worshippers to the assault. 'Blasphemy! Slay the desecrators of the shrine! Kill them, in the sight of the Living God!'

"With a roar, the whole mob poured off its earth benches and rushed for the three figures which ran slowly across the sand. Poole stood where he was, his hand raised in a curse, his face now wholly evil, working with madness in the firelight. Behind him some few yards, that unbelievable crustacean had paused, immobile, like a bizarre statue, motionless save for the moving, twitching mouth parts.

"I think to this day we would have been dead men, but for two factors. Joe, heavily burdened, Maxton and Oswald were still thirty feet from the path's entrance. Behind them, the horde of frantic, raving islanders were no more than a hundred paces. I had begun to shoot, forgetting Poole, firing at the foremost men instead, and hitting at once, but it did no real good. Those behind simply leapt the prostrate bodies and came on. One rifle simply could not stop this gibbering, animal horde. But something else could.

"Above the howling of the pack and the bark of my rifle rang out a scream so awful and agonized that I can still hear it in my sleep. No one could have ignored that dreadful cry. With three exceptions, everyone halted to see the cause.

"Brother Poole had momentarily forgotten his god, but his god had not forgotten him. As he stood there launching curses and hellfire, the monster, irritated no doubt by all the noise and movement, had come from behind and now clutched him in its titanic, larger claw, as firmly as its little brothers would hold a grasshopper. Suddenly, with no apparent effort, it simply closed the claw, and before our eyes, the two halves of the scream-

ing Shepherd of the Island fell to the sand in a fountain
of blood.

"The three below, however, had not halted nor seen
this sight, but were now steadily coming up the path. I
resumed my ineffective rifle practice, for with fresh
screams of rage, the mob of worshippers surged forward
again, and began to gain. But Joe changed that.

"He halted and allowed Oswald and Maxton to run
past. Dumping the girl, who had never moved at all, to
the ground, he reached for his belt and pulled out a
bulky metallic object which I now saw for the first time
in the firelight. It was the schooner's flare pistol.

"Aiming at the center of the oncoming crowd, he
fired straight into them, and then the flare exploded
somewhere in the mass in a blast of white incandes-
cence. At the same instant, I had a stroke of genius,
and almost without thinking, I shifted my sights and
squeezed off a shot at that incredible horror, the Soldier, aiming directly for the center of the head, and just
over the grinding mouth parts.

"In the twin lights of the flare and the still-blazing
fires, I caught a glimpse of Hell. Blackened figures
writhed in agony on the ground, and others, their hair
ablaze, ran aimlessly about, shrieking in pain and fright.
But this was not all. My bullet must have wounded the
Soldier in its tenderest parts. Raising its great shell off
the ground and snapping its giant claws, it rushed at
the nearest humans in a frenzy, not gripping and holding, but instead slashing and flailing about with its
colossal pincers. That a creature of its bulk could move
with such speed was a revelation to me, of an unsought
kind. I remember seeing a screaming child crushed flat
by a great leg.

"I was no longer firing, but simply watching the base
of the path with one eye and the terrible scene below
with the other. In only a few seconds, Maxton's and
Oswald's heads appeared just below me, as they climbed
panting from the inferno below.

"A little behind them came Joe, reloading as he ran and checking his backtrail as he paused at the bend in the path. The girl was gone.

"I rose and covered the path behind them as they reached level ground. 'That lunatic girl got up and ran back into the crowd,' gasped Joe. 'To hell with her. Let's get out of here.'

"With me to the rear covering the retreat, we stumbled off down the track to the main road. In a minute the edge of the cliff was lost to view, and only the red glow on the leaves and the appalling sounds remained to tell us of what we had left behind. Breathless with shock and fright, we ran on at our best speed under the stars and trees until we reached the road and only a far-off wailing came to our ears.

"As we ran, I tried to make some sense out of what I had seen. In only a few moments, a maze of jumbled thoughts poured through me. How had that incredible thing been grown? How long had it lived? How many people had died to feed it? As the sound of anguished voices died away, my brain simply gave up, and I devoted myself to breathing and moving. Thinking back now, I believe that somehow, through their insane religion, the islanders had created a miracle of biology, taking a tiny animal and forcing its size somehow until no natural sea shell would contain it, and then building artificial ones to house its increased growth. But now, of course, no one will ever know the answers.

"There was no pursuit, I must say. The whole population of the island had been in that shambles of a pit, and we simply walked, for we could no longer run, back to the town and along the beach to our piled and tied life preservers. Within an hour of leaving the Amphitheatre of the Crab, we were climbing wearily over the side of the schooner. It took us only a few minutes to start the engine and get in the anchor, and then we were underway. Checking my watch, I found it was 4:30 A.M., although it seemed that a week had gone by.

"At blazing dawn, the island was only a faint blur on the horizon, which soon sank into the sea, leaving us feeling that we had been in a bad dream.

"No, we never called at Dominica. The four of us talked it over and decided not to.

"Look here, you fellows, we had probably killed, at a minimum, twenty or so souls, directly by flare or gunfire, and more still through the agency of the Soldier. By the time any representatives of the law arrived, what evidence would they find in our favor? Whatever governing group or person took over from Poole would have the whole island behind him or it. Who would believe our story? No one.

"No, we did nothing, at least at the time. We sent an anonymous letter to the Colonial Office and a copy to the Dominican Administrator later on, saying nothing at all about giant crabs, but demanding an inquiry into voodoo murders and local affairs generally. I have never heard that anything came of it, and as I told you earlier, the people were almost entirely wiped out by the hurricane of the following year.

"But I don't eat lobster or crab. It came too close to being the other way round, you see? Anyone care for bridge?"

Williams managed to grunt. We would hear from him later on, no doubt.

I think that the question of what is Art has vexed almost as many people over the ages as Pilate's, "What is truth?," even though the latter is applied to religious and political questions.

Part of the problem is just a lack of a database with which to judge an artwork. Beauty is Truth, Truth Beauty? Not if you don't speak English. That sentiment and the painstaking structure in which it appears—one of the highest expressions of Art in its time and culture—is precisely as artistic as a page from a Chapel Hill phonebook to most Yucatan peasants.

The same is true in the plastic arts. A person who can appreciate a Goya painting doesn't necessarily have the background to understand why encircling an island with plastic sheeting is an artistic expression (and on this point, I speak from personal experience).

None of this would matter very much if people took a live-and-let-live attitude toward art. Well, I don't understand it, but he doesn't seem to be doing anybody any harm, that sort of thing. People aren't tolerant now about attempts to create new forms of artistic expression, they've never been tolerant; and that, at least, is one of the human attributes least *likely to change for the better as we expand among the stars.*

One needn't assume that humans are unique in their flaws, either.

BLACK CHARLIE

Gordon R. Dickson

You ask me, what is art? You expect me to have a logical answer at my fingertips, because I have been a buyer for museums and galleries long enough to acquire a plentiful crop of gray hairs. It's not that simple.

Well, what is art? For forty years I've examined, felt, admired and loved many things fashioned as hopeful vessels for that bright spirit we call art—and I'm unable to answer the question directly. The layman answers easily—beauty. But art is not necessarily beautiful. Sometimes it is ugly. Sometimes it is crude. Sometimes it is incomplete.

I have fallen back, as many men have in the business of making like decisions, on *feel*, for the judgment of art. You know this business of *feel*. Let us say that you pick up something. A piece of statuary—or better, a fragment of stone, etched and colored by some ancient man of prehistoric times. You look at it. At first it is nothing, a half-developed reproduction of some wild animal, not even as good as a grade-school child could accomplish today.

233

But then, holding it, your imagination suddenly reaches through rock and time, back to the man himself, half-squatted before the stone wall of his cave—and you see there, not the dusty thing you hold in your hand—but what the man himself saw in the hour of its creation. You look beyond the physical reproduction to the magnificent accomplishment of his imagination.

This, then, may be called art—no matter what strange guise it appears in—this magic which bridges all gaps between the artist and yourself. To it, no distance, nor any difference is too great. Let me give you an example from my own experience.

Some years back, when I was touring the newer worlds as a buyer for one of our well-known art institutions, I received a communication from a man named Cary Longan, asking me, if possible, to visit a planet named Elman's World and examine some statuary he had for sale.

Messages rarely came directly to me. They were usually referred to me by the institution I was representing at the time. Since, however, the world in question was close, being of the same solar system as the planet I was then visiting, I space-graphed my answer that I would come. After cleaning up what remained of my business where I was, I took an interworld ship and, within a couple of days, landed on Elman's World.

It appeared to be a very raw, very new planet indeed. The port we landed at was, I learned, one of the only two suitable for deep-space vessels. And the city surrounding it was scarcely more than a village. Mr. Longan did not meet me at the port, so I took a cab directly to the hotel where I had made a reservation.

That evening, in my rooms, the annunciator rang, then spoke, giving me a name. I opened the door to admit a tall, brown-faced man, with uncut, dark hair and troubled, green-brown eyes.

"Mr. Longan?" I asked.

"Mr. Jones?" he countered. He shifted the unvarnished wooden box he was carrying to his left hand and put out his right to shake mine. I closed the door behind him and led him to a chair.

He put the box down, without opening it, on a small coffee table between us. It was then that I noticed his rough, bush-country clothes, breeches and tunic of drab plastic. Also an embarrassed air about him, like that of a man unused to city dealings. An odd sort of person to be offering art for sale.

"Your spacegram," I told him, "was not very explicit. The institution I represent . . ."

"I've got it here," he said, putting his hand on the box.

I looked at it in astonishment. It was no more than half a meter square by twenty centimeters deep.

"There?" I said. I looked back at him, with the beginnings of a suspicion forming in my mind. I suppose I should have been more wary when the message had come direct, instead of through Earth. But you know how it is—something of a feather in your cap when you bring in an unexpected item. "Tell me, Mr. Longan," I said, "where does this statuary come from?"

He looked at me, a little defiantly. "A friend of mine made them," he said.

"A friend?" I repeated—and I must admit I was growing somewhat annoyed. It makes a man feel like a fool to be taken in that way. "May I ask whether this friend of yours has ever sold any of his work before?"

"Well, no . . ." Longan hedged. He was obviously suffering—but so was I, when I thought of my own wasted time.

"I see," I said, getting to my feet. "You've brought me on a very expensive side-trip, merely to show me the work of some amateur. Good-bye, Mr. Longan. And please take your box with you when you leave!"

"You've never seen anything like this before!" He was looking up at me with desperation.

"No doubt," I said.

"Look. I'll show you . . ." He fumbled, his fingers nervous on the hasp. "Since you've come all this way, you can at least look."

Because there seemed no way of getting him out of there, short of having the hotel manager eject him forcibly, I sat down with bad grace. "What's your friend's name?" I demanded.

Longan's fingers hesitated on the hasp. "Black Charlie," he replied, not looking up at me.

I stared. "I beg your pardon. Black—Charles Black?"

He looked up quite defiantly, met my eyes and shook his head. "Just Black Charlie," he said with sudden calmness. "Just the way it sounds. Black Charlie." He continued unfastening the box.

I watched rather dubiously, as he finally managed to loosen the clumsy, handmade wooden bolt that secured the hasp. He was about to raise the lid, then apparently changed his mind. He turned the box around and pushed it across the coffee table.

The wood was hard and uneven under my fingers. I lifted the lid. There were five small partitions, each containing a rock of fine-grained gray sandstone of different but thoroughly incomprehensible shape.

I stared at them—then looked back at Longan, to see if this weren't some sort of elaborate joke. But the tall man's eyes were severely serious. Slowly, I began to take out the stones and line them up on the table.

I studied them one by one, trying to make some sense out of their forms. But there was nothing there, absolutely nothing. One vaguely resembled a regular-sided pyramid. Another gave a foggy impression of a crouching figure. The best that could be said of the rest was that they bore a somewhat disconcerting resemblance to the kind of stones people pick up for paperweights. Yet they all had obviously been worked on.

There were noticeable chisel marks on each one. And, in addition, they had been polished as well as such soft, grainy rock could be.

I looked up at Longan. His eyes were tense with waiting. I was completely puzzled about his discovery—or what he felt was a discovery. I tried to be fair about his acceptance of this as art. It was obviously nothing more than loyalty to a friend, a friend no doubt as unaware of what constituted art as himself. I made my tone as kind as I could.

"What did your friend expect me to do with these, Mr. Longan?" I asked gently.

"Aren't you buying things for that museum-place on Earth?" he said.

I nodded. I picked up the piece that resembled a crouching animal figure and turned it over in my fingers. It was an awkward situation. "Mr. Longan," I said. "I have been in this business many years . . ."

"I know," he interrupted. "I read about you in the newsfax when you landed on the next world. That's why I wrote you."

"I see," I said. "Well, I've been in it a long time, as I say and, I think, I can safely boast that I know something about art. If there is art in these carvings your friend has made, I should be able to recognize it. And I do not."

He stared at me, shock in his greenish-brown eyes.

"You're . . ." he said, finally. "You don't mean that. You're sore because I brought you out here this way."

"I'm sorry," I said. "I'm *not* sore and I *do* mean it. These things are not merely not good—there is nothing of value in them. Nothing! Someone has deluded your friend into thinking that he has talent. You'll be doing him a favor if you tell him the truth."

He stared at me for a long moment, as if waiting for me to say something to soften the verdict. Then, suddenly, he rose from the chair and crossed the room in three long strides, staring tensely out the window. His calloused hands clenched and unclenched spasmodically.

I gave him a little time to wrestle it out with himself. Then I started putting the pieces of stone back into their sections of the box.

"I'm sorry," I told him.

He wheeled about and came back to me, leaning down from his lanky height to look in my face. "Are you?" he said. "*Are* you?"

"Believe me," I said sincerely, "I am." And I was.

"Then will you do something for me?" The words came in a rush. "Will you come and tell Charlie what you've told me? Will *you* break the news to him?"

"I . . ." I meant to protest, to beg off, but with his tortured eyes six inches from mine, the words would not come. "All right," I said.

The breath he had been holding came out in one long sigh. "Thanks," he said. "We'll go out tomorrow. You don't know what this means. Thanks."

I had ample time to regret my decision, both that night and the following morning, when Longan roused me at an early hour, furnished me with a set of bush clothes like his own, including high, impervious boots, and whisked me off in an old air-ground combination flyer that was loaded down with all kinds of bush-dweller's equipment. But a promise is a promise—and I reconciled myself to keeping mine.

We flew south along a high chain of mountains until we came to a coastal area and what appeared to be the swamp delta of some monster river. Here, we began to descend—much to my distaste. I have little affection for hot, muggy climates and could not conceive of anyone wanting to live under such conditions.

We set down lightly in a little open stretch of water— and Longan taxied the flyer across to the nearest bank, a tussocky mass of high brown weeds and soft mud. By myself, I would not have trusted the soggy ground to refrain from drawing me down like quicksand—but Lon-

gan stepped out onto the bank confidently enough, and
I followed. The mud yielded, little pools of water springing up around my boot soles. A hot rank smell of
decaying vegetation came to my nose. Under a thin but
uniform blanket of cloud, the sky looked white and sick.

"This way," said Longan, and led off to the right.

I followed him along a little trail and into a small
swampy clearing with dome-shaped huts of woven
branches, plastered with mud, scattered about it. And,
for the first time, it struck me that Black Charlie might
be something other than an expatriate Earthman—might,
indeed, be a native of this planet, though I had heard of
no other humanlike race on other worlds before. My
head spinning, I followed Longan to the entrance of
one of the huts and halted as he whistled.

I don't remember now what I expected to see. Something vaguely humanoid, no doubt. But what came
through the entrance in response to Longan's whistle
was more like a large otter, with flat, muscular grasping
pads on the ends of its four limbs, instead of feet. It was
black, with glossy, dampish hair all over it. About four
feet in length, I judged, with no visible tail and a long,
snaky neck. The creature must have weighed one hundred to, perhaps, one hundred and fifty pounds. The
head on its long neck was also long and narrow, like the
head of a well-bred collie—covered with the same black
hair, with bright, intelligent eyes and a long mouth.

"This is Black Charlie," said Longan.

The creature stared at me and I returned his gaze.
Abruptly, I was conscious of the absurdity of the situation. It would have been difficult for any ordinary person to think of this being as a sculptor. To add to this a
necessity, an obligation, to convince it that it was *not* a
sculptor—mind you, I could not be expected to know a
word of its language—was to pile Pelion upon Ossa in a
madman's farce. I swung on Longan.

"Look here," I began with quite natural heat, "how do you expect me to tell—"

"He understands you," interrupted Longan.

"Speech?" I said, incredulously. "Real human speech?"

"No," Longan shook his head. "But he understands actions." He turned from me abruptly and plunged into the weeds surrounding the clearing. He returned immediately with two objects that looked like gigantic puffballs, and handed one to me.

"Sit on this," he said, doing so himself. I obeyed.

Black Charlie—I could think of nothing else to call him—came closer, and we sat down together. Charlie was half-squatting on ebony haunches. All this time, I had been carrying the wooden box that contained his sculptures and, now that we were seated, his bright eyes swung inquisitively toward it.

"All right," said Longan, "give it to me."

I passed him the box, and it drew Black Charlie's eyes like a magnet. Longan took it under one arm and pointed toward the lake with the other—to where we had landed the flyer. Then his arm rose in the air in a slow, impressive circle and pointed northward, from the direction we had come.

Black Charlie whistled suddenly. It was an odd note, like the cry of a loon—a far, sad sound.

Longan struck himself on the chest, holding the box with one hand. Then he struck the box and pointed to me. He looked at Black Charlie, looked back at me— then put the box into my numb hands.

"Look them over and hand them back," he said, his voice tight. Against my will, I looked at Charlie.

His eyes met mine. Strange, liquid, black inhuman eyes, like two tiny pools of pitch. I had to tear my own gaze away.

Torn between my feeling of foolishness and a real sympathy for the waiting creature, I awkwardly opened the box and lifted the stones from their compartments.

One by one, I turned them in my hand and put them back. I closed the box and returned it to Longan, shaking my head, not knowing if Charlie would understand that.

For a long moment, Longan merely sat facing me, holding the box. Then, slowly, he turned and set it, still open, in front of Charlie.

Charlie did not react at first. His head, on its long neck, dropped over the open compartments as if he was sniffing them. Then, surprisingly, his lips wrinkled back, revealing long, chisel-shaped teeth. Daintily, he reached into the box with these and lifted out the stones, one by one. He held them in his forepads, turning them this way and that, as if searching for the defects of each. Finally, he lifted one—it was the stone that faintly resembled a crouching beast. He lifted it to his mouth—and, with his gleaming teeth, made slight alterations in its surface. Then he brought it to me.

Helplessly I took it in my hands and examined it. The changes he had made in no way altered it toward something recognizable. I was forced to hand it back, with another headshake, and a poignant pause fell between us.

I had been desperately turning over in my mind some way to explain, through the medium of pantomine, the reasons for my refusal. Now, something occurred to me. I turned to Longan.

"Can he get me a piece of unworked stone?" I asked.

Longan turned to Charlie and made motions as if he were breaking something off and handing it to me. For a moment, Charlie sat still, as if considering this. Then he went into his hut, returning a moment later with a chunk of rock the size of my hand.

I had a small pocket knife, and the rock was soft. I held the rock out toward Longan and looked from him to it. Using my pocket knife, I whittled a rough, lumpy caricature of Longan, seated on the puffball. When I was finished, I put the two side by side, the hacked piece of stone insignificant on the ground beside the living man.

Black Charlie looked at it. Then he came up to me—and peering up into my face, cried softly, once. Moving so abruptly that it startled me, he turned smoothly, picked up in his teeth the piece of stone I had carved. Soon he disappeared back into his hut.

Longan stood up stiffly, like a man who has held one position too long. "That's it," he said. "Let's go."

We made our way to the combination and took off once more, headed back toward the city and the spaceship that would carry me away from this irrational world. As the mountains commenced to rise, far beneath us, I stole a glance at Longan, sitting beside me at the controls of the combination. His face was set in an expression of stolid unhappiness.

The question came from my lips before I had time to debate internally whether it was wise or not to ask it.

"Tell me, Mr. Longan," I said, "has—er—Black Charlie some special claim on your friendship?"

The tall man looked at me with something close to amazement.

"Claim!" he said. Then, after a short pause, during which he seemed to search my features to see if I was joking. "He saved my life."

"Oh," I said. "I see."

"You do, do you?" he countered. "Suppose I told you it was just after I'd finished killing his mate. They mate for life, you know."

"No, I didn't know," I answered feebly.

"I forget people don't know," he said in a subdued voice. I said nothing, hoping that, if I did not disturb him, he would say more. After a while he spoke. "This planet's not much good."

"I noticed," I answered. "I didn't see much in the way of plants and factories. And your sister world—the one I came from—is much more populated and built up."

"There's not much here," he said. "No minerals to speak of. Climate's bad, except on the plateaus. Soil's not much good." He paused. It seemed to take effort to say what came next. "Used to have a novelty trade in furs, though."

"Furs?" I echoed.

"Off Charlie's people," he went on, fiddling with the combination's controls. "Trappers and hunters used to be after them, at first, before they knew. I was one of them."

"You!" I said.

"Me!" His voice was flat. "I was doing fine, too, until I trapped Charlie's mate. Up till then, I'd been getting them out by themselves. They did a lot of traveling in those swamps. But this time, I was close to the village. I'd just clubbed her on the head when the whole tribe jumped me." His voice trailed off, then strengthened. "They kept me under guard for a couple of months.

"I learned a lot in that time. I learned they were intelligent. I learned it was Black Charlie who kept them from killing me right off. Seems he took the point of view that I was a reasonable being and, if he could just talk things over with me, we could get together and end the war." Longan laughed, a little bitterly. "They called it a war, Charlie's people did." He stopped talking.

I waited. And when he remained quiet, I prompted him. "What happened?" I asked.

"They let me go, finally," he said. "And I went to bat for them. Clear up to the Commissioner sent from Earth. I got them recognized as people instead of animals. I put an end to the hunting and trapping."

He stopped again. We were still flying through the upper air of Elman's World, the sun breaking through the clouds at last, revealing the ground below like a huge green relief map.

"I see," I said, finally.

Longan looked at me stonily.

We flew back to the city.

*   *   *

I left Elman's World the next day, fully believing that I had heard and seen the last of both Longan and Black Charlie. Several years later, at home in New York, I was visited by a member of the government's Foreign Service. He was a slight, dark man, and he didn't beat about the bush.

"You don't know me," he said. I looked at his card—*Antonio Walters.* "I was Deputy Colonial Representative on Elman's World at the time you were there."

I looked up at him, surprised. I had forgotten Elman's World by that time.

"Were you?" I asked, feeling a little foolish, unable to think of anything better to say. I turned his card over several times, staring at it, as a person will do when at a loss. "What can I do for you, Mr. Walters?"

"We've been requested by the local government on Elman's World to locate you, Mr. Jones," he answered. "Cary Longan is dying—"

"*Dying!*" I said.

"Lung fungus, unfortunately," said Walters. "You catch it in the swamps. He wants to see you before the end—and, since we're very grateful to him out there for the work he's been doing all these years for the natives, a place has been kept for you on a government courier ship leaving for Elman's World right away—if you're willing to go."

"Why, I . . ." I hesitated. In common decency, I could not refuse. "I'll have to notify my employers."

"Of course," he said.

Luckily, the arrangements I had to make consisted of a few business calls and packing my bags. I was, as a matter of fact, between trips at the time. As an experienced traveler, I could always get under way with a minimum of fuss. Walters and I drove out to Government Port, in northern New Jersey and, from there on, the authorities took over.

Less than a week later, I stood by Longan's bedside in the hospital of the same city I had visited years before. The man was now nothing more than a barely living skeleton, the hard vitality all but gone from him, hardly able to speak a few words at a time. I bent over to catch the whispered syllables from his wasted lips.

"Black Charlie . . ." he whispered.

"Black Charlie," I repeated. "Yes, what about him?"

"He's done something new," whispered Longan. "That carving of yours started him off, copying things. His tribe don't like it."

"They don't?" I said.

"They," whispered Longon, "don't understand. It's not normal, the way they see it. They're afraid . . ."

"You mean they're superstitious about what he carves?" I asked.

"Something like that. Listen—he's an artist . . ."

I winced internally at the last word, but held my tongue for the sake of the dying man.

". . . an artist. But they'll kill him for it, now that I'm gone. You can save him, though."

"Me?" I said.

"You!" The man's voice was like a wind rustling through dry leaves. "If you go out—take this last thing from him—act pleased . . . then they'll be scared to touch him. But hurry. Every day is that much closer . . ."

His strength failed him. He closed his eyes and his straining throat muscles relaxed to a little hiss of air that puffed between his lips. The nurse hurried me from his room.

The local government helped me. I was surprised, and not a little touched, to see how many people knew Longan. How many of them admired his attempts to pay back the natives by helping them in any way he could. They located Charlie's tribe on a map for me and sent me out with a pilot who knew the country.

We landed on the same patch of slime. I went alone

toward the clearing. With the brown weeds still walling it about, the locale showed no natural change, but Black Charlie's hut appeared broken and deserted. I whistled and waited. I called. And, finally, I got down on my hands and knees and crawled inside. But there was nothing there save a pile of loose rock and a mass of dried weeds. Feeling cramped and uncomfortable, for I am not used to such gymnastics, I backed out, to find myself surrounded by a crowd.

It looked as if all the other inhabitants of the village had come out of their huts and congregated before Charlie's. They seemed agitated, milling about, occasionally whistling at each other on that one low, plaintive note which was the only sound I had ever heard Charlie make. Eventually, the excitement seemed to fade, the group fell back and one individual came forward alone. He looked up into my face for a brief moment, then turned and glided swiftly on his pads toward the edge of the clearing.

I followed. There seemed nothing else to do. And, at that time, it did not occur to me to be afraid.

My guide led me deep into the weed patch, then abruptly disappeared. I looked around surprised and undecided, half-inclined to turn about and retrace my steps by the trail of crushed weeds I had left in my floundering advance. Then, a low whistle sounded close by. I went forward and found Charlie.

He lay on his side in a little circular open area of crushed weeds. He was too weak to do more than raise his head and look at me, for the whole surface of his body was criss-crossed and marked with the slashings of shallow wounds, from which dark blood seeped slowly and stained the reeds in which he lay. In Charlie's mouth, I had seen the long, chisel-teeth of his kind, and I knew what had made those wounds. A gust of rage went through me, and I stooped to pick him up in my arms.

He came up easily, for the bones of his kind are cartilaginous, and their flesh is far lighter than our human flesh. Holding him, I turned and made my way back to the clearing.

The others were waiting for me as we came out into the open. I glared at them—and then the rage inside me went out like a blown candle. For there was nothing there to hate. *They* had not hated Charlie. They had merely feared him—and their only crime was ignorance.

They moved back from me, and I carried Charlie to the door of his own hut. There I laid him down. The chest and arms of my jacket were soaked from his dark body fluid, and I saw that his blood was not clotting as our own does.

Clumsily, I took off my shirt and, tearing it into strips, made a poor attempt to bind up the torn flesh. But the blood came through in spite of my first aid. Charlie, lifting his head, with a great effort, from the ground, picked feebly at the bandages with his teeth, so that I gave up and removed them.

I sat down beside him then, feeling sick and helpless. In spite of Longan's care and dying effort, in spite of all the scientific developments of my own human race, I had come too late. Numbly, I sat and looked down at him and wondered why I could not have come one day earlier.

From this half-stupor of self-accusation, I was roused by Charlie's attempts to crawl back into his hut. My first reaction was to restrain him. But, from somewhere, he seemed to have dredged up a remnant of his waning strength—and he persisted. Seeing this, I changed my mind and instead of hindering, helped. He dragged himself through the entrance, his strength visibly waning.

I did not expect to see him emerge. I believed some ancient instinct had called him, that he would die then and there. But, a few moments later, I heard a sound as of stones rattling from within—and, in a few seconds, he began to back out. Halfway through the entrance, his strength finally failed him. He lay still for a minute, then whistled weakly.

I went to him and pulled him out the rest of the way. He turned his head toward me, holding in his mouth what I first took to be a ball of dried mud.

I took it from him and began to scrape the mud off with my fingernails. Almost immediately, the grain and surface of the sandstone he used for his carvings began to emerge—and my hands started to shake so hard that, for a moment, I had to put the stone down while I got myself under control. For the first time, the true importance to Charlie, of these things he had chewed and bitten into shape, got home to me.

In that moment, I swore that whatever bizarre form this last and greatest work of his might possess, I would make certain that it was accorded a place in some respectable museum as a true work of art. After all, it had been conceived in honesty and executed in the love that took no count of labor, provided the end was achieved.

And then, the rest of the mud came free in my hands. I saw what it was, and I could have cried and laughed at the same time. For, of all the shapes he could have chosen to work in stone, he had picked the one that no critic would have selected as the choice of an artist of his race. For he had chosen no plant or animal, no structure or natural shape out of his environment, to express the hungry longing of his spirit. None of these had he chosen—instead, with painful clumsiness, he had fashioned an image from the soft and grainy rock; a statue of a standing man.

And I knew what man it was.

Charlie lifted his head from the stained ground and looked toward the lake where my flyer waited. I am not an intuitive man—but, for once, I was able to understand the meaning of a look. He wanted me to leave while he was still alive. He wanted to see me go, carrying the thing he had fashioned. I got to my feet, holding it and stumbled off. At the edge of the clearing, I looked back. He still watched. And the rest of his people still hung back from him. I did not think they would bother him now.

And so I came home.

But there is one thing more to tell. For a long time, after I returned from Elman's World, I did not look at the crude statuette. I did not want to, for I knew that seeing it would only confirm what I had known from the start, that all the longing and desires in the world cannot create art where there is no talent, no true visualization. But at the end of one year I was cleaning up all the little details of my office. And, because I believe in system and order—and also, because I was ashamed of myself for having put it off so long—I took the statuette from a bottom drawer of my desk, unwrapped it and set it on the desk's polished surface.

I was alone in my office at the time, at the end of a day, when the afternoon Sun, striking red through the tall window beside my desk, touched everything between the walls with a clear, amber light. I ran my fingers over the grainy sandstone and held it up to look at it.

And then—for the first time—I saw it, saw through the stone to the image beyond, saw what Black Charlie had seen with Black Charlie's eyes, when he looked at Longan. I saw men as Black Charlie's kind saw men—and I saw what the worlds of men meant to Black Charlie. And, above all, overriding all, I saw art as Black Charlie saw it, through his bright alien eyes—saw the beauty he had sought at the price of his life, and had half-found.

But, most of all, I saw that this crude statuette was *art*.

One more word. Amid the mud and weeds of the

swamp, I had held the carving in my hands and promised myself that this work would one day stand on display. Following that moment of true insight in my office, I did my best to place it with the institution I represented, then with others who knew me as a reputable buyer.

But I could find no takers. No one, although they trusted me individually, was willing to exhibit such a poor-looking piece of work on the strength of a history that I, alone, could vouch for. There are people, close to any institution, who are only too ready to cry, "Hoax!" For several years, I tried without success.

Eventually, I gave up on the true story and sold the statuette, along with a number of other odd pieces, to a dealer of minor reputation, representing it as an object whose history I did not know.

Curiously, the statuette has justified my belief in what is art, by finding a niche for itself. I traced it from the dealer, after a time, and ran it to Earth quite recently. There is a highly respectable art gallery on this planet which has an extensive display of primitive figures of early American Indian origin.

And Black Charlie's statuette is among them. I will not tell which or where it is.

There is probably a tougher job than working on your family's farm, but I'm not sure what it could be.

Agriculture is extremely dangerous. The fatality rate is well above that of firemen, who in turn have much higher per capita fatalities than the police. The number of ways to die and be maimed on a farm range from the standard ones—tractors rolling over; trousers getting caught in the power take-off—through the exotic (nerve gas was developed from agricultural insecticides; want to guess how much training farmers get before they mix and apply those insecticides to their crops?)—to the downright bizarre.

As a kid, my Dad was wiring bales behind a combine which rolled over a nest of yellowjackets. The scores of stings didn't kill him outright, but he still carries antihistamines with him throughout warm weather because the next sting might very well finish the job begun by that sensitization sixty years ago.

A six-year old boy slipped off the fence around the hog pen three miles down the road from my wife's family's farm (just outside Dubuque, by the way). The boy would have been killed if his mother hadn't jumped into the pen and thrown him to safety.

The pigs then knocked the mother down. And killed her.

I don't have romantic notions about farms or farming. I don't think anybody who's worked on a farm does. I'm afraid that's why this story, the only one I've set on a farm, is in some ways as bleak as anything I've written.

The farm is real. The Indian mound is real. The curio cabinet is real.

The characters aren't my in-laws; but the characters are real too.

THE RED LEER

David Drake

As he swung the tractor for a final pass across Sac Ridge Field, Deehalter saw that dirt had been turned on the side of the Indian mound. The big man threw in the hand clutch of the Allis-Chalmers and throttled the diesel back to idle as he glared at the new trench through the barbed wire. "That goddamn Kernes," he whispered. "If I've got to work with him much longer . . ."

He revved the engine and slammed the tractor back in gear. The farmer's scowl was as black as the hair curling up his arms from the backs of his hands to the shirtsleeves rolled at his biceps.

At the south end of the field, Deehalter raised the cultivator and drove the Allis down the long, looping trail back to the farm buildings. There was a way of sorts straight west from the top of the ridge, but it was too steep for the tractor. The more gradual slope took Deehalter through half a dozen gates and eventually back to the buildings from the southwest. To the left loomed the barn and the three concrete silos peering over its roof at him. The milking parlor was a one-story addition to the barn's east side, facing the equipment shed and the gas pump. And at the pump was Tom Kernes with his ten-year-old son, Deehalter's nephew, putting gas in the jeep.

Deehalter pulled up beside them and let the diesel clatter for a moment before he shut it off. Kernes, a short, ginger-headed man, looked up. His arms were not tan but a deep red, with brighter slashes where the straps of his undershirt had interrupted part of the sunlight. Kernes was thirty-five, five years younger than his brother-in-law, but his crinkly, sunburned face would have passed for any age. "Finish Sac Ridge already, Dee?" he asked in his pleasant, throaty voice. The tension in his muscles showed that he had correctly read Deehalter's anger.

"Kernes, what've you been doing with the Indian mound?" the bigger man demanded from the tractor seat. "You know to leave that the hell alone!" A pick and shovel lay in the back of the jeep. Deehalter noticed them, and a black flush moved across his face.

Kernes's skin was too red to show the blood, but his voice rose to the challenge. "When Old John owned the farm, he could say what he pleased; but he's dead now. I'm damned if I'm not going to get an Indian skull like yours." Gesturing eastward at the ridge, the little man added, "I own half this goddamn place, and I'm going to get a skull."

The curio cabinet in Deehalter's parlor had been assembled by his grandfather before the First World War. Among its agates and arrowheads, swordcane and ostrich plumes, was a brown human skull. The family had always assumed the skull came from a mound somewhere, but not even Old John had been sure. It fascinated Kernes, perhaps only because Deehalter had refused to give it to him. The main house and its furnishings, including the cabinet, had gone to Deehalter under his father's will—just as the new house in which his sister Alice lived with Kernes and their children had gone to her. The rest of the six-hundred-acre farm was willed to Deehalter and Alice jointly, with the provision that if either of them tried to partition the property, the whole of it went to the other. Deehalter had talked to a lawyer, and he was sure Kernes had done the same. The worst news either of the men had heard in a long time was that the will would probably stand up in court.

"There's a law against digging up mounds," Deehalter muttered.

"There's a law against keeping an Indian skull on display," the shorter man blazed back. "You going to bring the law in here, Dee?"

"Well," Deehalter said lamely, "you don't get everything in the mound. You've no right to that."

Kernes stood, arms akimbo, sweat from the June sun glittering on his face. "If I do all the goddamn digging, I do," he said. "And anyhow, I get the skull out first."

Deehalter wiped his face with his huge callused palm. He didn't like to fool with the mound. Old John had whaled him within an inch of his life thirty years ago, when he had caught his son poking into the smooth slope with a posthole digger. But Deehalter remembered also the nightmare that had awakened him for months after that afternoon, and that dream was of nothing so common as a beating by his father. Still, to let Kernes take everything. . . . "All right," Deehalter said, "I'll help you dig. But I get my pick of anything besides a skull. Wouldn't be surprised if there was gold in with a chief." Actually, Deehalter knew enough about mounds to doubt there would be anything that would interest a non-archaeologist—often the mounds hadn't even been built over a body. But that wasn't anything the big farmer was going to say to his brother-in-law.

"Dad," said the Kernes boy unexpectedly. "If Uncle Dee helps you, you don't need me, do you?"

Kernes looked at the child as though he wanted to hit

him. "Go on, then," he snapped. "But I want that goddamn tool shed painted when I get back. All of it!"

The boy took off running for the house. Wiener, the farm's part-collie, chased after him, barking. "Kid's been listening to his mother," Kernes grumbled. "From the way Alice's been carrying on, you'd think Old John was going to come out of his grave if I dug up that mound. He must've knocked that into her head with a maul."

"He was strong on it," Deehalter agreed absently. "I know when he was a boy, there was still a couple Sac Indians on the farm. Maybe they talked to him. But he was strong about a lot of things."

"Well, you ready to go?" Kernes demanded. He had hung up the pump nozzle and now remembered to cap the jeep's tank.

Deehalter grimaced. "I'll put the cultivator in the shed," he said. "Then we'll go."

Kernes drove, taking the direct trail through the east pasture. There was a rivulet to ford and a pair of gullies that had to be skirted, but the hard going didn't start until they reached the foot of the ridge. They had bought the jeep ten years before from Army surplus, and the sharp grades of the ridge slope made the motor wheeze even in the granny gear. Cedars studded the slope, interspersed with bull thistles whose purple brachia were ready to burst open. There was a final switchback just before the trail reached the summit. As Kernes hauled the wheel hard to the left, the motor spluttered and died. Deehalter swung out of the jeep and walked the last thirty yards while the smaller man cursed and trod on the starter.

The mound was built on the north end of the ridge. That part had never been opened as a field because the soil was too thinly spread above the bedrock. The mound was oval: about fifteen feet long on the east-west axis and three or four feet high. Though small, it was clearly artificial, a welt of earth on the smooth table of the ridge. Kernes's trench was in the center of the south side, halfway in and down to the level of the surrounding soil. Deehalter was examining the digging when the jeep heaved itself up behind him and was cut off again.

"We just kept hitting rocks," the smaller man explained. "We didn't get near as far as I'd figured before we started."

Deehalter squatted on his haunches and poked into the excavation with a finger like a corncob. "You didn't hit rocks," he said, "you hit *a* rock. One goddamn slab. There's no way we're going to clear that dirt off it without a week of work or renting a bulldozer. And even if we cleared down *to* the rock, that slab's a foot thick and must weigh tons. We're just wasting our time here—or we would be if we didn't go on back right now."

Kernes swore. "We could hook a chain to the Allis—" he began.

Deehalter cut him off. "We'd have to get the dirt off the top first, and that'd take all goddamn summer. This was a bad idea to start, and it got worse quick. Come on, let's go back." He straightened.

"What about dynamite?" blurted Kernes.

Deehalter stared at his brother-in-law. The smaller man would not meet his gaze but continued, "There's still a stick under the seat from when you blew up the beaver dam. We could use it."

"Kernes," Deehalter said, "you're so afraid of that dynamite that you'd rather leave it in the jeep than touch it to get it out. Besides, it'll blow the shit out of anything under that slab—if there is anything—and the slab's not flat on bedrock all the way across. What're you trying to prove?"

Kernes's red face grew even brighter with embarrassment or anger. "Look," he said, "I'm gonna get into this goddamn thing if I got to hire a contractor. I said I would and I will. You don't want to help, that's your goddamn business."

Deehalter eyed him a moment longer. "Oh, I'll do my part," he said. He gestured to the pick and added, "You see if you can cut a slot an inch deep and maybe eight inches long in the seam between the top slab and the bedrock. I'll get the dynamite ready." He grinned. "Unless you want to do that instead?"

Kernes's only response was to heft the tool with a choked grip and begin chopping at the stone.

Deehalter flipped the jeep's seat forward and lifted out the corrugated cardboard box beneath it. There was, as Kernes had said, still one stick of dynamite left along with a roll of wire and a smaller box of blasting caps. The explosive terrified Kernes in the way snakes or spiders do other men. Deehalter had deliberately refused to take the stick out of the jeep despite his brother-in-law's frequent requests. Finally Kernes had ceased to mention it—until now. Kernes was so stubbornly determined to have an Indian skull that he had overriden his fear of the explosive. It occurred to Deehalter that he was doing the same thing himself with his fear of the mound.

The big farmer leaned against the jeep as he dug a fuse pocket in the dynamite with a pencil stub. Kernes was chipping the soft rock effectively, even in the confined space. "Not too wide," Deehalter warned as he twisted the leads from the blasting cap onto the extension wire.

He didn't like what they were doing. Shapes from long-ago nightmares were hovering over his mind—unclear, but no less unpleasant for that. He'd never heard of Indians using stone in their mounds, and that bothered him, too. Still, why not? The Mississippi Basin was rich in soft yellow limestone, already layered by its floodings and strandings in the shallow seas of its deposition. So it wasn't the stone or anything else rational which was eating at Deehalter; it was just that something felt cold and very wrong inside him.

"That enough, Dee?" Kernes asked, panting. His sleeveless undershirt was gray with sweat.

Deehalter leaned forward. "It'll do," he acknowledged. Kernes was shrinking back from the explosive in Deehalter's hand. "Run the jeep over the crest of the ridge and get the hood open. There's enough wire to reach to there."

While his brother-in-law scrambled to obey, Deehalter knelt in the trench and made his own preparations. First he set the blasting cap in the hole in the end of the dynamite. Then he carefully kneaded the explosive into the slot Kernes had cut in the rock. The heavy waxed paper and its fillings of sawdust, ammonium nitrate, and nitroglycerin were hot and deformed easily. A lot of people didn't know how to use dynamite; they wasted the force of the blast. Deehalter didn't want to blow the mound open, but he'd be damned if he wouldn't do it right if he did it at all.

When the dynamite had been molded into the rock, the big man shoveled dirt down on top of it and used his boots to firmly tamp the pile. The thin wire looped out of the earth like the shadow of a grass blade. Deehalter hung the coil on the pick handle, using it as a loose spindle from which to unwind the wire as he walked to the jeep.

"This far enough away?" Kernes asked, eyeing the mound apprehensively.

"Unless a really big chunk comes straight down," Deehalter said, silently pleased at the other man's nervousness. "Christ, it's just one stick, even if it is sixty-percent equivalent."

Kernes bent down behind the jeep. Deehalter squatted at the front, protected from the blast by the brow of the hill. He held the bare end of one wire to the negative post of the battery, then touched the other lead to the positive side. Nothing happened. "Goddammit," he said, prodding the wire to cut through the white corrosion on the post.

The dynamite exploded with a loud thump.

"Jesus!" Kernes shouted as he bounced to his feet. Deehalter, more experienced, hunched under his baseball cap while dirt and tiny rock fragments rained over him and the jeep. Then at last he stood and followed his brother-in-law. The smaller man was now cursing and trying to brush dirt from his head and shoulders with his left hand; in his right he carried a battery spotlight.

Acrid black smoke curled in the pit like a knot of snakes. The sod walls of the trench looked as they had before the explosion, but the earth compacted over the charge was gone, and the exposed edge of the rock slab had shattered. Because the limestone could neither move nor compress, the shock had broken it as thoroughly as a twenty-foot fall could have.

Kernes bent down over the opening and grasped a chunk of stone to toss out of the way. The dynamite fumes looped a tendril over his face. Kernes coughed and quivered, and for an instant Deehalter thought the other man lost focus. Then Kernes was on his feet again, fanning the shovel blade to clear the smoke faster and crying, "By God, Dee, there's really something in there! By God!"

Deehalter waited, frowning, as Kernes shoveled at the rubble. A little prying with the blade was enough to crumble the edge of the slab into fist-sized pieces like a three-dimensional jigsaw puzzle. More dirt fell in, but that was easily scooped away. The actual opening stayed small because the only cavity in the bedrock was a shallow, water-cut basin. It sloped so gradually that even after a two-foot scallop had been nibbled from the overlying slab, there was barely enough room to reach an arm into the hollow.

The fumes had dissipated. Kernes scattered a last shovelful of dirt and gravel, then tossed the tool aside as well. Kneeling down with his face as close to the opening as he could get it and still leave room for the spotlight, he began to search the cavity. "God damn,"

Kernes said suddenly. "God *damn!*" He tried to reach in left-handed, found there was too little room, and shoved the light back out of the way since he had already located the object in his head. The spotlight beam touched grass blades shaded from the sun, a color rather than an illumination.

"Look at this, Deehalter!" cried Kernes as he scrabbled backward. "By God!"

"I've seen skulls before," the black-haired man said sourly, eyeing the discolored bone which his brother-in-law held hooked through the eyesockets. The lower jaw was missing, but the explosion seemed to have done little damage. Unless the front teeth . . .

"There's other stuff in there, too," Kernes bubbled.

"Then it's mine," said Deehalter sharply.

"Did I goddamn say it wasn't?" Kernes demanded. "And you can get it out for yourself, too," he added, looking down at his shirt, muddied by dirt and perspiration.

Deehalter said nothing further. He lay down carefully in the fresh earth and directed the spotlight past his head. He could see other bones in the shallow cavity. The explosion had shaken them, but their order was too precise for any large animals to have stripped away the flesh. Indeed, the bundles of skin and tendon still clinging to the thighs indicated that not even mice had entered the tomb. The stone-to-stone seal must have been surprisingly tight.

Metal glittered beyond the bones. Deehalter marked its place and reached in, edging himself forward so that his shoulder pressed hard against the ragged lip of the slab. He expected to feel revulsion or the sudden fear of his childhood, but the cavity was dry and empty even of death. His wrist brushed over rib bones, and he thought the object beyond them was too far; then his fingertips touched it, touched them, and he lifted them carefully out.

Kernes stopped studying the skull in the sunlight

from different angles. "What the hell you got there, Dee?" he asked warily.

Deehalter wasn't sure himself, so he said nothing. He held the two halves of a hollow metal teardrop, six inches long. On the outside it was black and bubbled-looking; within, the spherical cavity was no larger than a hickory nut. The mating surfaces and the cavity itself were a rich silver color, untarnished and as smooth as the lenses of a camera.

"One of them's mine," said Kernes abruptly. "The skull and half the rest." He reached for one of the pieces.

"Like hell," said Deehalter, mildly because he was concentrating on the chunks of metal. His big shoulder blocked Kernes away without effort. "Besides, it's all one thing," he added, holding the sections so that the polished surfaces mated. Then, when he tried to part them, the halves did not reseparate.

"Aw," Kernes said in disbelief and again put a hand out for the object. This time Deehalter let him take it. Despite all the ginger-haired man's tugging and pushing, the teardrop held together. It was only after Kernes, sweating and angry, had handed back the object, that Deehalter found the trick of it. You had to rotate the halves along the plane of the separation—which, since there was no visible line, was purely a matter of luck the first time it worked.

"Let's get on home," Deehalter said. He nodded westward toward the sun. Sunset was still an hour away, but it would take them a while to drive back. The ridge was already casting its broad shadow across the high ground to the east. "Besides," Deehalter added, almost under his breath, "I don't like the feeling I get up here sometimes."

But it was almost two weeks before Deehalter had any reason for his uneasiness. . . .

* * *

Despite the full moon low in the west and the light of the big mercury vapor lamp above the cowyard to the north of the barn, the plump blonde stumbled twice on the graveled path to the car. The second time she caught Deehalter's arm and clung there giggling. More to be shut of her than for chivalry, the farmer opened the passenger door of the Chrysler and handed her in. Naturally, she flopped across his lap when he got in on the driver's side. He pushed her upright in disgust.

It was 3 A.M. and there were no lights yet in Alice and her husband's house. Deehalter knew they had seen him bring Wendy home in the evening, knew also that Wiener would awaken them as he chased the car. Kernes had once complained to Deehalter, red-faced, about the example he set for his nephew and nieces by bringing whores home to their grandfather's house. Deehalter had told him that under the will it was his house, and that when Kernes and Alice quit doing it in *their* house, he'd consider quitting it in his.

When the car began to scrunch down the drive past the new house, Wiener came loping toward them from the barn. He barked once every other time his forefeet touched the ground. The noise was more irritating than even a quick staccato would have been. The car windows were closed against the night's damp chill. Deehalter's finger was poised on the switch to roll the glass down and shout at the mongrel when Wendy's scream snapped his head around.

The bank to the left sloped up from the drive, so the thing standing there was only in the edge of the lights. It was wire-thin and tall—twice the height of a man at a fleeting glance, though a part of Deehalter knew that was the effect of the bank and the angle. A flat lizard-snout of teeth glittered sharply. Then the beast turned and the big car leaped forward down the drive as Deehalter floored the accelerator. Wendy was still screaming, her face buried in her hands, when the car banged over the slotted cattle-guard and fishtailed onto the gravel county road.

Deehalter kept his speedometer dangerously above 60 for the first three miles, until they reached the tavern and gas station at Five Points. There he braked to a stop and turned on the dome light. The girl whimpered. Deehalter's big hands gripped her shoulders and hauled her upright. "Shut up," he said tightly.

"W-what was it?" she blubbered.

"Shut up, for Christ's sake!" Deehalter shouted. "It wasn't a goddamned thing!" He brought his face close to Wendy's. The girl's eyes were as fearful as they had been minutes before at the sight of the creature. "You saw a cat in the headlights, that's all. You're *not* going to get everybody and his brother tramping over my farm shooting my milking herd. You're going to keep your goddamn mouth shut, do you hear?"

The blonde was nodding to the rhythm of Deehalter's words. Tears streamed from her eyes, and when she tried to wipe them, she smeared the remains of her eye shadow across her cheeks.

Deehalter released her suddenly and put the car in gear. Neither of them spoke during the rest of the ride to town. When the big farmer stopped in front of the girl's apartment, she stumbled out and ran up the steps without bothering to close the car door. Deehalter locked it after he slammed it shut.

He drove back to the farm at a moderate pace that slowed appreciably as he came nearer. The night had only its usual motions and noises now. Deehalter was waiting in his locked car an hour later, alone with nothing but a memory to disturb him, when Kernes came out of his house to start milking.

After lunch—a full meal of fried steak and potatoes— Deehalter had cooked for himself and his father as well before Old John died—the big man walked down the drive and began searching the grassy bank to the left of it. Once when he looked up, he saw his sister watching him intently from the Kernes's kitchen window. He waved but she ducked away. Toward three o'clock, Kernes himself came back in the jeep from inspecting the fences around the northwest pasture. Deehalter hailed him. After a moment's hesitation, the ginger-haired man swung the vehicle up the bank and stopped.

"Come look at this," Deehalter said. The turf was marked fuzzily where he pointed. "Doesn't it look like three claw prints?" he asked.

Kernes looked at him strangely. "Claw prints? What do you mean, Dee?"

"It—oh, Christ, I don't know," said the big man, straightening and lifting his cap to run his hand through his hair. He looked glumly back past the barn to the long bulk of Sac Ridge.

"Haven't seen Wiener today, have you?" Kernes asked unexpectedly.

"Not since I took Wendy home this morning," replied Deehalter, his own expression odd. "Barked at the car as usual. You must've heard him."

"Learned to sleep through it, I guess," said Kernes, and the words did not quite ring true . . . though that might have been the blurred print on the ground and Deehalter's blurred memory of what had made the print. Kernes got into the jeep. "Usually he chases a rabbit, he gets back for breakfast. Kids've about worried me to death about that damn dog."

"I'll ride to the barn with you," Deehalter said. They did not speak about the dog—or the print—for the rest of the afternoon.

In the evening, after Deehalter had finished his turn at milking, Alice came out to the barn to help wash down the equipment. Alice Kernes was ten years younger than her brother. Though they had never been close, there was a thread of mutual affection despite Deehalter's reciprocated hatred for his brother-in-law. Alice hummed as she polished the glass tubing and stainless steel; a short woman with her black hair tied back by a kerchief and a man's shirt flapping over the waistband of her gray skirt.

"Wiener been back yet?" Deehalter asked with feigned disinterest.

"No, have you seen him?" Alice said, pausing to catch the shake of Deehalter's head.

"Susie's been crying all day. Tom went out to quiet the dog down this morning, and I think he scared him off. But he'll be back tonight, I figure."

Deehalter flipped the switch that would drain the water now being cycled through the transfer piping. "Kernes got up to chase him?"

"Uh-huh. Did you get the big tank?"

"Yeah, we can call it a night," Deehalter said. Bloodstains are hard to identify in heavy grass, harder even than footprints in the sod beneath, so he had made no mention of the splotches he had found thirty yards from the drive that afternoon. There had been no body—not even a swatch of dog fur torn off in a struggle.

But despite that, Deehalter guessed that the mongrel would not be coming home that night.

A cow awakened Deehalter with a blat like a cut-off klaxon. His Remington .30–06 leaned against the window frame, bathed in moonlight. Deehalter stripped a shell into the autoloader's chamber from the full magazine before he pulled on his dungarees and boots. Shirtless, his baggy trousers weighted down by the rest of the box of ammunition, Deehalter unlocked the front door and began running across the yard.

There were one hundred and sixty cattle in the barn, and from the noise they had all gone wild. Over their bellows came clatters and splintering as the frantic tons of beef smashed the fittings of the barn. Normally in the summer, the cows were free to wander in and out of the yard and to the pasture beyond, but tonight Deehalter had penned them for safety. He was a hundred feet from the electric fence of the yard, cursing his mistake in having concentrated the herd and then left it unprotected, when one of the black-and-white Holsteins smashed from the barn into the cowyard through both halves of the Dutch door.

There was something behind it.

The thing's tongue and the blood on its jaws were black in the mercury floodlight. Erect against the side of the barn it was almost eight feet tall, though only the shadows gave mass to its splindly limbs. It saw Deehalter and skidded on the slippery concrete, its claws rasping through the slime. Deehalter threw his rifle to his shoulder. It was as if he were aiming at a skeleton made of coat hangers, the thing was so thin. Deehalter's hands shook. The creature bent forward, cocking its hips back for balance. It opened its jaws so wide that every needle tooth seemed pointed at the farmer. Then it screamed like a plunging shell as Deehalter fired. His bullet punched neatly through the side of the barn ten feet above the ground.

With a single stride, the creature disappeared back within the building. Deehalter slammed another shot through the empty doorway.

Panting, the big man knelt and fumbled out the box of ammunition without letting go of the rifle. His shoulder ached. The empty cases shone silver-pale on the grass to his right. When Deehalter had reloaded, he shuffled forward again. He held his rifle out as if he were thrusting it through fluid. The yard was filled with milling cows. Deehalter moved past them to the low milking parlor and tried in vain to peer through the dusty windows. Then, holding the rifle awkwardly like a huge pistol, he unlatched the door and flipped on the light. There was nothing in the parlor, and its metal gates to the barn were still closed.

Deehalter turned on the lights in the main building. There were only a score of frightened cows still within. The half-loft eight feet above the bare floor had only a little straw in it. The loft door in the south wall hung askew. There were deep scratches around its broken latch. From the loft, Deehalter grimly surveyed the barn. The interior walls were splattered with blood. A heifer was dead in her stall; long gouges reddened the hides of several others of the herd.

It was almost dawn. The black-haired farmer stood at the loft door, cursing and staring out into the red sunrise which pulled the shadow of the ridge like a long curtain over the pasture.

The door to the milking parlor banged. Deehalter swung around and raised the muzzle of his rifle. It was Kernes barefooted and in torn pajamas with Alice, wide-eyed, behind him. Seeing the blood and the dead heifer, she shouted at her husband, "My God, Tom, have you and George been shooting cows?"

Kernes gaped. Deehalter couldn't understand why the question was directed at his brother-in-law. "No, it was a, a—" Deehalter began and stuttered to a halt, uncertain both of the truth and what he should say about it. To change the subject he said, "We got to phone Doc Jepson. Some of the cows've been—cut."

"Phone the vet?" blazed Alice—Kernes still had not spoken. She reached back into the parlor for the extension which hung on the wall higher than a cow carries its head. "We'll call the sheriff, we'll call—"

"Put down that goddamn phone!" Deehalter said, not loudly but too loudly to be ignored by anyone who knew him well.

Alice was in a rage herself, but she stepped back from the phone and watched her brother descend carefully from the loft. "What did it, George?" she asked.

"I didn't get a good look."

"God *dammit*, George," Alice said, letting go of her anger now that Deehalter had cooled enough not to shoot her dead in a fury, "why won't you let me get help?"

"Because we're in the milk business," the big man

said, sagging against the ladder in mental exhaustion. Kernes wasn't really listening; Alice's face was blank. "Because if we go tell people there's an eight-foot lizard on our farm—"

Kernes swore. Deehalter shouted, "All right, I saw it, what the hell's the difference? Something killed the cow, didn't it?" He glared at the others, then went on, "First they'll think we're crazy. And then when they learn it's true, they'll say, 'Strontium 90,' or 'What're they spraying their fields with to do that?' or, 'There's something in their water.' And we'll never sell another pint of milk from here as long as we live. You *know* what the dairy business is like!"

Alice nodded sharply. "Then we'll just raise hogs," she said, "or corn—or we'll sell the farm and all get jobs with Purina, for God's sake. Spring Hill Dairies isn't the whole—"

"Alice!"

Kernes's eyes were flicking from one sibling to the other, a spectator rather than a referee. Alice glared at him, then said to her brother, "All right, George. But I'm taking the kids into town to stay with Iris until you come to your senses." Then, to husband, she added, "Tom, are you coming too?"

"If you leave here, Kernes," said Deehalter quietly, "you'll never come back. I don't give a shit what the law says."

The men stared at each other. "I'll stay," Kernes said. Alice banged through the gate and into the milking parlor without a look behind her. "I'd have stayed anyway, Alice!" the smaller man shouted.

"Call Doc Jepson," Deehalter repeated wearily. "We can tell him it was dogs or something"—the tooth marks were too high and broad for that to be other than a transparent lie—"and hope we can scotch this thing before worse happens."

Numbly, Kernes made the call. As the little man hung up, they heard the rasping starter of the old station wagon. A moment later, gravel spattered as Alice rocketed down the drive. Almost as fast as he himself had driven the night before, Deehalter thought.

"It's because of what we took out of that mound," Kernes said in a small voice.

Deehalter shook his head in irritation. "This thing didn't come from a skull or a little bit of iron," he snapped. "It's big—big enough to kill a Holstein."

"It was there just the same," Kernes replied. "We've got to close that grave up with everything in it again. Then maybe we'll be okay."

"You're nuts," Deehalter said. But he remembered the thing's eyes and the gape of its jaws—and he knew that sometime that day he would help Kernes bury the objects again.

Deehalter walked to the mound and the parked jeep without speaking. In the field behind him, the crows settled noisily on the carrion again.

Kernes had lifted out a pair of shovels and the gunny-sack holding the objects. "Well?" he asked.

"Yeah," said Deehalter with a shrug, "it was Wiener."

Kernes began to undo the knot which closed the sack's throat. Without looking up, he said, "I think it's the moon. That's why it didn't come out when we opened the mound. It needed the full moon to bring it out."

"Bullshit," said Deehalter. "I *saw* the thing and it's not moonlight, it's as solid as you or me. Damn sight solider than old Wiener there," he added with a grim twist of his head. "Moonlight's just light, anyway."

"Fluorescent light's just light too," Kernes retorted, "but it makes plants grow like they don't with a regular light-bulb. Christ, Dee, don't you feel the moon on you at night?"

Deehalter did, but he wasn't about to admit that weakness even in the noon sun. Kernes had paused after opening the bag, unwilling either to dump the contents back into the hole without ceremony or to touch them again barehanded. The big man hesitated also. Then he glanced at the guns in easy reach, between the front seats of the jeep, and lifted out the skull.

The bone felt warm. Because Deehalter had not really taken a look at it before, he did so now at this last opportunity. The teeth were damaged in a way that at first he could not explain. Then the farmer cursed, set the skull down on the ground, and stretched out in the open trench. The angle was too flat for Deehalter to have been able to see anything even if he had brought a flashlight this trip, but his fingertips found the shallow grooves he expected in the undersurface of the slab.

"Christ," he muttered, standing up again. "That poor sucker was alive when they covered him up in there. He didn't have a damned thing to dig with, so he tried to scrape through the stone with his teeth."

Kernes stared at the skull and looked a little sicker than he had before. His finger traced but did not touch the front teeth. All four of the incisors were worn across the flats, as if by a file. They had been ground down well into the nerve canals. One of the front pair had cracked about halfway from the root. "Yeah, I'd seen that but I didn't think . . ." he said. "Jesus, what a way to go. He surely must've known he couldn't chew his way through a foot of rock."

"Maybe he didn't know there was a foot of it," Deehalter said. "Besides, he didn't have a lot of choice."

Carefully, the big man set the skull as far back into the mound as his arm would reach. The litter of bone and rock chips within scrunched under his shirtsleeve.

The rippled iron teardrop was still closed. Deehalter looked at it for a moment, then twisted it to split the halves because they had been separate when he found them. The metal divided with a soft gasp like a cold jar being opened. Deehalter set the halves under the slab as carefully as he had the discolored skull.

Almost before he rolled out of the way, his brother-in-law was tossing a shovelful of earth into the hole. Kernes worked feverishly at the spoil pile he and his son had thrown up in digging the pit. By the time Deehalter had brushed himself off and picked up a shovel, the blast-crumbled edge of the slab had been buried again.

They finished their work before noon, leaving on the mound's side a black scar that sealed off the greater blackness within.

The barn windows were green fiberglass which the western moonlight outlined sharply against the walls. The diffused illumination was weak and without distinct shadows. It made the loft floor an overlay of grays on grays which wobbled softly as Deehalter paced along it. The cattle penned below murmured, occasionally blatting loudly at their unfamiliar restraint. At each outburst, Deehalter would pause and lean over the loft rail with his rifle forward; but the bellowing was never for any reason that had to do with why two armed men were watching the barn tonight.

At the north end of the loft, Deehalter stopped and looked out the open loading door. The cowyard below was scraped and hosed off daily, but animal waste had stained the concrete an indelible brown which became purple in the mercury light.

To the left, within the fence of the cowyard and in the corner it formed with the barn, hunched Kernes with a shotgun loaded with deer slugs. From Deehalter's angle, the smaller man was foreshortened into a stump growing from the concrete. Nothing moved in the night, though the automatic feeder in the hog pens flapped several times. As Deehalter watched silently, Kernes looked up at the moon. Despite the coolness of the night and the breeze from the west, Kernes pulled out a handkerchief and wiped his forehead.

Deehalter turned and began pacing back to the south

end of the barn. He had finished his thermos of coffee hours ago, and it was only by staying in motion that he was able to keep awake. He couldn't understand how Kernes could huddle in the same corner since ten o'clock and still be alert; but then, Kernes wasn't a person Deehalter *wanted* to understand.

Deehalter peered out the south door. Nothing, nothing, of course nothing. A fox barked in the invisible distance, and the big man's grip tightened on his rifle stock. He caught himself before he threw a bullet out into the night in frustration; then he began to pace back.

But each time the creature had come, it was in the near dawn. As if it were striding to the farm from far away, or because it got a late start. The notch he and Kernes had blasted in the Indian mound faced southwest. Moonlight would not have entered it until nearly morning. But there was no living thing in that narrow rock basin—only a litter of bones and what was probably a meteorite.

Why had that Indian been sealed up alive?

Nothing but bones and iron in the mound. Briefly, Deehalter's mind turned over a memory of awakening to seize his rifle in the pattern of moonlight etched across his room by the venetian blinds. Now he held the weapon close and bent forward to look at his brother-in-law.

Kernes had moved slightly, out along the electric fence. The yard light colored his shirt blue, but could not throw a shadow forward into the glare of the full moon. Kernes was staring west at that mottled orb. His shotgun barrel traced nervous arcs, rising and slipping back to a high port. It was almost as if the smaller man were wishing he could fire at the moon, but catching himself a moment before he did anything that . . . crazy.

Kernes's body *slithered*.

"Kernes!" Deehalter screamed.

The man below turned and was a man again. The shotgun had fallen to the concrete. Kernes's clothing was awry from having something monstrously thin start to clamber out of it. Part of Deehalter's mind wondered what Kernes had thought in the mornings when he found himself naked in the pasture, his tangled pajamas outside his house.

Now the small farmer was looking up at Deehalter, his face as dead and horrified as that of the statue of Laocoön. Then he changed again, and the long jaws spread to hiss at the man above. Deehalter laid his open sights in the middle of the thing's breastbone and squeezed off the shot.

The bullet flew high because of the angle, but the big man was hunter enough to have allowed for that. The soft-nose spiked through the lower mandible and into the throat, exiting at last through the creature's back. The jacketed lead, partly expanded but with only a fraction of its energy gone, slapped the concrete beyond and splashed away in a shower of sparks and a riven howl.

The thing that had been Kernes hurtled backwards and slid until it struck the fence. Its stick-thin limbs thrashed, shredding remnants of its clothing with claws and the strength of a grizzly. Its jaws snapped. The hole in its throat was small, but Deehalter knew that the supersonic bullet would have left a wound cavity like a pie tin in the back.

The entrance wound had closed. The beast was scrabbling to its feet.

Deehalter screamed and shot it through the chest, an off-center impact that spun the creature again to the concrete. This time Deehalter could *see* the plastic flesh closing on the scale-dusted torso. He remembered Wiener and the gullied throat of the Holstein. With only that instant's hesitation, the big man braced his rifle in front of him and leaped through the window to his right. The fiberglass panel sprang out in a piece as the frame tore. Deehalter stumbled headlong onto the low roof of the milking parlor, rolled, and jumped to the ground. The jeep was only twenty feet away and he ran for it.

There was no ignition lock. Deehalter flipped the power on and stabbed at the starter button under the clutch pedal. The engine ground but did not catch. There was a tearing noise behind him, and despite himself, the big man turned to look. The creature was in the cowyard fence. The top strand was electrified. Blue sparks crackled about the thing's foreclaws. Its shape was in a state of flux so swift as to be almost subliminal. It was as if superimposed holograms of Kernes and the creature he had become were being projected onto the fence. Then the hot wire snapped, and the thing's legs cut the remaining strands like sickles through fog.

Deehalter fired one-handed and missed. He steadied the rifle, locking his left elbow on the tubular seat-frame, and knocked the creature back into the cowyard with no top to its skull. Then the engine chugged and the big farmer threw the jeep into second gear at higher revs than the worn clutch was used to. Spewing gravel but without the power to sideslip, the vehicle churned forward.

For choice, Deehalter would have run west for the county road as he had two nights before in his Chrysler. That would have meant turning and trying to race past the cowyard, where the creature was already on its feet again and striding toward him. Deehalter had small need of his imagination to picture that scene: the long-clawed arms hooking over the steering wheel and pluck-ing him out like the meat from a walnut half, leaving the empty jeep to career into a ditch. He was headed instead toward Sac Ridge and the mound from which the horror must have come.

Deehalter had the headlights on, but they were mounted too low to show up potholes in time even at moderate speed—and his present speed was anything but moderate. The jeep jounced so badly that only the big man's grip on the steering wheel kept him in the vehicle. The shovels in the back did spin out into the night. It occurred to Deehalter that the rifle which he had wedged butt-downward beneath the back seat might fire and end him permanently as it had been unable to do to the thing pursuing. He did not care. He only knew that he had looked down the creature's gaping jaws and would rather anything than die between them.

Despite his panic, Deehalter shifted into compound low to cross the stream, knowing that any attempt to mount the slippery bank in a higher gear would have meant sliding back into certain death. On the rutted pasture beyond, he revved and slam-shifted. He was proud of his skill only for the instant before the low moon flicked a leaping shadow across the corner of his eye. Fear washed away pride and everything else.

Despite the ruts, the jeep made good time in the pasture; but as the old vehicle began to climb the side of the ridge, Deehalter knew the creature must be gaining. There was no choice, nowhere else to run. If he turned either north or south, the thing's long shanks would cut it across the slant of his right angle.

Where had the creature come from originally? Perhaps the Indians had known; but even if the teardrop was the source, it could as easily have fallen a million years before and a thousand miles away, carried south on a glacier. Deehalter could picture a nervous band of Sacs dragging one of their number to the rock basin, bound or unconscious. Or would it have been a tribe from the pre-Columbian past? There was nothing in the mound to date it. Something had come from the cocoon of iron and had been trapped again between layers of rock. Trapped until he and Kernes had freed it in a vapor which merged with the black tendrils of dynamite.

As Deehalter neared the top of the ridge, he glanced sideways. The creature was a foot behind him and a foot to the left, its right leg poised to stride and its yard-long right arm poised to rip the farmer's throat open. Dee-halter slammed on the brakes, acting by reflex. It was the proper reflex, even though the jeep stalled. The beast's claws swept where Deehalter's head should have been, and its body belled and rebounded from the unyielding fender. For a moment, the thing sprawled backwards on the hillside; then it twisted upright, lizard-quick, and lunged.

Deehalter touched the muzzle of his Remington to the scaly ribs and blew the creature a dozen yards down the hill. The cartridge case sailed away in a high arc, the mouth of it eroded by the excessive pressures from the blocked muzzle.

And though Deehalter still had the part-box in his pocket, that had been the last round in the weapon.

In stalling, Deehalter had flooded the jeep's engine. He leaped out, winded already with fear, and topped the ridge with two long strides. The headlights were waning yellow behind him, where he could already hear the creature moving. The sky to the east was the color of blood. Deehalter ran for the mound as if its gentle contours could protect him. He tried to jump to its top, but his foot sank in the soft earth of the dig-gings. The big man windmilled forward onto his face in the grass beyond. His grip on the empty rifle had flayed his right knuckles against the ground. His twisted ankle gave a twinge; it might or might not bear his weight again.

Deehalter turned, trying to fumble another cartridge into the breech of the rifle. It was too late. Hissing like a cat in a lethal rage, the creature leaped delicately to the top of the mound.

It was even thinner than it had looked when flicker-ing shadows had bulked its limbs. It had to be thin, of course, with only Kernes's hundred and thirty pounds to clothe its frame. The curve of the mound made the creature's height monstrous, even though its legs were poised to lunge and it carried its flat skull forward like that of a nearsighted mantis. The narrow lips drew apart in a momentary grin, gray-white and then crimson as the first rays of the sun touched the creature over the rim of the next hill.

For a moment the leer hung there. Deehalter, on his back, stared at it like a rabbit spitted by the gaze of a hunting serpent. Then the thing was gone and the fear was gone, and Deehalter's practiced fingers slid a live round into the chamber of the ought-six.

"Wh-what's the matter, Dee?" Kernes whimpered. He was pitiful in his nakedness, more pitiful in his stunned surprise at where he found himself. Kernes really hadn't known what was happening, Deehalter realized. Perhaps Alice had begun to guess where her husband had been going in the night. That may have been why she had been so quick to run, before suspicion could become certainty.

"Dee, why're you looking at me like that?" Kernes begged.

Deehalter stood. His ankle only throbbed. If his first bullet had killed the creature as it should have, he would have buried the body and claimed that something had dragged Kernes away. Perhaps he would have buried it here in the mound from which the creature had escaped to begin with. Alice and Doc Jepson could testify to the cattle's previous injuries, whatever they might surmise had caused them.

The same story would be sufficient now.

"Good-bye, you sonofabitch," Deehalter said, and he raised his rifle. He fired point-blank into the smaller man's chest.

Kernes *whuffed* backwards as if a giant had kicked him. There was a look of amazement on his face and nothing more; but momentarily, something hung in the air between the dead man and the living, something as impalpable as the muzzle blast that rocked the hillside— and as real.

Deehalter's flesh *gave*, and for a startled second he/it knew why the Indians had buried their possessed brother alive—to trap the contagion with him in the rock instead of merely passing it on to raven and slay again. . . .

Then the sun was bright on Deehalter's back, casting his shadow across the body of the man he had murdered. He recalled nothing of the moment just past.

Except that when he remembered the creature's last red leer, he seemed to be seeing the image in a mirror.

WARNING: THIS SERIES TAKES NO PRISONERS

Introducing

David Drake has conceived a future history that is unparalleled in scope and detail. Its venue is the Universe. Its domain is the future of humankind. Its name? *CRISIS OF EMPIRE.*

An Honorable Defense
The first crisis of empire—the death of the Emperor leaving an infant heir. If even one Sector Governor or Fleet Admiral decides to grab for the Purple, a thousand planets will be consigned to nuclear fire.
David Drake & Thomas T. Thomas, 69789-7, $3.95 ____

Cluster Command
The imperial mystique is but a fading memory: nobody believes in empire anymore. There are exceptions, of course, and to those few falls the self-appointed duty of maintaining a military-civil order that is corrupt, despotic—and infinitely preferable to the barbarous chaos that will accompany it's fall. One such is Anson Merikur. This is his story.
David Drake & W. C. Dietz, 69817-6, $3.50 ____

The War Machine
What's worse than a corrupt, decadent, despotic, oppressive regime? An empire ruled over by corrupt, decadent, despotic, oppressive *aliens* ... In a story of personal heroism, and individual boldness, Drake & Allen bring The Crisis of Empire to a rousing climax.
David Drake & Roger MacBride Allen, 69845-1, $3.95 ____
